MOONSPAWN

by

BRUCE McLACHLAN

Published by **CHIMERA**
ISBN 9781780807034

PROLOGUE

Closing her eyes, she tasted the wind. The smells of the city were a palate of every description. The scent of exhaust, of food, of restaurants, of sweaty bodies dancing to the tunes of self-gratification. The hot lusts and appetites of the prey were rampant, concentrated into their brief span. But beneath these aromas were the darker traces, the hidden belly of the city released through this olfactory encyclopaedia - rot, decay, fear, hate, the true face beneath the shallow neon mask.

The night breeze pawed at her cold flesh, tugging at the vinyl veil of her trench-coat. The chase was underway, she could feel it. Feel the rush of adrenaline, the thrill of pursuit, the terror of the hounded fugitive.

Opening her eyes, she regarded the sprawling city below her. Amber radiance trickled up through the cracked valleys that were its streets and roads, the rooftops black, bathed solely in the glorious smile of the moon and the stars. This was her domain, her dominion; every brick, every pipe, every breath of tainted air was hers.

Beneath, the small park was a realm of shadows, barricading itself from the outside with a wall of spiked iron railings. A body lay slumped against this wall, lines of red running across the stone and into the gutter. Other than this stolid occupant, the street was empty.

Smiling, she casually stepped off the edge of the building. The air rushed around her, rippling her coat, the six stories plunging past as a blur until she struck the pavement, shattering the stone, the skyscraper heels and pointed toes of her thigh boots now surrounding themselves with a halo of zigzagging cracks.

Stepping from the craters, she walked casually across the thin road to the body. Putting her fingers to the puncture wounds that had ripped open its throat, she tasted the spilt life and gave a shudder of pleasure.

Spatters of crimson wound off to the right, dropped by the reckless diners as they fled. Straightening back up she turned and started to follow the path, the two distinct scents so pronounced that they might as well have painted arrows to mark their route.

It was time.

CHAPTER 1

The streets were choked with travellers, with people negotiating a route home after a club, a bar, an evening of food and merriment. Preened and dressed to impress, the denizens of the city failed to give her more than a second glance as she dashed past them. It was as though her grimy and bedraggled appearance

2

was some manner of urban camouflage, a concealing layer of filth that pushed her out of the human spectrums of sight and awareness.

Weaving through their ranks as an undetected breeze, Kira continued her mad bolt through the centre of the city. Her eyes flicked to every direction, her paranoia rampant, every shadow and every face a possible threat.

The neon signs and amber streetlights painted the scene of stone metal and glass with wild hues and numerous spectral shadows - places where her enemies might be lurking in wait. The scents of the city were strong in her nose, filling her senses with smells that no longer had purpose for her.

With her attention diverted to a suspicious figure at the entrance to a store, she slammed into a group of businessmen and their dates. Kira sent the startled travellers to the pavement and she dropped to her knees, before stumbling recklessly aside and into a foul smelling alleyway.

Their curses were lost to her. She had other far more pressing matters at hand than those of apologising to incensed office workers.

The alley reeked of rank food, of stale urine and long accumulated rot and grime. Cardboard boxes were piled in mouldering heaps, dank and sagging, leaning precariously upon one another for feeble support.

The passage led back to another main street, the streams of cars streaking past ahead, the flow of people like vessels through a vein. A soft silence existed in the thin corridor, the darkness smothering the sounds from without, absorbing them.

Limping forward, she cradled her arm, the limb aching from her fall. Shaking with fright and anxiety she looked about her surroundings as she walked. The windows were sealed, either bricked up or covered with bars and mesh to stop intrusion. Five stories arose straight up around her, and then parted to offer a slim view of the dark night sky. The stars sparkled and winked at her, the moon offering a crescent apparition and glowing with silvery wrath, seeking to emulate the sun it had replaced for an all too short period of time.

A flurry of motion snapped her gaze back to the world more immediately about her. A figure had entered the other end of the alley and was rushing towards her, his feet splashing in the shallow pools of fetid water. His clothes slapped against the air, a briefcase clutched grimly at his side.

With a squeak of shock Kira looked around for a way out, a way to continue her escape. Every second carried the man closer to her, and she knew his intentions well.

In the sombre light she saw him reaching into the case as he charged her. There was a wink of bright metal in the moonlight and Kira flung herself upward with a distressed squeak, the blade whistling with a sanguinary hack. The crates behind her were shredded, the contents splashed across the floor as Kira slapped her hands to the bars of the second floor window, vacating the area he had attacked.

Her body wrenched at the holds as gravity grabbed her and tried to bring her back to the ground. With jeopardy goading her on she scrambled upward, her body moving with the celerity of utter fear. Sparks lit the area below with a strobe pulse as her legs jolted up and away from another truculent slash, the metal edge screeching along the bricks.

A hissed imprecation of hate spilled from her pursuer's lips as she continued her assent, hauling herself up, grabbing the grilles, her arms aching from such exertion.

The lip of the roof beckoned and throwing a hand up, her fingers caught the ledge. With a scowl of labour she drew herself up and flopped over the perimeter and onto a crunching carpet of gravel.

A necessary moment of recovery gave way to a roll as she restored herself to her feet, every muscle and ligament raw within her.

Stumbling away, she wove amongst the pipes and ventilation ducts, the fans spilling warm dry air into the night about her. The other buildings of the area were an uneven landscape, rising and falling all about her, offering a possible route out, but one that would be difficult and exhausting to negotiate. No lights were on in any of the windows; the offices and businesses deserted at this extreme hour, testifying that she could move undetected.

Looking one way and then another she tried to figure where she was, which route to follow. But her meditations were cut short as there was a soft thud from behind her.

With a start she whirled to see the man slip over the ledge, dragging with him the rope of a grappling iron that had sunk barbed fangs into the stone.

'The hunt is over,' he stated grimly, and arose from his low crouch, revealing himself and his true purpose. He was a middle-aged man, his hair receding slightly at the front to reveal a few short scars. He appeared no different to any other mundane commuter, his loose suit clean and pressed, its edges like razors, his shoes polished to a mirror sheen but now spattered with mud and scuffed from his ascent.

The jacket lay open, revealing a harness over his white shirt and paisley tie, the hidden weapons now brazen in the rays of the moon - stakes, a pistol, a knife marked with eldritch runes.

In one hand he clutched a curved short blade, the small sword flickering with internal light, possessed of some eerie internal power. The other hand dropped the briefcase, leaving him holding what had been within. Stepping forward and leaving the case behind, he levelled the modified Uzi in her direction, the barrel rendered overlong and fat with a silencer and a laser scope. A red beam arced through the night and touched her chest, giving Kira a split second warning of his attack.

With a spasm she threw herself aside and behind a cluster of stout pipes. Hissing coughs rocked the air, mumbled from the assault weapon. Scintillating bursts erupted above her, bullets springing from the metal amidst dazzling plumes of radiance. Clutching her arms about her head she scurried onward, the deluge continuing to eat at her vicinity.

A pipe cracked before her and sent out a geyser of scorching steam, blocking her passage, herding her back, the sporadic bursts of her pursuer driving her, steering her one way and then another as he continued his hounding attentions.

Dropping onto her side she found herself in the corner of the building, open space on either side, places devoid of cover. She looked again and again, hoping she was wrong, praying that she not be trapped as she knew she was.

'Nowhere left to run,' stated a hateful voice, the tones harsh.

'Leave me alone,' she wailed, burying her face in her hands.

'Can't do that I'm afraid. You have to be cleansed.'

'Please, I haven't done anything,' she implored, looking over the edge at the drop into the street. A fall would cripple her, leave her defenceless against him. She had a better chance by choosing to fight him directly.

'No, but you will, you won't be able to resist your thirst,' he testified, the sound of his steady footfalls continuing to close in on her.

'Thirst? What do you mean? You're insane.'

'Maybe. But killing vampires is what I do, and killing you serves that vaulted purpose.'

'Vampires? You're mad, there's no such thing,' she cried, trying to convince herself he was in error. 'And even if there was, I'm not one. I work in a department store for Christ's sake. I have a mini, I have two pet tube mice called Mook and Chook!'

The footfalls started to draw close and Kira huddled into the corner. She didn't have the strength to flee any more, and her will to fight was flagging rapidly. She couldn't go on. Her life was shattered, broken and lost to her, and hounded for days, she just wanted it to end.

There was a crunch and the hunter stepped out from behind a stack of exhaust vents. Kira looked up with tears in her eyes, shaking with terror as he looked blankly upon her.

'Come on then, you fuck!' she growled, the salty trails from her eyes dark with dirt. 'End it! Get it over with!'

Kira caught the faint trace of blood and then her eyes snapped to his shirt, a pool of darkness creeping across the collar, spreading like a staining cancer. The weapons drooped in his grasp and then fell to the gravel with a crunch. He dropped to his knees, put fingers to his neck as his face drained of expression, and with a faint smile he keeled over and landed with an indolent thud. His legs twitched for a moment as the crimson pool continued to grow around him, and then he went still.

Eyes wide with confusion, Kira stared at the area he had emerged from, wondering who had performed this deed.

A heeled boot stepped out into the hesitant moonlight, the polished stiletto turning slightly as Kira's eyes flowed up the burnished thigh boot, following the shapely limb to find the rest of the owner.

The woman emerged with a graceful turn, one hand holding the pipes to steady her. She was an apparition of desire, the most gorgeous expression of feminine beauty Kira could have predicted, and what was even more startling, was that Kira had seen her before.

The milk-white skin of the woman shone like ivory against the night, her elegant face wreathed with long albino hair that shimmered in the soft breeze. Her dark eyes winked with ferocity and power, her lips were stained red, her bared incisors wet with the blood of the hunter.

Her tall and glorious physique bore a thin studded choker, a gloss trench-coat open and hanging behind her as a dark backdrop to her body. A strapless latex bra cupped her breasts together, offering a deep and inviting cleavage. Fishnet covered her thighs and reached into the tall boots. Fingerless leather gloves allowed her digits to emerge, each digit tipped with a wicked, ebony talon.

'Not bad, not bad at all,' she purred, wiping the excess from her lips onto the back of her hand.

Stepping over the body she sauntered forward, flowing like liquid towards the huddled and quaking form of Kira.

'You, but how, I—' she began, her mind muddled.

'Shhhh, my little one. Explanations are for later. First we have to get you somewhere safe. Dawn is on the way.' She extended a hand to Kira, her face soft and inviting, her tone seductive and irresistible.

With trembling fingers Kira gradually reached up and put her own hand in that of the woman's. With a soft pull she was brought to her feet and into the embrace of the female, the soothing familiarity making Kira melt. She closed her eyes, the stress visited upon her by the chase, the fight, and the last few days dragging her from consciousness. Riven with exhaustion and tribulation and now given solace, Kira drifted into a faint, falling as a slack mannequin into the awaiting arms of the woman of her dreams, the memory of her reviving and returning in full.

The equations and problems on the page before her were starting to merge and shift, writhing like serpents, unintelligible. Her eyes were heavy, her thoughts furious at having been preoccupied for so long with the extensive homework.

It was her last year of school, it was almost over. Just a little longer and she would be free. It wasn't even *her* homework, because once again she had been bullied into it.

Just the mere thought of the incident had her rubbing her injured arm and scowling with rancour. Why did they keep picking on her? Her life was hard enough, she didn't need others making it even more complex.

She wished she had the strength to stand up to them, but she was afraid, she just wasn't aggressive. Sure, she would spend hours afterwards brooding on all the things she could have done, all the vicious retaliation she could have undertaken, but when it came around to another encounter, she folded immediately, compliant and weak. She hated herself for that, hated being such a victim, yet here she was toiling into the middle of the night to do their homework for them.

There was a soft click behind her and she turned to see who it was, thinking that perhaps her parents had come home early. Looking to the side, she panned her gaze through the room. The second floor bedroom was large but filled with only two kinds of adornment, each in direct opposition to the other. Everything was either fuzzy animals, posters of boy bands and frivolous toys, or books and charts of pure science and learning, academic accessories complemented by exercise books filled with her own projections and work.

There was no one there, so she dismissed it as a product of sleep deprivation. As she regarded her room she caught herself in the mirror, the frame decorated with fluffy toys and simpering saccharine concessions to the image her parents held of what a wholesome young girl should find appealing.

Her ice-blue eyes were rimmed with red, a shade to match her curling ginger locks, the strands hanging in tight spirals but dishevelled from lack of trained attention.

She was still in her school uniform, having lacked the time and effort to change because of the workload she faced this night. Her parents were out again, socialising with their clique, bragging about how important they were, how much they earned, and all those who were subordinate to their every whim.

Kira would readily trade all their prolific and grandiose gifts and purchases for some actual genuine attention from them. They bought her such things just to make her more valuable, like adding a pool to a house to increase its intrinsic value. It was because she, like everything they had, was just another bauble to impress and add to their standing - the daughter in the most prestigious school, whose grades stood out over all others.

They didn't care about her.

'You're a total fuck up,' she accused at her reflection. 'You're going to be a doormat all your life. No one will love you, and death will end up being the only thing you'll look forward to,' she continued, and then closed her eyes tightly, tears welling in the corners.

'I hate you, I hate you, I hate you,' she chanted, and then sniffled back her distress.

It felt good to drop her eyelids, the orbs beneath them requiring a break. Kira decided to lay her head down, just for a while, just a few minutes so she could rest and then revitalise herself a little before finishing up.

A gust of wind rushed over her face, cooling her skin and making her jolt up from her slouch. Her eyes focused and she saw that the window was now open before her, the night breeze wafting through and making the curtains dance.

Leaning forward, she grabbed the handle and hauled it closed, the glass suddenly reflecting the image of someone standing behind her. With a squeak of shock she turned, catching a vague image of the woman before she was grabbed and hurled aside.

Careering across the room she collapsed onto the pink sheets of her bed, bouncing upon the mattress, disorientated by her brief flight and from being awoken so suddenly.

The woman dropped across her chest, pinning her down, her black-nailed hands snagging Kira's wrists and shoving them into the sheets. Kira whimpered and struggled weakly, her eyes fixed to the visage of the woman.

Her long snow-white hair was tied back into a ponytail, the silken locks fixed with a midnight ribbon. Her dark eyes were wreathed by a token application of brooding make-up and her lips were painted a deep blue, stretched wide upon an amused grin.

She wore a latex basque, the material hugging her body, presenting her breasts within sculpted cups. The suspenders reached beneath her high thong and grabbed fine denier stockings that poured across her legs and into knee high zipped boots, the patent footwear armed with a dagger heel. Opera gloves rolled along her arms, the fabric rippling as her muscles kept Kira subdued, the fingers of the gloves severed.

Kira opened her mouth to scream for help, but as she sucked in a deep gasp to unleash, the woman dove in and clamped her mouth across Kira's.

Panicked wriggling joined her squeal of protest and she fought desperately as her arms were hauled up over her head, her wrists being crossed before the woman's left hand ensnared the connection. Kira tugged fervently, but the strength of this woman was more than a match for her, and she could do nothing to resist.

The freed hand wandered down and cupped Kira's breast, gently hugging the budding flesh as a tongue reached into her mouth. A finger teased across her nipple and she gasped with pleasure, suddenly pausing in her battle to get free. Then her eyes rolled back as the hand continued its work, bringing forth a wonderful flood of sensation, washing away her resistance.

The pointed toes of the woman's boots reached in and hooked to her inner thighs, the stranger forcefully making Kira splay her legs wide.

Kira panted through her nostrils as the woman continued the kiss, curling against Kira's petrified tongue, seeking to bring it to life with such tenderness. She could not believe this was happening; she had to be dreaming.

Against reason she let her tongue emerge, stretching out to meet the intruder. They coiled upon one another, slippery and eager to play. She shivered as the stranger ran her tip across her lips, tickling the skin before slipping back in, probing deep.

The hand started to slip lower, releasing breast and migrating, making Kira's breath quicken with every second that passed of its voyage until she was panting frantically. Clawed fingers hooked the base of her skirt and started to haul up, raising the curtain of fabric to expose her panties. The same hand began to sneak under the front, stealthily entering and then letting a fingertip brush her clitoris. She was already damp with desire, the flames of a long-forsaken libido suddenly erupting into volcanic fervour.

The finger began to circle and tickle, caressing the tender bud. Kira almost swooned from rapture, her body breaking into a cavorting fit, the woman staying atop her body as though it were a bucking bronco ride.

Manipulating her loins, her legs held wide by the demanding boots of the stranger, pinned down and subjected to a passionate kiss, Kira surrendered herself in full, melting with prurient desire.

The hands left their captives and the woman sat up, arching her back, her breasts straining against the taut fabric, making Kira's eyes burn with wonderment.

'Who... who are you?' she whispered, licking her lips, the taste of another person's saliva strong upon her palette.

'No more than a figment of your imagination, Kira,' she purred, her voice silken, an enticing delicate sound with a hidden core of darkness to it.

The hands of the woman closed into the front of her shirt. There was a brief pause where her eyes met Kira's and kept a momentary exchange, then with a wrench she tore it open, sending the small buttons dancing across the bed. Reaching back in, she took the folds of her bra and broke the centre, allowing her to peel back the soft satin fabric and expose Kira's breasts in full.

'A luscious sight indeed, but not quite ripe,' she uttered, almost to herself, yet with her stark gaze fixed to her subject. 'Not yet, but soon.'

Abashed worry crept into Kira's mind and she moved to try and cover herself, unused to being put on display for others. But the hands of the woman flashed out and captured her wrists once more, stopping her in her task. Kira's breath froze, afraid that this encounter was to become a violent one, but the woman merely grinned her wicked grin and transferred Kira's hands to her own rubber coated mounds.

Kira felt the smooth fabric pass beneath her palms, the woman moving Kira's hands in circles across the delicious assets. It felt wonderful; it was a vision of awe that had her devoting herself to more substantial play, to indulge this encounter to its fullest extent. Dream or not, a charm had been laid upon her and she was helpless to resist.

The woman let Kira feel her hardening nipples lurking within the basque, and then slowly drew the young hands down her sides, following her contours until they cleared her hips. The latex gave way to soft flesh, the skin cool, almost cold to the touch. It enforced that this was a dream, for no normal person had such a body temperature.

Kira felt the firm buttocks, squeezing the skin, her own loins moist with complete intoxication.

'That's it, go on,' crooned the woman, as though Kira were a student who had finally succeeded in learning an elusive lesson.

The woman released Kira, letting her continue as she wished, running a hand around and across the latex of her stomach, holding to a breast as she sought to fill her senses with the physique of the stranger.

Her enigmatic partner leaned back, presenting an open plate for Kira's hands to dine upon, her taloned hands peeling back the obstructing cloth of her underwear. Letting one set of fingers explore Kira and tickle her clitoris, the other captured a sheen of moisture and used it to steal entry into her rear. A finger kissed the puckered opening and started to slither in, causing Kira to gasp at the alien sensation, the woman probing in and out, circling as Kira sobbed with rapture. The steady stimulation of rear and sex had Kira throwing her head from side to side, striving to endure such intensity while also seeking to try and keep her eyes on the portrait of beauty before her. She was determined not to miss a second of it, not even to blink, for to do so might dispel the dream.

Kira's hands were wild and random, groping and fondling with passion, the smooth panes of midnight fixating her fingers, the scent of the rubber sifting through her nose.

The woman lifted up and started to shuffle back, removing herself from Kira's stomach and instead settling between her splayed thighs. A moment of hesitation struck and Kira tried to close her lewd pose, only to have firm hands slap to her thighs and keep them there.

Looking up from her reclining position, Kira saw the woman lowering her head, an iniquitous smirk ruling her features. Kira could see what was going to happen, her breath once more breaking into chaotic fits. 'Oh God,' she whispered with trepidation.

A cool tongue burrowed into her loins, taking a flitting kiss of her clitoris that made her jolt, her legs tensing and fighting the restraining hands of the woman. Kira immediately cried out, dropping her arms and taking firm fists of the blanket, hauling at the fabric, every muscle and ligament taut beneath the skin as she shook with bliss.

The cunnilingus had her mind melting with sheer rhapsody, her thoughts scrambled and insensible, everything pushed from her mind and body save this unprecedented bliss. It was as though the woman knew every part of her, knew exactly how and where to achieve the best results, even more so than Kira herself. To label the oral attention as unparalleled would have been an injustice to it, and Kira bit her lip until she feared it might bleed, so pressing was the need to shriek her glory and shake the heavens with it.

Kira's legs were released and the fingers reached up, tracing light routes up her body until they were once more upon her breasts, tickling them, applying swift pinches to the nipples, the sharp sensation melting into the hedonistic hurricane.

Time melted amidst the woman's expert attention, the tongue continuing to burrow and fawn upon her, the fingers treating her breasts to treasured manipulation.

Without word the woman retreated and lifted one of Kira's legs, flipping her over onto her front. Reaching up, the female grabbed Kira's wrists once more, one hand capturing both extremities and pulling back, lifting her front from the bed, her breasts thrusting, her shoulders aching from the contortion, the limbs used as reigns to control the girl.

Her eyes bulged and she released shocked purls as the woman's face burrowed between her buttocks. She tensed in alarm, but the stranger gave a

10

jerk to the captured arms, sending a chastising flare of pain into the joints to correct her behaviour. A resounding smack from the other hand dropped to her rear, the spanking hand adding four more strokes, the applause ringing out, sending stinging shocks through her buttocks.

Kira whimpered and did as she was instructed, releasing the barring flesh so the woman might enter and kiss her rear, the lips peeling back to let an eager tongue stab through her orifice. Kira set loose a prolonged moan, pulling weakly at the armlock just to feel its existence, of being so ruthlessly controlled but so gloriously pleasured. The feel of the organ pouring into her, lapping at her insides, was a sensation more delightful than she would ever have thought possible.

'Please, please let me taste you too,' she mewled through racing gasps.

The face withdrew for a moment.

'You are sure?' it quizzed, making Kira commit herself with greater dedication.

'Yes, I do, please let me,' she rasped, her most pressing wish now being to attend this woman, to do the things that had been done to her, to explore further, to know another woman as she herself had been experienced.

'You'll do anything for me then? To earn this reward?'

'Yes, yes, anything you want, anything,' she blurted.

The stranger rose from the bed and stood beside it, hands on her hips, her glower dropping down on Kira as she lay huddled and in shock from the session.

'First, stand over here, and take off all your clothes before me,' she stated with authority. 'I want you to perform.'

Kira sprang from the bed, stepping into the middle of the room, her hands jumping up to her tie to begin tearing it off with harsh yanks.

'Slowly,' warned the woman, settling back onto the bed, seating herself and crossing her legs, propping herself up on her arms as she regarded Kira with exquisite menace.

Kira reduced her speed, stifling her impetuous haste. It was suddenly harder to comply; the deliberate displaying of this strip something that was less easily acceptable to her. But the sight of the woman, her beauty, the promise of being able to attend her, outweighed and eased her troubled young mind.

The only other token against performing was that her efforts would be as nothing compared to her partner's. She had never done this before, so would the woman become frustrated or mocking as to her feeble efforts? She wanted to please her, but did she have the necessary skill? Beginner's luck was her only hope, and it was a cliché she doubted would assist her.

The knot unravelled and she dropped the tie aside. The torn folds of her shirt slipped from her arms and fell to the floor, leaving her torso bare save for the ruined bra. Removing the straps from her shoulders, she dropped the white underwear and reached back to the button of her pleated skirt.

Keeping her eyes lowered for a moment, she opened the fastening and let the material sheath drop to her feet. Stepping from it, her bare feet touched the carpet and she folded her arms about herself, stood only in her panties, displayed for the viewing pleasure of the woman.

What was her body compared to that of the female before her? How could she hope to please her, either visually or through amateur sexual antics?

'Look up at me, Kira,' demanded the woman, causing a reluctant obedience. 'Now, remove your underwear and put your hands by your sides,' she commanded, the words brooking no intolerance, possessed of an edge that made Kira hopelessly obedient to them.

With sloth she hooked her thumbs into the damp material and drew it down, revealing herself in full before stepping out of the flimsy garment.

Straightening up, she returned her eyes to those of her enslaver and put her hands to her sides, covering nothing.

The woman continued to keep her eyes to Kira's, and after a prolonged stare started to let them wander down across the presented girl, following her supple form, admiring it, concocting the deeds she wished her to perform. Goosebumps flashed across her skin as Kira felt the glare, as though it was a physical touch, caressing her skin with the lightest of ethereal brushes.

'Touch yourself, Kira,' she bade with a smile.

Kira swallowed and paused, her hands rising a little and then freezing.

'Go on, start with your breasts and then work your way down,' she commanded, clearly aware of how difficult it would be for her subject to comply.

Kira relented to the force of will emanating from the woman, and almost of their own accord her hands reached up to her teats, brushing them with her palms before closing to the flesh. With gentle effort she started to please herself as she had done many times in the night - lying beneath her covers, hidden from view, exploring, treating herself to the only real pleasure her life granted.

'Very good, keep going,' commented the woman, continuing her scrutiny.

Kira's hands started to descend, dropping and nestling between her legs. She shuddered at the first touch, the feeling of being watched, of being humbled by this forced display of something that was always so completely secret.

The woman pulled down her thong and removed it, twirling the slender fabric on a raised finger as she re-crossed her legs to hide her naked sex.

'You still want to kiss me?' she asked softly.

'Yes, please, I'll do my best, I promise,' rashly stated Kira, the pleasure she was cultivating for herself with the onanism eroding any concerns. The woman was making her do this to have her rendered more amiable to cunnilingus. The woman was playing Kira like an instrument, plucking strings to have her obey.

'First, an appetiser. Kneel before me, but don't stop your performance, it pleases me,' she stated, the confirmation that this goddess was being entertained making Kira even more eager to be compliant.

Kira settled down, her mouth watering with anticipation. The woman reached forward and pulled the thong down over Kira's head, straightening it so that the crotch hung over her nostrils. Hooking it over her ears to keep it in place, the woman leaned back, the latex clothing adorning her releasing teasing groans with the stretch and pull upon her sumptuous anatomy.

'We are going to go through the senses,' she murmured. 'You are currently working on touch, so now we shall try smell. Smell and continue, and think of what it will feel like and taste like when it comes to the real thing, Kira.'

Closing her eyes, Kira filled her mind with notions of what was to come, drinking in the smell via deep draughts, the scent of the woman's sex pouring through her like a tidal wave. Her masturbation was bringing her closer to orgasm, the stimulation of this scenario speeding the effects. The creak of latex and vinyl reached her ears again, the sound of the woman moving making Kira's heart stamp in her chest with hunger.

'It's time for sight now, so open your eyes and look while you continue.'

Kira found herself staring at the splayed legs of the woman, her pudenda on display before Kira's straining eyes, the stockings coating her pale thighs, the basque shimmering above. Looking down at her, the stranger watched with fascination as Kira stared into the cleft of the presented sex, teasing her own as she continued to drink in the smell of the underwear.

'Now, its time for taste, Kira,' she decreed, reaching over and pulling the thong from the girl's head and enclosing a fist to her hair as a reign. Using this mooring, she was steered into the awaiting meal, nuzzling in, the subtle smell infinitely stronger now simply through hunger and proximity, the flavour spilling across Kira's taste buds as she started to lap.

Looking across the stretched midnight plains of the basque, Kira peered through the twin peaks of black latex breasts and to the face of the woman. The image of her lounging back, her eyes rolling, her mouth broad with a wanton grin burned itself indelibly into Kira's mind.

The closer she brought herself to climax, the more energetic her tongue became until she howled into the sex of the woman, the orgasm more potent than any she had previously enjoyed. Thrashing on the floor, she tried to keep her actions steady, but it was so difficult, the pleasure was crippling.

As the heat withdrew all life seemed to dribble from her body and she dropped back, collapsing onto the carpet, shaking with wild spasms.

The woman arose and settled beside her, lovingly stroking Kira's hair as she shook with residual bursts of feeling.

'Shhhh, my sweet one, everything will be fine, just you wait and see,' she purred, the lullaby promise causing Kira to drift into an exhausted snooze. 'Be patient, and be ready when I come for you.'

With a shout she jerked upright in bed, throwing her gaze around to try and find the woman who had filled her to the point of overflow with glorious pleasure.

But the room was empty. Seeking conformation, she jumped from the sheets and dropped to her forsaken school uniform. Her heart sagged in her chest as she lifted up her shirt. The buttons were all in place. With a furious burst of effort she rummaged through the rest. The bra was still intact, her underwear still clean and fresh.

She wondered if it had all been nothing more than a dream. Torn by the vivid nature of her memories and the physical evidence denying the event, she dropped back into bed, dragging the covers over her.

Dwelling on what she had done, and what had been done to her, she let a hand snake between her legs and once more start to tickle her loins. As she masturbated to a new but lesser climax, she filled her mind's eye with the image of the woman, the latex-clad succubus that had ambushed her in the night and seduced her with wicked vice.

She had never before thought of herself as inclined sexually in any particular way, it was not something that ever seemed pressing in her life, but now she had tasted another woman and been reformed by it, even if it had only been a phantasm in her own mind.

CHAPTER 2

The air was thick of moisture, and when she breathed in she could feel the damp pouring into her. Strong light was seeping through her eyelids, and as she tried to open them the intensity proved too painful to tolerate.

She had dwelt solely in darkness for several days now, and any sort of light was alien to her eyes. The exact time she had been on the streets was unknown, her recall hazy and corrupted, affected by the savage delirium that had taken over her psyche.

Awakening suddenly from sleep, she had been afflicted with a hunger the likes of which she had never known. Once, when she was a child, she had been placed in hospital to have her tonsils out. The sentence of nil by mouth had left her mad, her awareness of her surroundings lost as she begged and lied, tried any deceit to gain water. She had burbled a need to go to the toilet so she might steal water from a tap, steadfastly refusing bedpans, unable to rise, needing help but gaining none. The new thirst that had torn into her was similar, though far more intense and consuming.

There were a few recollections of stumbling recklessly through slum areas, of finding herself caked in grime from her dizziness. Blood was found upon her without explanation so she hid, and when she felt the sun kiss her body she scrambled into sewer, drain or stinking festering pit to evade it, the merest lick of golden light instantly searing her skin.

What had happened to her life? She was no doubt fired. Her rent would be well overdue if she had been away long enough, and she could well be evicted.

Lifting herself up, Kira found her body stiff from lack of use and overlong rest. Her eyes had accustomed a little better, and rubbing them, she started to peer through the dazzling sheet of white, bringing the blurred images into greater focus.

Looking down she discovered herself in a loose white gown of silk, all her other clothes removed. The hastily compiled layers of coats and scarves that helped hide her from view and from the agonising touch of the sun had been lost, removed while she slumbered.

Squinting, she discerned movement and as her eyes gathered full strength once more, she found herself located in opulent splendour.

The circular hall was a vast pool chamber that had been modified steadily towards being some sort of gallery, for the tiled walls were set with flowing mosaics of incredible detail and artistry. The walls had marble pillars placed along them, hiding sections of the spiralling Celtic patterns that curled around equally spaced silver wall sconces. Clusters of candles were set upon the elaborate baroque arms of these fixtures, helping spread an amber haze along the outermost perimeter of the hall. It was this light that had pained her so much, a level of illumination that should have ordinarily been gloomy to her, but because of her recent nocturnal lifestyle and her dwelling in absolute darkness, even this had been an estranged sight.

The pillars rose to the base of the domed ceiling, the serpentine tendrils of dark pattern reaching up to gather and weave about a vast ideogram that dominated the centre. It could have been a Japanese character, but it was far more geometrical, almost like an advanced rune of some lost and forgotten culture.

The barbed symbol hung over the circular pool that filled almost the whole hall. The crystal waters were still, undisturbed, releasing shifting murky banks of scented mist that spiralled through the air, lit from within by the aura of the candles.

There was only one exit, a pair of large ebony double doors set in one portion of the wall, the ornate handles and lock comprised of polished silver. Hooks in the walls supported rows of dressing gowns similar to hers, telling her that this place could cater to many more than just a singular visitor.

Kira herself was lying on a cushioned plinth, one of six placed around the pool, set back a few feet from the lymphatic waters. The raised slabs were all adorned with a padded surface, like massage tables, but in addition they were some sort of long cabinet, with drawers and cupboards beneath each.

Intrigued, she opened several of those below her, pawing through the towels, soaps, perfumes, and oils she found within. Clearly the top was to serve for the purposes of sensual recreation.

Sliding from the slab, she dropped her feet to the warm tiles and took a few faltering steps. Against the aromatic tides of the air she could more clearly smell her own unwashed flesh, and was tempted to immediately slide into the pool to cleanse herself. Crouching by the side she reached down and tested the waters, etching some circles and watching the ripples spread out across the surface. Was she dreaming still?

With a shout of shock she jumped back and onto the plinth as the clues of movement rose again, strangely emanating straight from the pool. Two heads emerged slowly from the middle, the short hair of the women dark and flat upon their heads. Beneath these were silvery bands, the chokers fitted about their throats and seemingly without lock. Four rings were set around them, the one at the front being flanked by the symbol that adorned the ceiling, as well as another more detailed symbol, this being different for both women. Was it a personal identification?

Both were slender and gorgeous, their slim faces serene and passive as they stood up and started to walk forward. Lithe of frame, like delicate models of the catwalk, their sublime breasts acted as prows, the waters reaching no higher as they paced forward.

The naked women drew close and then stopped before her, keeping their alluring pale eyes to Kira as she maintained an aghast expression. How had they been breathing down there? No bubbles from oxygen supplies had corrupted the surface, and they had been down there for ages. Were they even human?

'Will you not come in and join us, miss?' asked one of them.

'We are here to attend you,' added the other, their voices like silken purrs, enticing and hypnotic.

Kira paused, looking at the duo with worry, wondering what was going on. Would they drown her the moment she entered the waters? Should she run? Try to flee? Her paranoia ebbed as they lifted marble smooth arms from the waters, the hot fluids dripping in sparkling trails from their limbs as they extended welcoming hands and opened into inviting smiles.

'Please, let us help you,' said one of them, her soft tones velvet in Kira's ears. 'Her majesty commanded it.'

'Her majesty?' quizzed Kira, closing her robe more tightly to her, feeling somehow inadequate compared to these sensual beauties of the waters.

'The one who brought you here,' replied one of the nymphs.

'Our mistress,' added her partner.

'The Queen of the City,' finished the first, running off the titles this mysterious woman was known by to her subjects.

Feeling more secure with this knowledge, Kira slid from the soft surface and back onto the tiles. Taking the belt of the robe, she started to unfasten it and then froze as she realised she was naked beneath. The women read her shame and smiled with amusement at such a display of shame.

'No need to be bashful, miss,' whispered one of them, the delicate voice a beguiling tune that lured her, as though these were sirens and she was powerless to resist their supernatural song. 'Remove your robe and come in.'

Opening the soft sheet she dropped it behind her and stepped to the edge, trying not to look upon them, for to meet their eyes was to acknowledge her nakedness.

'What is there to be ashamed of?' asked one.

'Come in and look at yourself,' stated the other, indicating the floor of the pool, the surface being a huge polished mirror, shimmering with the refractions of the agitated waters pressing upon it.

Settling down, Kira sat on the lip and then flipped in, letting loose a sudden gasp of awe as the warmth flowed into her, the sweat and the grim sloughing away like an unloved skin. Sinking down her head dropped beneath the waters, submerging her in full, and with a kick into the wall she launched herself forward. As a dart of motion she drilled through the halcyon sea, the waters streaming through her hair, peeling away her angst, soothing her very soul. It was such a simple pleasure, but never had she found one quite so profound.

As she flung her outstretched arms back to force herself onward, she opened her eyes and caught sight of her reflection. Immediately a cloud of silver bubbles burst from her lips and she hurled herself up, erupting from the surface with a yell.

'What the hell!' she exclaimed, kicking back to try and escape the sight, thinking that another person had been swimming beneath her, taking her by surprise with a parallel course.

Realisation dawned and she put hands to her face. It was still the one she recalled, but it had been changed. It was as though she'd been drained. Her features and body had been siphoned from within to reveal a new body beneath. She had never been really thin, but likewise she was not actually fat, yet somehow something had removed that last stubborn layer that helped hide a natural beauty beneath. Was this real? was this the creature that had been lurking beneath her skin all these years? Had she truly been such a delightful sight, just one hidden from view until now?

Dropping down she hung in the waters and stared across her naked loitering form with wide eyes, wondering if she had seen correctly. Perhaps the ebb and flow of the waters had tricked her like a fun house mirror, deceiving her eyes with a false vision.

Still she could not believe what her senses told her to be true. She recognised every feature, every part of herself, but it had been drawn in, tightened, bringing out a salacious angel.

Breaking from the surface she turned to the women, her red hair limp about her features, the warmth running down her form, her breasts standing proud and firm, all excess weight removed.

'What's happened to me?' she questioned with a mixture of elation and unequivocal terror. 'What did this?'

The women started to pace towards her, having armed themselves with soap, sponges and other instruments to attend her needs, to further enhance her beauty.

'Maleficence changes the body both inside and out,' whispered one of the women.

'Maleficence? What the hell is that? What's going on? What? Who was that woman? Is that this queen? How did she? I mean—'

Her words were ended when female lips reached forward and connected with hers. The kiss was soft, tempting, delicate and delicious. Her questions were blown away like loosed leaves in the arms of autumn and all thought and concern drooled from her mind.

The limbs of the woman encircled her and the lips parted, opening as the servant's tongue solicited entry by running its tip along Kira's lips.

Answering the call, Kira returned the exchange, their tongues emerging to lock together, to writhe against each and explore the cavern of each other's mouths. The waters that still ran their features made the kiss glide and slip with their passion, while the other nymph chose to explain, running a cake of soap across Kira's shoulders.

'Maleficence. Or the Malefic Kiss, as others call it. Having a malignant influence, the doing of evil to another. It is what we have termed our transformation from fleeting life to eternal undeath.' The lather made Kira shudder as more hands brushed her nipples, the other woman continuing her kiss while also applying herself to the cleansing of Kira's front.

'We have been reborn into the ranks of the Homo Nocturnus,' continued the other female, applying a sponge and drawing circles across Kira's back and onto her shoulders. 'The Nosferatu. We are vampire. We live by night, we never die, we devote ourselves to pleasure and fulfilment.'

The nymph before her slipped a hand around the back of Kira's neck, drawing her in close to make their kiss all the deeper as she started to work the soap across Kira's body with her free hand.

Kira could do nothing save be consumed by the pleasure of being serviced thus. The distraught concern at such revelations of what she was failed to break the prurient mood.

'Our queen is undisputed ruler of the city. She controls everything you have ever known, working from the secretive depths. This is her palace, we are her servants. Our existence is unknown to almost every mortal. Only the privileged or damned knows of us. Our kind created the myths, turned them into Hollywood legend to hide ourselves further, to protect us. We give our enemies false weapons against us, portray ourselves as we wish, and make our very existence seem so incredulous that even when discovered, we are ignored.'

The woman ceded her place to the other, letting her continue the kiss, the two of them taking turns to taste of Kira's lips. All the while they continued washing away the dirt, running a brush through her hair as it was gently and methodically shampooed and then conditioned.

Once she had been cleansed they drew her to the side, leaning her against the edge of the pool. Kira locked her arms to the tiles, holding to the slick stone, her head drooping back as a tongue slithered into her sex, making her croak and gasp at the intensity of the pleasure, something she had not experienced since the dream.

But had it been a dream? The woman was real, she existed, and Kira had seen her with waking eyes and was now her guest. The visitation that had haunted her since its occurrence had been no product of her subconscious or imagination.

Razors drifted along her legs, the heat having coaxed the follicles forth, letting her be shaved smooth. The women tended her body, and then proceeded with a more intimate shearing of their charge. Kira stiffened and ensured she kept as still as she could, the worrying drift of the blade around her belly frightening her. She knew she did not really have to worry, for these women were expert in their skill, and not once was she even nicked.

It took a short while to dawn, but it soon became apparent that her beauticians were staying beneath the water for an inordinate amount of time. When they were shaving her legs they never once came up for air, and no bubbles emerged. Did they need to breathe? Was speech the only cause for them to draw breath?

The old saying of 'live fast, die young and leave a good looking corpse' made her giggle to herself, because now it had been indelibly set in a far different order: 'die young, be a good looking corpse, live fast and forever'.

Was it true? Was she actually... dead - or rather, undead? She put a hand to her chest where she felt a slow, almost non-existent heartbeat. Stopping her breath she held it, and found no effects of starvation. It was not easy to hold on and persevere with the experiment, for instinct and tradition were hard laws to break.

She had been performing these biological processes for nineteen years, and the lingering memory made it tough to just quit. But even so, it was true: she didn't need to. Her mind was numbed by the revelation. She had to be dreaming. She just had to be. Vampires didn't exist, so she couldn't possibly be one.

The women arose from the waters, steam slinking into the air from their soaked skin. Taking a wrist each they steered her to one of the poolside plinths. With graceful motions they slipped up and helped her from the waters, rubbing her with luxurious towels and then laying her face down on the pliant surface.

Oil was slipped across her skin, and Kira sighed contentedly as they began to massage her back and legs, working in unison, their hands soft and caring, their expertise sterling.

The mundane pampering began to take a new route once she had been rendered utterly limp beneath their hands.

Slender fingers opened her rear and a face slipped down, reaching under with a long eager tongue to tease her sex with calm and rhythmic attention. Kira closed her eyes, panting and clutching to the front of the slab, quaking on occasion from flares of bliss.

The other woman appeared before her eyes and lowered, settling onto her knees and without expression, moved forward to kiss Kira. Their lips met, and once more passion was set free, the woman stroking Kira's hair, running manicured nails down her cheeks and across her back. On occasion she would pause and offer up a breast to Kira's ravenous mouth, letting her suckle and lap at the unblemished flesh before her.

Only once they had treated their charge to numerous orgasms did they stop, slowing their play, toning it down, bringing Kira slowly from such heady heights, considerate of her every need.

As Kira lay listless and weak, they gathered another robe and helped her into it.

'What's going to happen now?' she asked, staring at the pool as it shuddered and flickered in the feeble light of the hall, her eyes so accustomed to it that it could have been the full glare of the sun.

'You will be taken to an audience with our queen,' replied one of the women.

'What's going to happen to me though?' she asked, concerned as to what her fate was to be.

'That all depends on what you want, miss.'

CHAPTER 3

A sole figure walked with hesitant sloth down the decrepit streets, eyes flitting from shadow to shadow, her senses piqued. The area had been deserted for many years, the buildings and warehouses left to rot until someone bothered to decide their fate.

The sheet of clouds scampered across the sky under a strong wind, affording fleeting glimpses of the heavenly vault beyond. Few streetlights were in operation, rendering the industrial ruins a belated and sinister realm.

Drawing her long coat closer she sniffed the breeze, catching the wafting scents that ruled the air - rot, decay, filth; the stink of pollution and the by-products of the factories, the sickly odours of the tramps who had populated this ideal dwelling ground and then moved on once their number had started to mysteriously disappear. Also, as a faint insidious presence in the air, a hidden spy lurking just at the limits of her senses, was the indisputable rank stench of undeath.

The foul breed were here somewhere, lurking in the shadows, hidden in this graveyard of obsolete machinery. The smell testified that they were present, and with night holding dominion on the skies they would be awake and active.

She needed them awake so she might drag out their secrets, to find her brother. Thanos had been missing for two years now, but she would not give up. She needed an answer, and she would have it.

CHAPTER 4

The women stepped to the pool and with the elegance of professional divers flipped into the air and dove like swans. Their ivory forms moved like knives within the crystal waters, slipping to the walls and vanishing through secluded trapdoors.

Kira watched the waters settle in their passing, wrapping her arms around herself, rekindling the feeling of their embraces, the ghosts of their touch haunting her.

The doors broke open, the foot thick panels drifting apart at a touch to reveal a small escort and a wide corridor beyond.

The two men were tall and sculpted like seasoned athletes, their limbs possessed of brawn, but not distorted into grotesque muscular Goliaths. Not one hair remained visible on them anywhere; their skin was smooth, their chests hairless, their heads utterly bald.

One was white, the other black, but both were equally handsome and both were dressed identically. Heavy boots adorned their feet, rising to their knees, with lacing riding over the zipped front. Latex leggings hugged their anatomy, the close-fitting polished material emphasising their muscles, and showing that their height, looks and muscles were not the only impressive factors about them.

The waistbands of the opaque hose were buried beneath a wide leather belt, almost like that of a weightlifter, except that it was armed with studs, with rings riveted at front, sides and back. The steel circles chimed as they walked, accompanying their stride.

A featureless steel band with a similar collection of four small rings equally set around it enclosed their wrists, and another was locked around their throats. The collar was marked with the symbol of this domain and another identifying mark.

The two brutal sentries accompanied a shapely woman who was slightly more powerful of build than the nymphs of the pool, but her face was far less flippant. Her young features were beautiful, but they were thin, feral and harsh. This intimidating aura was concentrated by a brutal cut of her hair. Shaven at the sides, the top was short, spiked upward and bleached a pure white. Her cosmetics assisted to give her a fierce glower, applied to darken and heighten her malevolent appearance.

Her body was encased within a mesh catsuit, the tight netting making her skin seem darker than the pale white her face decreed it to be. The catsuit left her breasts exposed, her nipples painted to make them almost black, contrasting her surrounding paleness. A collar identical to the others circled her throat, hiding the neck of the catsuit beneath it and giving the woman her own identity mark.

Opera gloves and thigh boots of latex rolled up her limbs, coating each extremity with featureless sheaths or wicked heels. At the top of each two bands tightened them to thigh and bicep, the twin buckles locked into place, trapping her within.

A stern latex corset collected beneath her breasts, riding down to lock over her hips and throw a triangular pane down between her legs. The strap bisected her buttocks as a slim buckled belt that connected to the rear of the corset, allowing her sex and rear to be freed simply by unfastening it.

In her hands she clutched a long crop, the slender woven length ending in a pair of leather tongues. The handle was ivory, carved with whirling designs and embossed with silver.

The procession stopped before Kira, and the woman looked up and down her form in assessment before speaking, her voice stern.

'Kira?'

In reply, she nodded, wondering what was going on.

'I am Cassandra, seneschal for her majesty,' stated the woman, the two men continuing past and turning on their heels to stand on either side of Kira. Meekly she looked up at each of them, towering over her like mountains, their eyes fixed forward with militaristic precision. 'Please come with us, the queen wishes to see you.'

'What does the—' she started and then let out a yelp, jumping onto tiptoe as the crop connected sharply with her flesh. Dropping down Kira rubbed her left buttock, a hot trench pulsating across it.

'You are not to speak without permission,' stated Cassandra with firm authority.

Walking past the trio, she emerged before Kira, looking into her eyes as she continued to nurse the welt. Satisfied that Kira was going to remain mute, she turned and took the lead.

Kira began to step forward, the guards steering her as they trailed behind the seneschal and left the hall. Kira looked to the scenery as it presented itself, but more often than not her eyes dropped back to study the wiggling enticing rear of the seneschal; the fishnet that smothered the perfect cheeks, the thin strap separating them, tight against her anus, the thigh boots twinkling like jet mirrors as she sauntered with fluidity.

Outside the pool chamber the structure of the domain was spacious and extravagant, constructed from pale marble and polished to an ice-like sheen. The wide passage had a domed ceiling, supported further by the pillars running the walls. Sconces such as before provided scant illumination, the candles letting long trickles of frozen wax hang from beneath them.

A black carpet ran the central route, wedged between the base of the avenues of pillars, soft and sumptuous underfoot. Gaps in the pillars offered doors and access to other passages that snaked out into the labyrinthine coils, and as she was led through the halls she started to see fleeting glimpses of the denizens of this dark maze.

Caught in the corners of her eyes they were adorned with latex and leather, sealed within fetishistic attire, watching from the depths, the light flickering on their silver collars and from wicked incisors. They watched covertly, as if afraid to bring themselves to the attention of the seneschal.

The passage ended with a spacious chamber, the walls lined with deep accommodating leather couches and armchairs with ebony tables arranged before them. Standing against the walls were women servants, bound into uniforms designed to restrict and punish their salacious bodies. Sealed within a thick latex leotard, the long sleeves bore the customary metal shackles, allowing their arms to be folded back and then placed up their spine so that their wrists could be locked to their metal collars. The leotards incorporated hoods, the opaque helmets compressing their heads, leaving only a visor for their sorrowful eyes, as well as an aperture for their nose and the silver septum ring piercing it. Their mouths were also given freedom from the hood, but only so that a black ball-gag could keep their jaws wide, a black strap fixing about the hood and keeping it in place.

Also, circles had been removed from the chest of the leotard, allowing their breasts to be forced through, the garment clinging tightly to make them swell. Their nipples had been transfixed with thick silver rings, each ring releasing a silver chain, just as their nose rings did. These strands reached down and grabbed the lip of a silver tray at their waist.

The platter had a raised edge and an indentation that accepted their belly, leaving it resting on their hips. With their nipples connected to the corners and their nose to the centre, the women were forced to bear the tray and were to suffer discomfort whenever they were brought to carry refreshments for whatever guests might be reclining here.

Their lower half was no less untroubled, for tight latex thigh boots held their legs, forcing them to walk on towering ballet boots. Fetters about their ankles connected to the base of a metal pole that lanced straight up and burrowed into their womb. The implement was of a length to prevent them getting free of it, their legs unable to reach out far enough to have the tip fall free, yet similarly it prevented them from sitting down or otherwise slacking in their servile caste. Kept upright by the intruder, locked in irrevocable bondage, the women were a sight as striking and darkly erotic as they were frightening.

A set of doors presented themselves directly before the seneschal, their entire face covered with the symbol she had seen in the pool, the emblem forged from silver and set with gems to make it wink with rainbow colour. On either side of these doors, set in the floor, were two circles of obsidian from which sprouted a female head. Encased in a rubber hood there were no concessions for their eyes or nostrils, only a slit for their tongue to emerge, for they were shoe polishers, held in underground coffins, their heads left free to serve this purpose. Kira wondered what additional bondage had been applied to them beneath the trapdoors, for surely this was not the full measure of their caste.

The seneschal graphically illustrated the truth of their vocation by placing one of her shoes to the obsidian, the clack of the sole landing upon the glass-like material alerting the slave that their services were required. As the servant began to fawn and lap, Cassandra placed a hand beside the portal, spreading her latex-coated palm across an area of blank stone no different to any other. There was a compliant click and a strip of light projected across her face, running vertically and then switching to a panning horizontal assessment.

With her identity confirmed, the doors gave several weighty clunks as the heavy bolts and locks drew back with mechanical whines, and then the portal itself started to crank back, retreating into the wall.

The reinforced vault doors were a metre thick, and revealed a plain box room, the walls and ceiling mirrored, the floor coated with the same black carpet.

The seneschal stood back and stepped in last, turning around to present her back to Kira's gaze once more. The slave below her licked her lips and struggled a little against her confinement, unable to escape, only continue to languish in a position she did not seem overly distressed by. Was she a willing supplicant? Were they all? Was this the nature of the queen's realm? Was this to be Kira's fate?

The doors started to crank shut, and sealed with a damning clang. The polished interior surface of the barrier started to drop away, the lift bearing them down, a smooth stone wall before them rising steadily as they descended.

Kira looked to the mirrors and met the eyes of the seneschal reflected there. The woman released a fleeting smirk, revealing that she had been aware of Kira's licentious study. Immediately Kira looked down at her feet, blushing as she discovered a new intense study of her toes.

With a steady deceleration they came to a halt and a new set of equally secure doors parted, this time revealing a black velvet curtain. As they walked forward the drapes parted at the centre, being hauled back to expose a hall that had Kira gasp with astonishment.

Stepping onto obsidian flagstones, her eyes fluttered about the titanic chamber. The vast oval cathedral reached up with thick pillars to grab the arched ceiling, where detailed frescoes depicted the woman of Kira's dreams surrounded by vampire slaves of every description.

Massive chandeliers hung from the roof, constructed from living people and each identical to the other. A large central ball accepted the eight heads of the slaves, swallowing them as it hung by a thick silver chain that reached back up to the roof. The hub spat free sixteen curling silver tendrils that reached back and grabbed their ankles, stretching them out and spreading them lewdly.

The stretched poses allowed their flesh to be used to hold the huge black candles that provided illumination. The midnight shafts were set on their legs and back, the drool of the lights having reached down and formed about the base, anchoring it to their physique. Excess ran around their bodies and legs, hanging as dark icicles from their underside, reaching down towards the floor in bulbous clusters. Hung in perpetual bondage, revealed by the light that they carried, they also served another function. Their wrists were connected together beneath them by uniform metal bands and a chain dropped from the shackles, the eight chains of each slave congregating under the hub and to a heavy censer. The burden kept their limbs stretched out, stopping them from lifting it even with the cumulative effort of them all.

From the ornate censer wafting blue trails of incense spilled in soft lines, filling the air with a heady aroma. It was a skulking cloying smell, one that tickled the nose, almost undetected, but which lurked through the senses, hiding from more discernible detection, a delicacy even amongst subtle perfumes.

Set against one wall was a dais, the regal stage accessed by a semi-circle of ten steps. The platform atop them held a large exquisite throne, the dark stone affair crafted to resemble flowing organic forms, twisting and cavorting upon each other as they offered velvet cushions for the comfort of its occupant.

The woman had not changed in countenance since Kira's schoolgirl dream, or the previous night. The queen was timeless, without age, save that now she exuded an almost tangible ambience of power; an authority that had not been apparent on the previous occasions Kira had encountered her.

A warped crown of silver and jet curled across her hairline, holding back her hair and flicking out cruel horns and barbs. It was the imperious throne of a tyrant, a dark empress.

Settled on her throne she was sealed within the smooth folds of a rubber outfit. It was a mixture of sleeveless halter neck dress and leotard, the polished skin-tight shell parting at her navel into an ankle length skirt, the missing front section letting a high cut crotch cover her loins. Sculpted thigh boots clung to her legs, and matching opera gloves clung to her arms. The fingers were armed with a detailed armoured claw, each silver articulated digit reaching from knuckle to tip before extending forward another three inches as a curved serrated fang of metal.

It took Kira a moment to notice that other people were present, for the queen was such a vision that Kira's sight had locked to her immediately and had remained unbroken during her long voyage across the throne room to the foot of the steps.

At her left crouched a monstrous form, half hidden behind the throne, dwelling in shadow, revealed more by glowing red eyes than anything else. It was a rabid juxtaposition of wolf and man, its monstrous frame equipped with titanic muscles and a pelt of dark fur. The elongated snout held rows of lethal fangs, a studded leather muzzle strapped in place to ensure safety and reveal subservience.

The clawed hands and feet of the beast were fitted with segmented restraints, a form of manacle that was copied by his spiked collar. A leash reached forward to be slipped over a hook on the arm of the throne, keeping the terrifying pet at the heels of his mistress.

Further back on the right, two men in attire identical to Kira's own guards held a flowing cloak of black latex between them, holding it in readiness for their ruler.

As Kira reached the first step her escort stopped, and she saw another set of forms to her left, these having been previously hidden by her devotion to the strange and marvellous sights offered at the top of the steps.

The male was in the middle era of his twenties, his face light and jovial, but it was an amusement offset by eyes that were cold and consuming. A cigarette drooped from his lips, his deep blue hair swept back over his head with several loose tufts hanging over his face.

Slender of build, he was clad in a dark and extremely expensive looking suit, the cut giving a powerful impression of wealth and the power spawned from it. The pinstriped outer layer was radically opposed by an interior lining of sparkling silver, the material available only through the most furtive clues. A silk shirt of equal darkness lay beneath, loose at the collar.

He could have passed for any mundane idle millionaire save that he held a set of four leashes, each of them connecting to a submissive human hound.

The women were kept on all fours, a belt about their waists throwing chains from the underside to grab their fetters and shackles, stopping them from rising. Plugs were crammed into their bared rears, the toys flinging up moulded tails that stood erect and waggled with their slight motions. Moulded hoods were drawn over their heads, leaving only an oval area free about their eyes. The hoods lifted two triangular points in mockery of ears, and the semblance of a snout pushed from their face to complete the transformation.

The hounds were completely silent, so Kira guessed that the masks were probably also elaborate and effective gags. Then she realised that the muzzles offered no breathing holes. Without the means to steal air, the captives could not spend such currency of words on cries. Was each of these hounds actually a debased vampiress?

Turning her eyes up from this bizarre display, she returned them to the sovereign of this vast domain.

'Your majesty,' stated the seneschal, and bowed deeply until she had dropped to one knee. With the creak of latex the guards followed the motion. Unwilling to cause offence, Kira copied them all, waiting there until she knew whether or not she should rise.

'Arise, my most trusted seneschal,' she announced, her voice rolling through the air as an irresistible wave, her very voice a force of utmost influence. 'Come and join me.'

Cassandra straightened and strode up the steps to stand at the right hand of the woman, pivoting on a heel and fixing her stare down at Kira.

'Guards, you may stand at ease,' attested the woman, leaving Kira the only one still humbled.

'Welcome, Kira, I trust you have found my hospitality to your liking,' said the vampire ruler.

'Yes, your majesty,' replied Kira.

'Then stand up and show us the results,' requested the queen.

Kira looked up with a start to find the woman grinning with wicked intent. Her eyes flitted to the seneschal, the pet, and then the man nearby. The thought of standing nude, on such display, was more than daunting.

'If you wish to insult me with your refusal, I shall have my guards do it and then have you thrown back out on the street,' warned the woman, her tone light but deadly serious. She was no longer the lover who had come to her that night, not the saviour who had rescued her on the rooftop. Here she was empress of the city, and here she could not be questioned.

Standing erect, Kira locked her eyes to those of her queen and opened the belt, staring at nothing but the captivating eyes of the woman. Opening the folds she let the smooth curtain slip down her arms and puddle about her feet.

She stood defiant of the stares, refusing to try and cower or conceal herself.

The queen smiled, her eyes winking with satisfaction before she too joined the rest of the throng in assessing Kira's new appearance. A faint and deep growl reached the outermost extent of Kira's hearing, a sound of longing that slipped the throat of the beast.

'Steady, Thanos, you'll frighten her,' stated the queen, petting his head while the incarnadine eyes of the creature widened as they bored into Kira's revealed frame.

Cassandra shifted uneasily as she examined Kira, something about her appearance setting the woman on edge, her hands furling into fists.

'And what do you think, Duke Khardekk?' she asked the man in the expensive suit. 'Is she not a fine addition to my house?'

'Indeed she is, my queen,' he replied. 'I take it the Malefic Kiss has been given to her?'

'Of course.'

'What is your intention for her?' he asked, an edge of lascivious thirst slipping through his words.

'You want her for yourself? Is that the truth of it, my dear duke?'

'Who could resist such a temptation? I have not seen Maleficence bring out such a beauty in at least a century.'

'Maybe some day, duke. I have plans for this nubile young vampire.' She arose from her throne, stepping forward and letting the two males shift forward, clipping the wide shouldered cloak to her, the voluminous folds trailing behind as she descended the steps, the rubber trickling down like molten coal.

'Of course, that all depends on her decision, doesn't it?' she stated.

'You are giving her a choice, your majesty?' quizzed Cassandra with a start, taken aback by what Kira assumed was an unprecedented offer.

'Yes, though I think I am confident in the reply, no matter what I say. Isn't that so, my little Kira?' She beamed, reaching up one of her talons and hooking it under Kira's chin, lifting her gaze before trailing the cold dagger down and through her cleavage, the chill metal making her shiver.

'Now, if you agree to become my subject, you will also become my slave. My realm is vast, and I have numerous guests and many more slaves. These may use you, they may abuse you, but you will always be mine. Time means nothing to our kind, and should you agree, you will spend eternity knowing what it means to be my property,' she declared, and continued with her speech as she paced around Kira.

'There will be pain and hardship, but there will also be pleasure. If you agree, you will know both in abundance. But before you answer I will enlighten you further. If you agree, you will be taken away and prepared for service by my seneschal. She will see to your initial training, and she may well be cruel if you do not perform as her expectations demand. Your will shall be superfluous. Whatever you say, whatever you regret, it will matter not. You shall have submitted yourself of your own choice, and there will never be any retreating from that decision. Have you any questions before you decide?'

Kira turned and met the eyes of the queen, her lips trembling with eagerness, but there was something she needed to know first, to reassure her that she was doing the right thing.

'What if I refuse your offer?' she asked.

'You will be released to continue your existence on the surface world,' she stated flatly. 'You will take your chances with the herds, the hunters, and the rivals.'

Kira knew she wouldn't stand a chance in the normal world. Here she would be protected and loved, taught to please the queen. She did not know what the details might be, but she was eager to learn. The sight of the other slaves had awoken an interest, kindled a perverse desire to be forced into these lots, and she knew what answer she had to give.

'I want to be your slave,' she declared.

'You are sure?'

'Yes, your majesty.'

'Then we shall seal our bargain with a kiss,' she revealed, and as Kira moved forward, puckering her lips, the woman stepped back and pointed to her booted toes.

'No, not there, here,' she stated.

Kira smiled with satisfaction and folded onto her knees, crouching before the ultimate ruler of her fate and placing devoted kisses to the footwear. The taste of the latex upon her lips would be her comfort in the time of training she was about to face.

'Take her away, seneschal,' the queen ordered, her smile wide, her face filled with delight as Cassandra marched back down the steps.

'Guards, bring her here,' she commanded, and instantly strong arms grabbed Kira's biceps, bringing her to her feet and marching her roughly towards the side of the room. All trace of civility had gone the moment the words of acceptance left her lips. She was a slave, and was to be treated as one.

CHAPTER 5

Taken to a section of wall, the woman placed a hand to it and with a sudden groan the stone blocks started to swing inward, the secretive portal opening onto a bleak corridor.

The passage was painted blue, with neon strip lights overhead and a lush black carpet. Led down the corridor Kira observed other doors set in the walls, the black featureless slabs reflecting her as a distorted ghost while she was driven deeper into the bowels of this domain.

The seneschal slapped her hand to the wall beside a door and the portal whirred aside, exposing a plain chamber beyond, a set of cabinets placed against one wall. Carried in, she was taken to the centre of the room and released. She slouched immediately, rubbing her upper arms, the grip of the sentries having been fierce.

'Return to your posts, guards,' ordered the woman.

'Yes, seneschal,' they humbly replied, bowing deeply and then withdrawing together.

'Assistants!' exclaimed the keeper of the queen's servants, and at this mere verbal demand four panels on the wall opposite the cabinets suddenly revolved, revealing four bound forms.

They could have been women, but they could have been either gender for there was no flesh to be seen to confirm which they were. They were like rubber golems, creatures forged from the smooth impermeable material that seemed to be so prevalent in taste in the queen's ranks. Were these fellow Nosferatu, or something else? Were they mortal? If so, such sweltering folds would be even more unbearable. But even to those without body heat, they would be terribly restrictive and uncomfortable.

A catsuit of the fabric encompassed every aspect of them, enclosing arms, hands, and head, the hood offering two tiny eyeholes, their faces a little overlong and telling that they were radically gagged beneath. Another pair of vents at the nostrils let them wheeze softly through the openings, revealing that these were not fellow undead, they were some other sort of being. Could they be mortals?

Holes at the wrists let their rings emerge, so that the restraints could be used even through the dense fabric.

A larger collar had been set over their normal displays of ownership, and like a neck brace it kept them up and to attention, unable to move.

A brutal corset compressed them into an absurd hourglass, crushing them before a hobble skirt squeezed their legs together, dropping to their ankles where a vague glimpse of their leggings remained before the incorporated high-heeled boots took over.

Each of them was held in place by metal bands that emerged from the walls, pinning them down. The bonds flashed across their wrists, neck, thighs and waist, leaving them unable to get free as they languished in their dismal storage compartments.

'You, furniture duty!' she snapped, pointing at one of the anonymous forms, and simultaneously all the bands jolted back into their housings, freeing the serviles.

The rubber spectre shuffled forward with tiny hampered steps and then settled onto her hands and knees before the seneschal.

Used as a seat, the slave remained motionless as the woman settled into her back, crossing her thigh booted legs and reclining slightly, her crop across her lap.

'Now Kira, before we start your lessons, we had best get you ready and into your lot,' revealed the seneschal. 'The first part of your initiation will be the addition of your basic uniform. Once applied, these items will be with you for the rest of your existence and will mark you as the property of the queen.

'Perform the fitting,' ordered the woman, and the slaves started to shuffle across and past Kira.

Opening a cabinet they removed collar, fetters and cuffs, the items prepared in readiness for Kira's enslavement.

'Present your wrists,' commanded the woman, and Kira lifted them to receive their decorations. The solid cuffs were in two halves, each having a slot and a notched lock protruding from one side. It was clear that once the barbs were slipped into the waiting housing and closed, the only way to gain freedom from the shackles would be to destroy them. The foam rubber interior was closed about each of her joints, and the moulded items locked to her, the fit absolutely perfect so that it gripped firmly and could not be removed. The four rings around each jingled as she shook them and put her hands by her side, readying to gain her slave collar.

The restraints for her feet were identical, and two of the women awkwardly settled by her ankles to snap them in place.

'Lift your hair,' ordered Cassandra, and as she complied the steel band was fitted in place by the third woman, encircling her neck, marking her forever as a slave.

'Also, until you are deemed trustworthy not to interfere with the property of her majesty, you will be kept enforceable chaste,' she added, glaring at Kira.

'Put her in the belt,' she said, and the controlled servant who had applied the collar scampered back to the cabinets to retrieve a set of polished steel bands.

With a worried expression Kira watched as the intimate incarceration was prepared. What would chastity do to her if she were held in this sexual slavery? To be constantly aroused and tormented and denied was perhaps the worst torture she could conceive of. But what could she do? There was to be no denying this imposition.

The jaws of the waistband were opened and enclosed around her. A shove had it snap shut, compressing her waist and resting on her hips.

The same woman responsible for this then lifted her hands, saving her comrades the extreme difficulty of rising to help her. Producing a short length of chain with locking clips at either end, she threaded it through the ring at the back of Kira's collar. The women beside her took her wrists and started to fold them up her back, presenting the ringlets on the cuffs to the waiting anchors. With her arms contorted and her shackles resting at her shoulder blades, the locks captured them, keeping her in this vexing pose, unable to do anything save wiggle her fingers and shrug her arms from side to side.

Once this restriction was applied, the other pair used deft fingers to locate hidden panels in the floor. These small pits flipped up their lids and the women drew out clips that were affixed to stout chains. The holes paid out slack and with a snap, the hooks were set to her ankle bands.

Immediately there was a cranking grind of movement from within the pits and Kira was alarmed to see the chain being devoured by them. With some panicked tugs she wrenched at her collar and feet, trying to get free, but there was nothing to be done.

The slack was lost and her feet were slowly drawn apart, spreading her legs as she toppled and swayed, the third woman remaining to assist her should her balance fail completely.

Spread wide, Kira wriggled impotently as fingers brushed her rear, applying a gelatinous sludge, greasing her rear and womb. With squeaks of shock she felt the fingers slide in, the latex smoothed digits lubricating her both inside and out. The hands were warm, the body heat and its long companionship with the rubber had left the latex contrasting Kira's own cool flesh. These women were not Nosferatu.

'What's going on?' she protested, worried at what was to follow.

'Hold!' berated the woman, rising from her seat and walking behind Kira. She tried to look over her shoulder to see what was being done, but any attempt affected her balance too greatly.

There was a hum of displaced air being thrown around a speeding stalk, and Kira released an agonised screech of shock. A searing line had been placed across her rear, connecting both buttocks, filling them with fire.

The assistant before her grabbed her shoulders before she fell, her equilibrium crippled by the fierce stroke.

'What was that for?' she complained, and then screeched again as another stroke was applied.

'Stop, please, stop!' she wailed, and then screeched as a third truculent hack sank into the soft flesh of her rear, rippling the tissues and filling them with harrowing.

'What do you want of me?' she wailed, sobbing, tears running down her cheeks as she battled vainly against her bondage.

Again she yelled as she was punished, gritting her teeth, leaning into the arms of the assistant and weeping onto the woman's warm rubber skin.

'Are we finished?' commented the seneschal.

Kira was too beset by the havoc in her rear to answer, a failing that served her well as the reason for the attack was divulged.

'You speak only when given permission or addressed. And when you do, you refer to me as seneschal. All others of stature shall be lord, or lady.'

Again the crop scorched her rear, making her jerk and croak with misery.

'Understand, slave?'

'Yes, seneschal,' she grizzled.

'Much better, now continue with the fitting,' she demanded, pacing back before Kira, and before re-seating herself on the other humble slave she treated the servant to a virulent hack, the broad sweep and ferocious strike offered so it would eat through the absorbing folds of the latex. The slave flinched and a moan slipped through her hood, her eyes remaining tightly closed for a long minute as she rode the storm of pain.

The two women below her shuffled inward and set the crotch band in place, whereupon Kira felt the two slim rods aiming inward into her womb and anus. With a brutal shove the device rammed upward. The staffs slammed into her and the rubber interior clapped between her legs. Lifted from her feet by their strength, the chains stopped her ascent and the band slipped its teeth into the awaiting holes. With clicks they were grabbed and she dropped back onto her feet.

Gasping, she tried to bite back her words, the petition of its removal riding through her thoughts. It was terribly tight, crushing her abdomen, but this had to be because of her splayed pose; once she was free of it the belt would be less strenuous. And besides, she had to be quiet; she had to be a good slave, to accept her training. It was what she had to do in order to once more be with the queen. She had to be perfect, to gain a position close to the queen, so she would never be apart from her again.

With the creak of her latex garments Cassandra arose and strolled before Kira, the assistants withdrawing and leaving her standing alone, spread by her bondage, her abdomen flicking with pangs of distress. Her arms were aching from their warped configuration, but even with stern hauls she could do nothing to break their containment.

Kira looked slowly up, her gaze moving across the firm thigh boots of her captor, the fishnet, the strip of latex concealing her crotch, the corset compressing, worn like armour to protect from submissive slaves like her. Longing flashed through Kira's dead heart as she crossed Cassandra's breasts, dreaming of touching the mesh-sheathed mounds, to hold them, to grovel and kiss the inviting black painted tips. After this alluring vision, she turned to meet the woman's gaze.

Cassandra's eyes were cold, intense, locked to hers, a thousand motives and thoughts rushing through her mind. The woman was most agitated, that much was certain, but why? What had Kira done? Had her disobedience irked her already to a point where the woman was furious with her performance?

A hand reached up, the midnight stems of her fingers grabbing Kira's chin and holding it tightly. She was being scrutinised, her face studied as the woman concocted rationales, plotted and schemed, setting down paths and avenues to explore or thwart. It was a scary but strangely reassuring notion, to have her life set down in stone for her, taken away and left in the utter command of another, subject to whimsical twists and turns.

'Gag her,' came the decree, and the spectres of latex were once more brought to action.

A hood was grabbed, the latex bag without any feature or vent, its neck armed with buckles to make it airtight. Kira started to panic at the very sight of it, for she was still having trouble accepting her lack of need to draw breath. To be introduced to it so forcefully was frightening. But fortune smiled as Cassandra saw the distress riding beneath her thin veneer of calm and decided to show clemency.

'Use a normal variety for now,' she ordered, and instead of the helmet, a thick contraption was delivered to her face. As she panted and wriggled against her bonds, her mouth was forced open by latex fingers. The thick plate at the front was moulded to gather in her chin and her lower face, and flung buckled rubber strips out from its perimeter. Two flaccid bulbs hung on the inside and led the path into her maw, laying slack on her tongue as the plate was pressed to her lips. An inverted Y ran the sides of her nose, joining and rolling over her head to connect first to straps riding over her cheeks and temples, and then to one that traversed the back of her head.

Using forceful hauls the buckles chimed and with a murmur the elasticised straps were drawn terribly tight, making the entire apparatus squeeze her skull in an uncompromising hold. Oval bulbs were forced onto the twin nozzles protruding from the front, and in the eager fists of the women they started to inflate.

Her tongue slapped at the swelling balloons, and was slowly deprived of space in which to move. Caught under the swelling orbs they grabbed it and forced it into the floor of her mouth, stamping it down and making Kira gag and retch as their tips touched the back of her throat and then stopped. Choking on the forceful gag, her eyes bulged and she flashed her gaze about. The sensation was disturbing yet delightful, the feel of being treated so casually, gagged, her voice taken from her by her owners.

'Use the trapeze on her,' the seneschal softly said, and walked away without further word, returning to her seat and observing Kira's continuing bondage lessons.

The assistants moved in and fingers slid into the small pits that held her ankles. A soft muted click reached out and identical fixtures located above her sprung open. Two chain lengths dropped and with a chatter of metal on metal they jerked to a halt, swaying steadily, both lines of chain bearing a locking clip.

One of the assistants went to the cupboards with hampered steps and retrieved a length of rope and a short pole, the stout length fixed with a hoop at either end and just wide enough to slip between the chains. Snapping the anchors to it, the stern trapeze was set in place.

Kira resisted as her collar was grabbed, a woman threading rope through the fastening at the front and dragging it out to the rings of her feet. Taking in the excess she drew it in, pulling Kira over the pole.

The cold steel touched her belly and she started to wriggle, trying to get her arms free, snorting in fright. She wanted to submit, to prove herself to these veterans of perversity, but she was afraid and inexperienced.

The pull continued, and folding at her belly she was drawn over the hovering strut. Her feet left the floor, pulled tight, her collar being the other anchor. Stretched over the pole, her arms twisted up her back, she was rendered immobile with her breasts hanging and her hindquarters struggling in the air.

The discomfort in her stomach was great, but her trepidation as to what other treatment she was to receive was a far greater matter weighing upon her immediate thoughts.

'Bring me a paddle,' ordered Cassandra, rising from her seat and pacing slowly behind Kira's vulnerable bottom.

An assistant shuffled to the drawers and removed a leather paddle, the weapon broad and fitted with a gripped handle. At the sight of it being delivered past her to the awaiting woman, Kira's breath was rushing in and out, her body shaking and trembling, tears welling in her eyes and slipping down her cheeks as saliva gathered into a pool in her mouth.

A long pause followed where Kira closed her eyes and shuddered, then came the steady beat of stilettos on the floor as Cassandra walked around to her front, patting the implement into her palm. The woman again squatted before the suspended prisoner, and an eyebrow raised in questioning at the sight of Kira's obvious dismay.

'What is the matter?' Cassandra wondered, and followed Kira's eyes as they flashed to the paddle. 'You've never been punished before?' she quizzed.

Kira shook her head as best she could with the collar dragging her down and towards the floor. There had been other occasions, but not ones that counted. Sure, she had been savaged by a bully with a ruler, but that was far different to this brand of erotic punishment.

Cassandra smiled and tutted, reaching up and running soothing knuckles down the tear-streaked face of Kira. 'Don't worry, it is necessary,' she crooned, continuing the gentle touch, a strange consideration considering the havoc she was about to apply to Kira. 'I won't be too harsh with you, but you need to be taught your place. Discipline is very important for slaves.

'Do you want to be punished?' she asked.

Kira stalled for a moment and then nodded. She needed it, she needed to feel that she was owned, and the paddle was a certificate of authenticity she would gladly invite and then revile.

'Good slave,' attested Cassandra, rising up and walking behind the girl, continuing to clap the stern device into her gloved palm as she went.

The smooth material of the treated hide laid itself gently to Kira's rear and started to rub in steady swirls, sliding easily against her rounded rear, the cheeks spread by the intruding metal path of the chastity belt.

The weapon jumped back, and suddenly the interior plugs of the belt sprung into life, tickling her clitoris, surging into her, filling her as they swelled and contracted like living things. Kira wailed from the pleasure, and there was a hum as the wide weapon beat the air with a deep tone and then sounded sternly against both of Kira's buttocks. A blast of heat and shock rolled through the skin and Kira spasmed, wriggling and choking into her gag.

The stinging flashes started to dwindle and the paddle again started to draw soothing circles on her rear. The teasing caress of the belt continued, settling to a slower rhythm, drawing out her pleasures. Squeezing her muscles to the plugs she closed her eyes, snorting in fits, her pain melting into exquisite pleasure.

'So you are a virgin?' Cassandra purred, and a hand came in to join the instrument, her fingers running down the smooth steel strip between her buttocks. 'You've never tasted the sting of a weapon across these delicate little mounds?

'It's true, isn't it?' she pondered, and the paddle swept out before slamming back again, causing Kira to fling herself against her bonds and struggle in the restraints.

As the pain dwindled so did her fight to get free, and as Cassandra returned to bestowing caresses Kira panted and braced herself for the next stroke, the chastity belt still toying with her most tender zones.

'Well, it matters not, it changes nothing,' she stated, and slapped another ferocious stroke into Kira's rear. 'You see, I saw the way her majesty was looking at you, and the time she spent arranging your seduction, and I've seen it before.'

Kira's skin was now hot, flicking with prickly riots of mayhem, but the belt was making her start to seep into the ordeal, to relish it, the heady heat of her lust accepting the fires of the paddle's impacts.

'When that damned lupine came into her hands she forgot all about me, and devoted all her time to training it,' she spat, her temper rising, making her strokes fall with more severity than before. The initial pleasant façade of tolerance she had displayed had snapped, the issuing of punishment had let it escape and it was starting to run rampant.

'So now I have another rival for her attention? No!' she hissed, and applied another swat, making Kira choke and squirm, the intensity of the pain making her ecstasy all the sweeter. 'I won't tolerate it, not again. I already have that damned werewolf, and now some fledgling vampiress? You think you'll take my position? You think you can be seneschal and take Dana from me?' Another sweeping slap was delivered, and another. The woman sent resounding smacks through the room, each one making the slender bound frame of Kira thrash and writhe in jeopardy, totally unprepared for the severity of the castigation.

'Well think again, little Kira. I'll not let you usurp me without a fight. Tangle with me and you'll regret it for eternity.' She continued to spank Kira with all her might, driving her deeper into harrowing. The influence of the belt continued to steal her towards climax, offering her a paradox of whether to hate or love this abuse.

'Come on - weep, cry, suffer, this is what you wanted!' she shouted, her arm flashing back and forth. 'This is what you deserve!'

Screeching into her gag, unable to get any sound save gurgles through its defiant walls, Kira was lost to panic as she was punished. The strokes eluded her count as all she had was suffering to dwell on and the rapture blooming within her loins, vying for control over her mind.

Slapping kiss after slapping kiss fell, and Kira started to pray that the woman continue, hoping that the belt and the punishment were related, for if the woman stopped, then would the belt not stop to? She was too close to climax, the relief offering itself as just moment's away, growing closer with every vibrating thrust of the dildos within her.

Choking into her gag she closed her eyes, screwing up her face beneath the tentacles of the gag, wailing for her final release. A stern spank of the weapon made her rear ripple and with an orgasmic detonation every muscle flung to attention, straining against the bonds as her battle for freedom became a wild dance within them. Flying into paroxysms, each swat of the paddle added to the effects, the toys still dragging out every measure of her pleasure, her mind boiling from the intensity of the sensations.

The attack stopped and she went limp, hanging over the pole, her body touched with a sheen of sweat, her rear throbbing with an internal fulgent pulse. She had not felt an orgasm of such intensity since her night with the queen, aeons ago during another life. Was she already attuned to such algolagnic vices? Was this the reason for the interest of the queen? Had she seen some untended seed within Kira, one she intended to nourish and let bloom?

Sobbing and elated at the same time, Kira was overcome with the strangest sense of purging, of having received justice and been set free of a guilt she bore but had not ever realised. The beating granted the oddest sense of exorcism, one that had her head wafting in giddy heights of intoxication. It was like being drunk on pain, as though the heady brew of her torment was a drug more powerful than any manmade pharmaceutical.

The queen wanted her to suffer for a reason, because she wished it. All the slaves being tormented here, all the people in bondage and terrible incarceration, it was so her majesty could know that it existed. She could lay back and think about all the pain her slaves were undergoing, just for her, just because she wished it. It was a reassuring thought, one that soothed Kira even in the face of Cassandra's jealous tantrums.

What was she to do? What was this woman planning? Could she fail in her training? Could she be rejected if this woman made her fumble in her goal to be a slave for the queen? She doubted that Cassandra would allow her an opportunity to be one of the queen's personal servants, but there had to be a way.

'Put her in an isolation suit,' ordered Cassandra, and walked back to her waiting seat. Handing her paddle to an assistant she settled in, brushing a few dislodged strands of hair from her face. 'I want this little viper to think about her fate.'

The assistants moved in immediately, their rubber gloved hands working with haste. The chains and rope were set free, the pits drawing them back out of the way but not removing them from view, hinting that they were still to play a part in her sorrow.

A cabinet was opened and piles of rippling black latex were removed and set beside her as she was extracted from the trapeze.

Kira collapsed to the floor, her legs weak and trembling, her arms resonating with internal havoc from having been kept under control for so long. Every shift of her abdomen made her sensitised openings move against the intruding dildos, bringing new flicks of sharp bliss through her body. Drained, she gently rubbed her scorched rear and watched the assistants prepare her for her encasement.

Manoeuvring her as though she were a lifeless mannequin, the women started to thread a set of tight latex stockings up her legs, the material more dense than any normal clothing, making any movement a battle.

The rings of her fetters were pulled through slots at her ankles, and a severe straitjacket of uncompromising rubber was drawn up, its sealed arms flapping, the many buckles and straps chiming and swaying like reeds.

'You have a lot to learn here, slave, and I'll be glad to make sure you learn your lessons flawlessly,' promised the seneschal.

Intimidated by the sight of the awful garment, Kira started to shuffle away, only to have her hair grabbed and used as the means to keep her still and deliver her into the garment. As she was held the strands were gathered up into a high ponytail and fixed with a stern elastic band, keeping them there and making the roots growl as they were stretched by the pull upon them.

The fist forced her forward, and wincing she followed it, her arms still too weak to offer any real resistance.

The back of the attire was unzipped and opened, and her arms slipped into the waiting sleeves. The jacket slithered back, the cool latex interior riding along her limbs. Then she saw the hood that hung before her eyes, the sight of the loose bag growing immediately more close as it was taken up and forced over her head, the back of it opened from neck to crown.

The helmet offered her nothing, not even nostrils, and she started to panic as she was forced to draw restricted breath through the meagre chinks of the garment. Once they sealed it though, there would be no such access, and even though she knew she had no physical need to breathe, the idea of suffocation still frightened her.

With a groan of debauched passion Kira answered the feel of the smothering jacket being zipped up. Two of the spectres drew it in, making the latex stretch across her front, squeezing her breasts as the other zipped it up. The compression onto her torso made it distinct with every hampered breath she stole, the latex compressing her ribs and squeezing her belly inwards as the jacket served another role - that of a stringent corset.

'I'm going to make you adore being utterly submissive. I'm going to make it so that the very thought of control never enters your head.'

One woman each helped themselves to an arm, holding it firmly and tightening the buckled straps that ran the length of the limbs, the strips placed only to make the embrace of the jacket more forceful. The third woman busied herself with the laces of the back, the criss-crossing path of the thick cord laid over the zip, adding further to the power of this fist of a garment.

Kira's breath hissed out as the jacket drew ever tighter, the feel of it stoking a libidinous haze. When they started to draw her arms in she almost fainted from the pleasure of being bound thus.

The women crossed her arms and pulled them back behind her, each hauling at a limb while the third kept hands in Kira's back, fighting the strength of the other two so as to stop Kira from falling.

'I'm going to break you, Kira, turn you into the most grovelling simpering vampire slut the world has ever seen,' said Cassandra, and there were two soft snaps as she was locked into the classic configuration of this most non-standard straitjacket.

Two of the women began to apply the chest straps that ran around her body, adding even more stretched belts to her sentence, enclosing her within a terrible cocoon of compressing bands.

Whimpering from a mixture of fetishistic glee and actual discomfort, Kira was suddenly thrown into jeopardy as the helmet was zipped up, pressing tightly to her face. The zip ran straight down after leaving a small hole through which her red hair exploded forth as a curled plume.

Instinctive panic took over and she flung herself against the numerous bars of her prison, trying to get free and haul this asphyxiating mask from her face. As she felt the laces being tightened over the zip, further compressing her skull, she started to settle, the burning angst of her denial fading away as no ill effects manifested.

'When I'm finished her majesty will congratulate me on a job well done, and whatever plans she has for you will have to be forgotten, because all you'll be able to do is crave punishment and bondage.'

The women loosened their hold on Kira, and once she had calmed down they continued their task of transforming her into a latex zombie such as they.

The hood was sealed tight, the zip of her spine and her head being connected by a padlock. Then a stout collar was applied, the rigid walls of the band propping her head up, craning her neck out and keeping it there where she could do nothing save maintain the position. Blinded by the latex, her nose still bloated with the smell of it, unable to breathe or speak, her skin able only to feel the pressure of this latex tomb, her only sense left was hearing, and even that was muffled by the thick sheet stretched over her ears.

Kira was lifted onto her feet, the crimp of the latex to her legs as they sought to support her making her shiver with delectation. There were clicks of metal on metal from directly above her as fastening grabbed an anchor atop her hood she had not noticed before, its existence hidden by the voluminous folds of the jacket. Other clicks again grabbed her ankle bonds.

'Now, I'm going to leave you to this entrapment. The smothering arms of this bondage are extensions of my own. You suffer here because I wish it, and when I return, we'll see what else I can do to bring you down, my pretty little slave.'

The whirring effort of engines started to seep through her latex hood, and the chains started to again withdraw, pulling at her head and feet. The hood pressed more ferociously to her face as the summit was pulled at, and then she was being lifted into the air by this point. Struggling as her feet left the floor and were again pulled apart to splay her, she fought the brutal clench of the jacket, trying to do something to aid her plight as the chains continued their drag, racking her in the air.

There was the sound of a door shutting and silence fell as she was left suspended and helpless, no sound reaching her save her own stolid heartbeat.

Lost in the dark world of her own latex prison, Kira dwelt on all that had happened of late. How radically her life had changed from that which she had known.

But her meditations were cut short as the chastity belt once more sparked into frenetic activity. With a hiss of rhapsody she shook within the stringent bonds, expelling the last of her air and leaving herself unable to draw in any more, effectively muting any noise she might attempt to make.

Going slack within her bondage she felt the swell of pleasure slowly growing to a peak, being cultivated by the continuing toil of the belt. Closer and closer she was carried, opening her arms to the imminent orgasm.

Without warning the belt stopped, having been taught through her previous session exactly the behaviour to expect before she succumbed to release. Sensors upon the dildo had gauged that she was on the very brink of climax, mere seconds from it, and thus it had spitefully shut down.

Unable to scream, Kira flew into distraught spasms, her most fanatic thrashing barely being noticed because of her stretched position. Squeezing her orifices to the rods she tried to gain the last shuffle, the last mere wiggle that would carry her over the brink. But instead she merely teetered on the edge, hanging for a moment before she started to trundle back down the slopes of ecstasy. Sobbing, she felt herself calming, every moment of delay carrying the final result further and further from her clutches.

Only once she was utterly subdued again, hanging helpless, the pain of her predicament punishing her limbs, compressing her terribly, did the belt restart. Once more it started to tickle her clitoris, the shafts thrusting in and out of their own volition as she flexed within the rubber tomb, revelling in its delightful crushing hug upon her.

She hoped this time she would gain the release she craved, but as she again neared the potent end to her molestation the accursed machine shut off, mindlessly obeying its programming. Venting curses through her mind she again tried to finish herself off, but the belt was just too tight, she could do nothing save hang and sob as the pinnacle of her pleasure again started to slip through her fingers. Every time the belt did this to her it fed the swell of her lubricious hunger. Every denied orgasm dropped another potion of weight, making this ravenous appetite grow and grow, and as it swelled, so to did her love of vice. She was being relentlessly attuned to be addicted to her bondage, for as her frustration grew so did her relish for being confined, sealed in bondage, making her fantasies of freedom turn slowly to dreams of having Cassandra come back and apply a harsh hand to her rear.

It was a frustration that had her furious, but also delighted. Cassandra was a cruel mistress, someone with a grudge against her, someone who would abuse her without relent, make her commit the most heinous acts of degradation. With the promise of being made to relish such distress, Kira was intently happy. Life with the queen would have been wonderful, but to be the property of such a diabolic mistress as the seneschal, to be her property and treated with disdain and constant punishment, was a fate she was besotted with. The paddling, the threats, and now her bondage, it had shown her her true lot. Was it part of the training? Had it brought this trait out in her already as Cassandra had intended? Or had she already been well attuned to such vices, and Cassandra had merely awakened what had always been there? In such a case, what would her eventual fate be? If training to turn a normal person into a grovelling sex slave were applied to one who was already well inclined to it, what sort of beast would it create?

The belt started its work once more, and Kira sighed and resigned herself to being frustrated again. Images of Cassandra clad in latex, her slender body pale and full of power, her cruel smile as she stood with a cane, a crop, a paddle, any weapon Kira could conjure in her mind. As the belt continued, Kira dreamt that she was being punished again, the searing flash of pain through her rear as the weapon was applied. But as the pleasure began to mount, another sensation started to creep into her. There was a cramp in her chest, eating at her insides and occasionally tightening her limbs. Her throat ached as though dry and requiring water, and there was a tickling in the front of her jaws.

CHAPTER 6

A faint rustle of movement snatched Corin's attention, causing her to hold her reactions in check and pretend she had failed to notice the near inaudible clue to the proximity of another.

They were intending to defend themselves instead of flee. Excellent. She wanted to face them head on instead of chasing them down like the vermin they were, and besides, a direct confrontation might give her access to their leaders, a capture that could let her question as to the whereabouts of her brother.

The elders had still not decided what course of action to take and were still discussing it, calling in representatives from the other tribes to make the choice. It was taking a long time. Some sort of epoch was dawning. The tribes of the Wyrm were growing, mounting some sort of plot. Prophecy and omen spoke of something dark brooding on the horizon, the dawning of an age of darkness only hinted at in their oldest and most venerated texts. With such matters occupying them, the running of internal matters of the tribes was all but forgotten and low on any agenda.

But while her fellows prepared for an apocalyptic war, Corin had remained to exact her blood vengeance on the Nosferatu. She was going to slay as many as she could in the hope of uncovering her lost sibling, or by forcing the vampire kind to cut their losses and give him back lest the genocidal female butcher them all.

Throughout the days since Thanos had vanished, she had tracked them down and entered their lairs, hacking down their ghouls and protectors before entering their precious sanctums and rending the occupants as they slept the sleep of death itself. But she could not find the major powers, the ones who were more likely to be responsible for the kidnapping than the small pockets of fledglings she unearthed. The oldest monsters were well hidden and protected and she would need the help of her tribe to find them and mete out their well-earned and long deserved fate.

But as she hunted, so too had others, and not all of them were without success. Occasionally she ran into human vampire hunters, and when she could she communicated with the less zealous - trading information.

There had been an uprising amongst the vampire ranks. A beast was loose, butchering those of the great vampire houses, the ones who had carved up the city and who ruled it from the darkness.

The lowly groups and individuals were going untouched, these vampire citizens of the city being forsaken as some sort of demon assassin was shattering the great vampire lords. There were numerous rationales to support what was doing it - a hater of vampires, someone betrayed by them, or a blundering sorcerer who had conjured a Wyrm demon that had got lose and which now wreaked such havoc. Or perhaps it was a renegade follower of Gaia, a shaman taking the fight to the darkest of enemies. Also there was the possibility of a dark lupine or tribe of such aberrations allied to the Wyrm, seeking to overthrow the vampire kind and take the city as their own.

Until she knew what was going on she would continue to exorcise her choler through murder, though it was not really a crime to give the breed the death they had cheated for so long. The shells she faced had died many years ago when first fed the blood of their sires, and to slay a walking corpse who flaunted the laws of nature to extend its cancerous existence was no felony, it was richly exacted justice.

The shadows began to seethe with movement, the occupants keeping out of sight, the vaguest minutiae being enough to warn her of their presence.

Subduing a smile of glee she tensed her body, regulating her breathing as she anticipated the rigors and joys of close quarter combat.

With a hiss of displaced air the enemy emerged and charged, seeking to catch her by surprise with an attack to the rear, sweeping in from behind, fangs bared, weapons drawn and readied to kill.

Keeping exact track of their whereabouts through sound alone, at the last moment she whirled, unleashing the unstoppable raw power of her full form. Her flesh rippled and rode out, unfolding its secret stores of muscles and skin, making the seams of her clothing shriek as it was pushed beyond tolerance to explode into rags and sundered strips. Bones bucked and solidified into struts as dense as hardened steel. Razor-edged claws ripped free of her fingertips as flesh-rending fangs sprung from an elongating snout. A deep crimson glow lit

41

up from within her eyes, the wells of light flashing with rancour.

The leading vampire was wrenched aside as her talons ripped into his throat, tearing open the meat and gouging open the entire area. After a brief moment of flight through the air he struck the street, bounced, and rolled into the gutter, clawing at the massive crater as a deluge of blood drooled through his fingers, the white glistening bone of his vertebrae clearly visible.

The two behind him did not waver in their fanatic assault. Their ragged attire gave the rough appearance of vagrants, a disguise to let them move and feed unopposed and unnoticed amongst this most uncared for social caste. Their resources were frugal, and thus could not gather a decent arsenal of silver weapons, therefore knives were their armaments, the weapons crafted from the metal so inherently caustic to her body.

They looked ferocious with wicked incisors and snarling faces, but she could see fear in their eyes. Their ranks were under attack, and they perhaps thought her to be the assassin that had felled so many noble houses. Were these really a lowly group, or were they lofty vampire elite, in hiding, trying to evade the fate so many of their fellows had already been given by this anonymous arch-nemesis of the undead?

A vicious stab lanced at her ribs from the left. A deft weave had the gleaming tip dancing through nought but air. Clapping a fist to the outstretched wrist she locked the other to his throat and ripped him into the air and into an overhead arc that smashed him face first into the ground. His body jolted with a violent throe as he crumbled, the violent signal of his features into the hard rock eclipsing the growl of the second opponent as he slashed at her in a wide arc.

'I'll drain your carcass dry, wolf bitch!' he roared.

Dropping into a crouch she let the thin knife speed overhead, caught upon its own momentum to sail far past its target.

'You want blood? Try your own!' she hissed, and a truculent upward kick from her retained position drove her heel into his ribs, the ferocity casting him up and into the air as the bones parted with a moist pop, her clawed toes marking his chest with deep scratches.

The vampire touched down and sought to recover his balance with a few staggered steps backward, fighting off the pain as his ancient flesh started to heal the trauma.

'Bitch whore,' he rasped with venom, a punctured lung bringing thick lines of meagre red drool over his lips.

With the immediate threat negated for a brief moment, Corin raised an elbow and dropped back into a retreating roll, smashing the poised joint to the neck of the fallen undead, shattering the discs and wringing a violent paroxysm from the stirring creature, vastly delaying his rise to regenerated normality.

The tumble brought her to her feet on the opposite side of the felled beast. The other vampire was still recovering his balance, so she opted to end the beast at her clawed feet. An underhand thrust slipped her talons into the soft viscera of his belly before sliding upward upon a savage slash, eviscerating the carcass. Immediately, it started to putrefy at an incredible rate as its undead life faded.

The second vampire charged with an ascending growl of fury upon seeing the wash of glistening offal pour free of the opened abdomen, the entrails slipping around the feet of the lupine.

Behind this creature she could spy the first attacker rising to his feet, the torn hole of his throat already congealed and starting to heal, his animated frame able to function fully even with this horrendous damage to a vital area.

Focusing upon the two creatures she almost failed to hear the twin hums of spinning blades as they cavorted through the air. Instinct kicked in as soon as her ears detected it, flicking her aside and turning the lethal assault into a nick from one pointed ear. The arctic pang from the silver made her wince and she turned her attention back to the fray.

Two dull thumps sounded a second after she had dodged, the silver tipped shuriken having sunk into the chest of the vampire before her. The creature choked, blood slipping over his lips as he started to pull the barbed teeth of the star from his ribs.

'Charltos, you fucking idiot!' he cursed, scowling as the metal fangs tore at his flesh, the process of removing the deeply embedded weapons little more than picking a splinter from his flesh.

Corin ran forward into their midst, to make their comrade pause lest he hit his fellows again.

'A feeble attempt, night soil, and it'll cost you!' she growled, and as the vampire stabbed at her again she swatted her forearm to his wrist, knocking the stab aside before her other arm jolted forward with a pile-driving punch. With clawed fingers leading the way she gouged through his torso, the talons erupting from his back amidst a plume of crimson.

An almost unheard whisper of motion arose behind her and she whirled to exchange places with the cavorting body. Another shuriken thudded into the skull of the vampire, and Corin wrenched her limb free and ran for the other creature.

The beast lost all willingness to fight and ran, having already been grievously wounded by the battle. Corin sprung, her powerful muscles kicking into the road and sending her high through the air.

Lost to a killing frenzy her claws raked down his back, shattering ribs and causing him to arch with a shriek, throwing his neck into her poised jaws. Snapping them shut and twisting, the sound of rending flesh poured out, and his cry became a gurgling high-pitched mewl before being abruptly cut off.

The headless cadaver ran on a few steps and collapsed, his head bouncing into the gutter, depositing a trail of red to mark its route.

Another hiss of motion came and Corin whirled, her hand slapping out, catching the side of the twirling death star and altering its trajectory in mid-flight. The star struck a wall and spat sparks from the bricks with a bright chime before bouncing across the pavement.

Corin dropped a claw behind her, pulling a dagger from a scabbard, her belt and tools for murder designed to accommodate her full form, allowing her to remain armed for her crusade of genocide. Peering into the night she saw the sniper hanging in a second-storey window.

'Fool undead!' she muttered irritably as the creature fumbled for another star. 'If you're going to throw a weapon, throw it right!'

Potent muscles, enhanced and fuelled by the power of the earth instantly flashed with inhuman force. The dagger moved at a speed beyond mortal vision, the sound of is passage reaching out only once it had already reached its target. The slender stiletto bored through skin, muscle and bone, sheathing deep, the point puncturing the beast's heart. Only the wide cross-guard stopped the weapon drilling all the way through and escaping from the other side, but the imbued velocity tore the beast from its feet and sent it hurtling back through the air. Smashed violently into the opposite wall its body crashed through the plaster and timbers, dropping through and onto the stairs beyond.

It bounced down, arms and legs flailing, its body starting to crumble. With its heart pierced, the creature joined the other vampires in true demise, and their decay was swift and merciless.

The head in the gutter, the decapitated body, the transfixed corpse, all started to wither and crack, the stolen years finally taking their revenge and pouring back in. In moments the bodies were restored to their true age, the onslaught of decades turning them to desiccated shells, and as these years became centuries, their blackened skeletons began to shatter and crumble into dust.

The sniper started her fall as a woman, was a mummified ruin a third of the way down, and amidst dust clouds of dry flakes of flesh, she crumbled to a skeleton near the base. When she struck the landing her form burst out into a pool of fine motes, a few bone shards fossilised within.

Corin stood alone in the street as the stink of fetid particles curled around her, the remains of her opponents drifting away on the wind. Again she had failed to find answers, her impetuous wrath having cost her possible informants. But she was warrior by nature; she killed, she hunted, she fought. Subterfuge and strategy were for these foul beasts, and until she found Thanos she would be glad to simply hack their numbers to final depletion.

CHAPTER 7

Shuddering from being deprived of release yet again, Kira was in abject torment. Her sex was dripping with lust, her heart aflame from within with terrible hunger. She was chewing on the gag, fighting to get free to sate her needs.

The sound of the door opening made her immediately go still, listening to the faint traces of stiletto heels approaching her. It was Cassandra, her soft menacing voice trickling through the latex prison and reaching her ears.

'Are we hungry, my slave? Does your thirst burn in your heart or your loins? Which starvation is of greater importance to you? If you had a choice, which one would you have fulfilled? Your vampire heart wails for blood. It's an interesting sensation, isn't it? More powerful than anything you've ever felt before. Nothing comes close to such a thirst. But then again, there is the constant tease of that belt, bringing you so close and then cheating you. That must be terribly frustrating. Your aching desire for release must be at unprecedented levels. I bet you'd do anything, perform any indignity, accept any man, woman or beast to find release. Wouldn't you? But not yet. I think you can wait a little longer. First, we'll have to punish you some more.'

A cupboard opened and the woman was furnished with a weapon before she walked back and around Kira's helplessly splayed form.

'Are we ready for our chastisement, slave?' she quizzed, pausing, holding off as she waited for the belt to start its next cycle of teasing.

In the soft quiet Kira could only wait and dwell on what was to come. Then the belt started to thrum with animation once more, drilling into her, making her quake with ecstasy.

A shock of warmth was applied to her rear as Cassandra's hand swept down and clapped to Kira's buttock. The hand held there, squeezing the flesh, caressing it before the spanking continued with celerity, the woman slapping each buttock in turn, imparting warmth with every swat. The impacts were minor torments, but as they continued they started to gather, conspiring together, making the new ones more and more distressing until Kira was riven with harrowing.

The clapping echo of the beating stopped, Kira's rear aglow from within, the muscle flicking as the washes of burning sensation continued to flow through it.

Dangling by her hood she was on the verge of relief again, the belt's assault drawing her ever onwards, the spanking having only accelerated it by arousing her further.

Suddenly a ferocious line of force crossed her rear, the welt exploding a moment later with additional pain. The cane descended again across the other buttock, making Kira strain at the latex, to try and gain air so she might set it free as screams to accurately describe her agony.

Again and again the woman chastised Kira's rear, leaving her lost within a whirlpool of excruciating travail, unable do anything. She fought to block the blows, to throw an arm down and shield the harried regions, but the jacket prevented it. She tried to get free, but was too well bound; she could do nothing save hang and be subjected to the cruel whims of the woman.

The savaging of her buttocks paused, leaving her exhausted, drained by her fanatic fight to get out. The abuse had eroded her wanton urges, driving them back under the intense pain, leaving her once more at the foot of her build up to relief.

The belt was tickling her within, making the hate she had levied against this treatment start to melt into relish. Under the delicate vibrations and soft stabs she was soon once more inundated with the need to have more of the cane. While it was applied she loathed it, would have done anything to escape it, but in the cosy afterglow where the belt drew out her bliss and fuelled her frustration, she craved it with all her heart. To be trained like this, to be held in bondage and to suffer so she could attain servile perfection was a dream come true.

'Would my slave like to be set free now?' the woman asked. 'Have you dwelt on what I've told you long enough?'

Kira nodded as best she could, fighting the effects of the collar to beg for release.

'You are sure? Perhaps you want to stay in bondage awhile longer, to really learn your lesson? Is that it?' she teased, making Kira thrash her head from side to side, barely able to offer the most minor sway against her bonds.

'Very well... assistants!' she commanded, and again the swivel of panels allowed the bound women exit to serve the seneschal.

Lowered to the floor, Kira crumbled into an enervated heap, scarcely capable of moving her wearied limbs. Chains were removed, and the bonds of the skin-tight latex tomb were unfurled, the straps opened, the laces set free, and then peeled from her skin.

At Cassandra's feet Kira kept her eyes closed, her long sentence of being kept in utter darkness making the meagre light of the room terribly bright. Through a tight squint she could see Cassandra's thigh boots, the black material winking in the light. She could barely move, every part of her raw and tender. But with a strain she managed to get her arms to her loins and try and open the chastity belt. She needed to give herself relief, but as her fingers slipped and slid against the polished steel it became painfully apparent that there was no hope of even getting a finger under the oppressive crotch-band.

The straps of the gag were released as the bulbs deflated, finally letting her aching jaws close as the saliva-sodden implement was drawn free.

A gloved hand cupped her chin and lifted her jaw from the floor before a finger drew her lips back and then tapped her incisors.

'Oh yes, you are hungry all right, you must be going insane with the thirst,' crooned the woman.

'Please, please seneschal,' Kira croaked, after drawing her first breath in what seemed like decades.

'Wait, what have we here?' she pondered, pulling back her lower lip, and then tapping two pronounced lower teeth. 'Now this is unexpected. Who would have thought it? We will most definitely have to keep this little secret under wraps,' she pondered, refusing to explain as she simply let go and backed away.

'Assistants, pin her down.'

The women moved in and leant their cumulative strength and weight to Kira. One sat across her calves and held to her thighs, the other applied herself to Kira's rear, and the last two folded her arms across her back before dropping rubber-coated seats onto them.

Grimacing from the strain, Kira watched impotently as Cassandra removed an opaque glass flask from the cabinet. With a twist she removed the cork and stepped forward, passing the lip before her nose and sniffing deeply. Closing her eyes she gave an icy shudder and smiled, her fangs emerging with a creak as she hissed softly and licked her lips.

Coming to her senses from the trance she had seeped into, the seneschal smiled and crouched before Kira, wafting the end under her nose. The scent of blood emerged and entered Kira's nostrils like a flash flood, the soft smell pouring through her because of her need for it. With a screech Kira launched into paroxysms, trying to get free, her jaws wide with her cry, her twin sets of fangs extending further, anticipating the rending of flesh and tasting of warm blood.

'Not yet, slave,' the seneschal purred, and tilted the bottle, pouring a trickle onto the floor. The sight of the thick crimson fluid stretching from the end of the bottle and spattering on the floor increased Kira's struggle, the assistants having to fight to hold her such was the berserk fury of her need.

Cassandra started to walk away, leaving a dribbling incarnadine trail behind her. Then, straightening up, she poured the rest of the contents down her legs. The sparkling life shimmered as it flowed down the burnished latex thigh boots, winding down, shimmering over the wrinkles in the fabric until it slipped down her heels and across her toes, forming a puddle about her feet.

Kira was insane with hunger. The image of what she needed most slipping down that which she worshipped was too much. With a bellowing howl she threw herself up, flinging off the serviles as though they were straw, her body imbued with new and incredible force. The women collapsed and skidded, tumbling back as they looked up with shock at having been so easily dislodged.

Kira did not even notice as the seneschal waved a hand to stop them from retrying to capture her. Flopping onto the floor, Kira's tongue spilled forth, lapping the liquid with fanatic speed.

Shaking with pleasure she felt stolen power siphoning through the blood and into her body, charging her nerves, making it feel as though her very structure were renewing itself into a potent form.

Scampering slowly forward she left not one drop behind, fuelling her motions with the blood she stole before reaching the feet of the seneschal. The woman stood with legs slightly apart, her muscles taut and rippling the fabric as she stood tensed and defiant, hands on hips, looking down with a wicked glower upon the grovelling form of Kira.

Her tongue fawned on the latex, the tang of the erotic substance mingling with the copper taint of the blood, creating a cocktail that had her delirious with rapture.

'That's it slave, worship me,' she hissed sibilantly, entranced by Kira's performance. 'Worship your mistress!'

Circling around the tight boots, paying slobbering homage to them as she fed, Kira ached to touch herself. Her only recourse was to covertly tickle her nipples, caressing her teats to bestow herself a meagre bliss, her loins growing humid within the chastity belt as they ached for release from sexual starvation.

The rhapsody pouring across her palate was unbelievably intense, and she was panting with lust as she continued to lap and lick, the feel of the seneschal under her tongue adding immensely to the experience. Her lips kissed up and down the calves and thighs, suckling up the blood, removing the streaks and stains, stealing every droplet as she relished being humbled so acutely.

Once the last of it was stolen she dropped aside, content beyond measure, even though her enforced abstinence was still a fury beneath the chastity belt.

As she lay and recovered from the feast, Kira felt one of the seneschal's boots settle onto her shoulder, holding her down as another display of power. Kept underfoot, Kira watched the assistants tidy up in her wake.

A touch to the internal controls had the pits stealing back the manacles and fetters and sealing over once more, their existence lost by the craftsmanship of this room. The bar was put away, and her latex clothing folded up and placed back in storage.

Standing in a line and to attention, like shadows on parade, they awaited inspection and new instructions by the seneschal.

'Bring me a leash,' she ordered, causing one of their number to scamper back and remove a short chain link length with a black leather hoop at one end, a clip at the other.

Cassandra accepted the item and snapped its tip to the front of Kira's collar.

'You are all dismissed,' she stated, and Kira watched as the four trained women returned to their alcoves. Placing their backs to the revolving panels, the metal bands flicked up and locked with sharp tones, returning them to their bondage. They stood idle within their bonds, struggling a little as the straps started to pull slowly in, tightening to them, pulling them forcefully back against the panel.

Cassandra removed her foot from Kira and placed it before her inert features.

'Kiss,' she said succinctly, allowing Kira to place a single peck onto the tip of one of her owner's magnificent legs.

Without further word the woman strode to the assistants, pulling a tube from the wall and forcing it into a self-sealing socket in their gags.

'You have served adequately and shall be rewarded with the blessing of her majesty. Accept a renewal of your lives by tasting of living death. Let the blood of the undead restore you as slaves,' she testified with practised rhythm, the words said naturally, so often had this litany been repeated. But what did it mean? Were they being fed the essence of vampires? What effects did drinking such a potent brew have? These assistants breathed, they were warm, they had the semblance of normal mortals. But did the ingestion of vampire blood have some other effect on them? To be made one of the undead in full, she assumed the victim had to be drained to the brink of true death before the fresh infusion came. But to simply drink it?

Threading the tubes deep, the seneschal turned a valve at the base and watched as the tinted pipe darkened with the flow of liquid. When it entered their maws, each assistant started to shake and quiver in her bondage, either through discomfort or pleasure, Kira could not tell which.

Stepping back, the slabs whirled around and snapped back into position, removing the females from view. The wall appeared to be totally featureless now. Behind it though, strapped in place, were rubber-bound slaves sealed within tight prisons, unable to do anything as they awaited another chance to break the monotony of their confinement.

The seneschal wandered back to Kira and took up her lead. 'Come with me, slave,' she uttered, pulling upward, bringing Kira back to her feet where she swayed like a sapling, her body weak but charged with vitality, 'we have some new lessons for you.'

She walked from the room, the door opening at her mere approach and bringing them back into the winding passages of the queen's private domain.

Escorted down the paths, Kira trailed obediently behind her owner, watching with a burning desire the soft saunter of the woman, the latex stretching and winking upon her luscious curves. The entrancing rear tempted her greatly, making her ache to just reach forward and touch it, to bury her face between the perfect cheeks. She knew she would be horrendously punished for it, and her lack of familiarity with such retribution was the only thing that made her resist the urge.

A new door opened, revealing a long rectangular hall. Along each face were numerous doors, all with a plaque of gold embossed with the strange symbols Kira had seen before, and which marked the collars of all here. Beneath this was another panel, an LCD display, upon which lay one or more of the circular ideograms.

In each corner was a chained male, the slave bound head to foot in tight latex, with their ankle cuffs and collar locked to the wall. Only their forearms and heads were free of the imprisoning shell, and while free of the restriction they had other torments afflicting them.

Shaven bald, a large black candle was set upon their crown, the long burning shaft having spilled wax down its side and onto the features beneath. The faces of the slaves were almost hidden beneath a cascading frozen waterfall of jet wax, the rivulets streaming down their face and hanging from their chins. It looked as though they had indeed been wearing latex hoods, and now these were melting under some fierce heat.

On each upraised palm was another candle, a black rod trickling its molten issue down to coat their extremities, hiding all fingers and leaving long coal-black stalactites drooping from the underside. Also, a single insulated red cable emerged from their hands, snaking out to the wall where a large version emerged and reached into their loins, connecting to the subdued clues of their chastity belts. They were clearly straining to keep up with their duty, the weight and the perpetual pose something not easy for them to bear, and Kira started to see that they were not going unpunished for any moment of lagging.

Should the candle wilt or rise for any reason from its determined height, the sensors of the cables would betray their crime and they would shudder within their cocoons, their legs crossing and folding as their loins were punished until they reacquired the correct form.

The light from these harried unfortunates bathed the hall with nebulous shadows, the gloom consuming, the dark smooth walls armed with silver rings between each set of doors. The carpet was thick and soft, a deep crimson shade that turned to a matching linoleum panel where it reached the slaves, each of them standing on a metre square where their ever trickling flows of wax could visit no vandalism.

In the middle of the room was a large sturdy table, clearly an antique, its stout legs engraved so that they flowed up and poured into the dense wood of the surface. Matching chairs each lay on one side of the furniture, their high backs and deep cushions designed for luxury and matching the style of the table perfectly.

The seneschal walked over and slouched into one of them, the red cushions sagging to accept her sultry form.

'Get on all fours, slave,' she ordered, jabbing an angry finger directly before her.

Without delay, Kira folded down, and with rigid pride adopted the required position. She closed her eyes with satisfaction as she felt the smooth thigh boots settle onto her back, using her as a rest while they waited, the chain links attached to her collar reaching to the hand of her owner.

The minutes of silence continued to waft by, marked only with the almost inaudible hum of electrical charges being distributed to the faltering living candlesticks.

One of the doors opened, releasing the previously hidden sounds from the room beyond; the creak of latex and rattle of chains and a keening gurgle as someone was tormented.

A young woman emerged at a spry pace, her long blonde tresses flapping against her body. She was small, with detailed contours and a compassionate face with intense green eyes. Her entire body was encased within a moulded catsuit of bright red, the material clinging to her with devotion, moulding her small but well-formed breasts.

Elbow length gloves of black rubber were matched with knee high zipped boots, the two midnight garments emphasising each extremity. Her silver collar lay beneath the high rubber neck of her catsuit, its rings again slipping through accommodating slots.

Behind her came a girl naked but for a pouch fastened around her waist by a thin belt. She was slender and reedy, an almost malnourished vision, her short brown hair cut to her scalp.

'Greetings, seneschal,' the blonde said with elation, walking over and accepting the woman's hand before kissing it.

'How is your night, Head Slave Strafe?' quizzed Cassandra, the red-clad woman pulling out a chair and joining her.

'May I?' she asked, indicating Kira.

'Go ahead,' replied Cassandra, and the woman placed her booted feet onto Kira as well.

'I've just finished changing some of the slaves around, and have been trying some new ideas,' she said, clicking her fingers and having the wiry girl reach into the pouch and producing a cigar and a match that she obediently handed over. 'Yourself?' Running the wooden stem along the wood, the head erupted with flame and the woman placed the fat brown length to her lips before sucking in rapid mouthfuls, releasing them quickly to ensure the tip remained alight.

'Not bad. That new slave the queen has had her eye on was brought in.'

The woman released a final plume of grey smoke that billowed forth and dissipated before she removed the cigar from her lips. Shaking the match she extinguished it and extended her arm with a regal wave. The girl emerged beneath it and opened her maw, the match being dropped into the open cavern, extinguishing its heat with a hiss. The girl closed her mouth and swallowed the small stem, the stick clearly causing discomfort as it trailed down her throat. The woman smiled at the sight and clasped the cigar in crooked digits, the removal allowing her to speak more clearly.

'And this is her? Not bad. What are you going to do with her, seneschal?' she wondered.

'As current head of the Pain slaves, I want you to take her for a while, teach her the usual neophyte rota. But she is not to find any relief, I want her kept frustrated while you use your inventions on her.'

'As you wish, seneschal,' she stated, placing the burning stem into her lips with a grin, taking a deep drag and then blowing a geyser of curling silver tendrils into the air.

Kira closed her eyes with dismay at the revelation that she was again to be teased with torment and not granted any hope of release from her pent-up desires. And being assigned to the lot of a Pain slave did not sound too reassuring either, but she was property, it was not her place to question, just accept, and that in itself made her feel better. She no longer had any choice - she did as commanded.

'By the way, expect an influx of Asian ghouls into your care,' added Cassandra. 'The Tsuki-Yomi Clan arrive later today.'

'Already? How many representatives are coming here?'

'We have various Wyrm covens, heads of the major houses, some demon hosts are coming in, it's going to be insane to try and keep them all content.'

'What's the queen up to?' asked the woman, reaching out with the cigar and holding it ready for a moment. She then absently tapped the end of the length and shed the ash, the girl having presented her open maw to catch the hot drizzle. It landed on her tongue and she winced, fighting to remain dedicated to her task either through lust or through fright. Again she made a revolted swallow once her startled organ had cooled the ash a little.

'I have no idea. Maybe she is trying to appease them, allay any suspicions that she'll come after them after the city is hers. Maybe she is forming alliances and pacts, getting ready for what's coming.'

'The apocalypse? She really believes it's coming?' she said, the revelation causing her to pause before taking another drag and letting the smoke roll within her mouth and impart its flavour before she expelled it.

'The signs are all pointing to it. Whether or not it'll occur, everyone seems to be getting ready for something big,' pondered Cassandra, and then removed her feet from Kira's back before continuing with her words.

'Well, I'll leave you to it. I'll be back to collect her in a few days or so.'

'Anything I should know about her?' questioned the trainer, looking from the seneschal to the slave.

'I think she's brood.'

'Really? You're sure?'

'Maybe. It'll be a while before we can see whether she turns in full.'

'I've never seen brood before. Will she need special consideration?'

'Not for a while, but she will if she becomes full brood. But for now I want it kept secret, I don't want anyone to know what I suspect, is that understood?'

'Yes, seneschal.'

The head slave rose as well and went down on her knees to kiss the gloved hand of her superior. After accepting the homage, Cassandra stroked the soft mane of her servile, handed her the lead and then turned to depart, leaving Kira to the mercy of this new owner.

'Come with me, slave, and we'll get you all nice and trussed up before we start your education,' she announced, pulling on the leash, the cigar lodged between her lips.

Kira started to rise, only to have the woman shove her back to the carpet. 'Did I say to rise? You will crawl, slave,' she snapped harshly, and then yanked the leash to bring Kira forward. 'You've just earned yourself extra punishment for that, slave,' she stated, walking towards a door, leaving a thin trail of smoke, her rear tensing and stretching the firm red rubber sheath, mesmerising Kira's starved vision. The girl scampered close behind, following to serve as Strafe's personal ashtray.

Presented to a door, the woman removed a small tab from the frame of the LCD and passed it over Kira's collar. Looking back and replacing the object, Kira's symbol appeared on the panel and the door started to shuffle aside. It was thick and solid, amply fortified to contain creatures of abnormal strength and to stifle their yowls.

Drawn within, the chamber was small. Every surface was a mirror - the walls, floor and ceiling reflecting them in dozens of ever diminishing images. A fat candle lay in each corner, the flickering light rippling, making the refracted shadows and glow shift and move as though alive.

A pile of latex garments was set to one side, and from the centre of the ceiling a heavy chain hung to waist height.

The door was already starting to grind closed when the woman hooked a finger into Kira's collar and brought her beneath the chain. She began her work with eagerness, her hands deft, her love of smothering slaves beneath rolls of latex brazenly displayed. As she worked Kira began to see her teeth elongating as they clamped to the cigar, her lust rising with her work.

The girl shifted into the corner, remaining in a huddled crouch, watching for sign that she was to be summoned.

In the mirrors of the chamber Kira watched herself being dressed. Thigh length boots were threaded onto her legs, compressing them, setting her atop absurd ballet boots. Next came a stern jacket, the sleeves ending in furled mittens. The garment was forced onto her, slotting her arms in the tight material, her hands entering the mittens, making her gather her fingers into fists and depriving her of all manual dexterity. The woman pulled her wrist rings through the slots, and continued.

The back zip was pulled up, squeezing her within, her breasts slipping through two open rings. As the garment was tightened the hoops forced her breasts through, making them swell with sensation.

A buckled strap was set between her legs to hold it down, and the final part was the forcing of a ball-gag over her lips, the large sphere spreading her jaws wide and keeping them there as the strap was buckled to the back of her head. With the basic uniform in position, the woman lifted Kira to her feet where she wobbled on the painful footwear, finding it hard to keep upright against their demands.

The cigar was removed and she looked over her handiwork with a grin, blowing free a mouthful of smoke and presenting the cigar. The girl scuttled forth and positioned herself beneath, catching another ashen downpour before returning to her position in the corner.

Slotting the dwindled stub back to her lips, the woman clapped her hands together and rubbed them, the latex squeaking before she recommenced her work.

Folded at her middle, Kira's arms were dragged around her thighs, and two fastenings by her armpits snagged her wrist rings, the locking clasps stopping her from straightening up, confining her to this extreme stoop, her arms wrapped around and hugging her thighs. Wobbling on her toes and heels, her rear in the air as her body draped down her thighs, breasts pressed against them, further straps were applied. The wide elasticised bands of dense rubber rolled over the top of her thighs and the small of her back, helping to keep her in the stringent pose.

Another of the secret pits was opened just behind her, allowing the woman to remove a length of black cable. The socket at the end snapped to her chastity belt, locking into place and feeding new energy into the toy.

Swallowing as best she could, she felt the chain being attached to the base of the jacket, taking hold, stopping her from descending.

Clicking her fingers, the woman pointed to the floor before Kira, causing the girl to trot over and get down on all fours, accepting the trainer's buttocks onto her spine. The girl shuddered with pleasure at the feel of the latex smoothed cheeks resting on her, and ate another tap of ash while the trainer addressed Kira.

'Now, we have some lectures for you, slave,' she declared, rising and walking to the wall. 'These will come in three parts. The first will be instruction as to what you are. The next will be a brief history of her majesty, and the last will be the most important - the rules and law of the queen's domain.'

Touching a section of glass wall, the pane pivoted and revealed three long canes of various thickness. Her gloved hand closed about one, the material rippling over her knuckles as she removed it from its hooks and closed the hidden compartment.

'You are a vampire,' she purred. 'You were drained of life until it was almost extinguished, and then, by feeding you a large amount of her blood, the Malefic Kiss of her majesty turned you to us.'

Wandering behind Kira, waggling the bamboo strut, she made it thrum against the air as its fibres were limbered up in readiness for their exercise.

Kira watched the woman with wide eyes, craning her neck back to observe the many reflections that offered the woman and her own bound form from every angle. Taking another draught of the cigar, she washed the smoke about and tilted her head back, blowing some smoke rings. She watched them rise and fade, smiling at her success while she continued to speak.

'We have existed since the dawn of time itself, and shall exist to the end of all things. We never age, we cannot be stricken by illness, and we can never truly die. Though we still feel pleasure.'

Moving closer, she ran a hand down the metal band of Kira's crotch band. As though in answer the device sprung into life, resonating within Kira's womb, making her dance on tiptoe, skipping from one foot to the next as the intense flare of feeling started to pour back into her.

'And pain...' the woman chuckled, and thrashed through the air, slamming the cane across Kira's rear. Instantly Kira jerked and let her scream spill around the gag as her legs gave out beneath her, leaving her momentarily suspended by the jacket. The rings at her breasts seemed to tighten, afflicting them until she dropped her feet back to the mirrored floor and helped alleviate the stress.

'I shall now address some of the issues relating to your un-life. Your heart is your life,' she stated, and applied the sceptre of chastisement again, crossing the previous, marking Kira's rear with a flushed X, the skin rising into a raised trench, like the sting of nettles. Kira screeched and danced for the woman, the pain slowly withdrawing, letting her give herself back to the pleasure of the belt.

'It is the organ that pulls the stolen vitality you imbibed through your veins, keeping the years you steal at bay, regenerating your body, giving you strength, stamina and speed beyond any mortal equal. We feed on the souls, on the essence of the living, drawing on it through the attachment to the physical form. Via the bodies of our prey we gain the energy that we use to sustain us. Drinking the blood is the quickest, easiest and most efficient way of doing this. While you feed, you will never age.

'But without blood you will eventually lapse into coma, and finally, your body will die and you will start to return to your true age,' continued the stern lecturer, adding another slash of her weapon. She caught Kira near the base of her buttocks, the join between thigh and rear where she was most vulnerable. Airing a squawk of suffering Kira drew her shins up, trying to soothe and protect the burning welt as she cried and tried to break free. The effects of the stroke started to again subside, and her feet slowly sank back down.

The woman removed the cigar and checked its length before holding it out, making the girl accept another barren meal before it was restored to her lips.

'Damage to your heart will disable you, but we regenerate swiftly, and unless the organ is pierced by a non-conductive weapon that is left there to prevent restoration, you will recover. Thus stakes are the most lethal tool in the arsenal of our enemies,' she said, and applied a pair of swift hacks, eating into Kira's rear, making tears trickle from her eyes, tumbling out to spatter against the floor.

'Sunlight will make you immediately assume your true age. The science we have levied to this matter has yet to determine why, for it is not UV, or radiation, it is some as yet undiscovered solar trait.

'The effects are not limited to daytime either, for an extremely radiant full moon will have sufficient power of reflected sunlight to cause you pain,' came the next revelation, and the cane came with it to make sure she kept her attention firmly to them. Grizzling, she tried to beg for mercy, but nothing intelligible could get through the cruel ball-gag.

'Silver can be toxic to us, depending on your blood. The rest of the fables are conjurations we have cultivated and encouraged, to have enemies wield them in the hope of them proving useful and thus give our number an advantage. However, there is an exception. The myth concerning our inability to cross running water has some vague basis. Sea crossings and voyages are avoided by the paranoid, for should an accident occur our lack of need to respire gives us no buoyancy, and thus we sink until pressure crushes us, or we have to spend laborious hours trekking undersea towards land while dawn looms and threatens our destruction.'

In the reflections of the mirror Kira could already see the earlier strokes deepening to a vibrant purple and some were already fading to a mottled yellow, her body erasing the contusions, working at a speed that made minutes into what ordinarily would take days.

'The work of nature and man are not the only threats to our un-lives; the attack of occult forces will visit the most grievous damage to us, and I will tell you a little about them,' she stated, and thrashed Kira's rear again, beating back the tide of bliss the belt was conjuring. The rising relief and the session of punishment, the sight of the mistress, were all making the cane a more treasured companion, one she was almost welcoming.

The woman paced back and forth as she spoke, the cane-wielding arm placed around her abdomen, the other crooked, her wrist limp to let the cigar dangle, leaving wafting trails as she walked and continued the lecture.

'The Lupine. Lycanthropes, shape shifters, werewolves, they can summon forth the power of the earth, a power they deify and call Gaia. They use this energy to transform themselves through various stages towards that of a man-beast. They act as guardians to nature, and as such, will kill any vampire they come across as an affront to the natural order of things. Because we do not age, because we pilfer life to sustain ours, and because we expand our city empires at the expense of their lands, we are arch enemies. The corporations and businesses we control and use to protect and fund ourselves pollute their land in a conscious effort to weaken them, for in a direct conflict we are little match for such beasts.' She stopped to launch a trio of harsh thwacks into Kira's rear. They made her screech and shake, then as the flashing torment started to fade she was wriggling her rump, savouring the pain as the belt continued to play her innards like an instrument, conducting a song of ecstasy.

The woman watched for a moment, drawing another drag of the cigar, holding it as she looked over Kira's rear, and then expelled it to continue talking.

'Their claws and fangs will cause trauma we find exceedingly laborious to heal, and they can prove fatal by disrupting our own sustaining dark force,' added the trainer, teaching Kira's rear another sharp lesson in pain, save that now she was inviting it, her hunger for the abuse being cultivated the longer the belt worked against her.

'They also have a dark side to them. These fallen tribes of Lupine follow the Wyrm, an antithesis of Gaia, a power of malevolence they tap to conjure their transformations. They will attack vampire-kind just as readily. Some tribes call vampire houses allies, but only ones that have proved themselves to these dark brethren,' and again the cane echoed its cruel signal through the room, making Kira sob, her legs shaking as she drank in the sensation, feeling the scorching warmth flow through her.

'Then there are the Shaman. These are mortals who have assimilated the powers of manipulating the earth forces. These are forces derived from life, and thus are beyond our control. Shaman cults owe fealty to either Gaia, or the Wyrm, and battle constantly for supremacy. The Lupines prey upon either just as fanatically, deeming the use of earth force for acts of sorcery a violation against that which they seek to protect and honour.'

Again Kira relished the impact of the cane across her chastised rear, the first weals almost having vanished without trace.

'Their spells can be devastating to us, but they are mortal and fall easily to vampire-kind. However, they can craft weapons of occult configuration, imbuing objects with power so they can harm us in the same way the natural weapons of the Lupines do. These artefacts again disrupt undead life force and can readily kill our bodies.

'Should any of these methods result in the ending of your un-life, either through making you assume your true age once your body is too old to endure such years, or through the infliction of grievous trauma, you can be restored. Blood poured onto your remains will heal the flesh, giving you back the lost years until you regain awareness. The more years that you have been a vampire, the more blood is required to push them back and allow you to regenerate. At the present time your corpse will be little different to that of a mortal, and the affliction of your true age by the sun will not prove fatal, although the process will cause extreme distress. But as the decades pass, when you perish, the accrued years will reduce you in moments to that of a skeleton, or if you reach extreme age - dust.' She finished with a final series of swinging underhand attacks that lifted Kira to her toes, crying out in delight and pain as she was savaged.

Kira swayed, her tears still flowing, the position growing uncomfortable, her back aching from being kept folded thus.

'I will now leave you to dwell on these lessons,' stated the woman, replacing the cane and putting the short stub of the cigar in her teeth.

With a snap of her fingers she summoned the girl to follow, and sidled equably from the room, her face broad with merriment, her desire to cause pain one that brought her the most profound satisfaction in her work.

With a final glance across the elegant rubber anatomy of the woman who had trained her, and the naked shaven rear of the crawling girl, Kira was left to isolation.

CHAPTER .8

The belt continued to build her towards climax, the loss of dissuading outside stimuli having her devoting her mind to it, filling her thoughts with lecherous dreams about Cassandra.

As she hung on the edge of relief, awaiting the sudden stop that would only feed her angst, the belt turned from a beloved though irritating companion, to a far more mordant comrade.

Sudden flicking shocks started to apply their voltage teeth to her womb and anus, scratching at her clitoris with painful jolts. Squeaking in distress, she winced as the sporadic gnaw of the belt was fired into her loins, making her jerk and cry out as she was ruthlessly and efficiently chastised. The electrical discipline shoved her back away from release at a fervid rate, and once sufficiently calmed by the abuse, the shocks gave way to thrumming bliss once more.

Kira struggled against her bonds, unable to discern what she should do. She wanted to get out, to break free, the prospect of being continually subjected to delectable caresses and then savaging shocks was too much for her to cope with.

Again she was drawn to the brink of release, and again the electrical flashes were sent careering through her most sensitive areas, making her squeal in abject dismay as she was subjected to this terrible maltreatment.

The unrelenting ordeal left her little option but to focus on her lessons, for it was the only and best way to distract herself, to avoid dwelling on the eventual fate as the belt built her towards climax once more, the offer of orgasm a cruel joke, the relief actually being hidden sexual mayhem.

Werewolves, wizards... it all sounded so ridiculous. Yet here she was, a slave of vampires, a vampire herself. And if they fed on the soul of their victims via the flesh, did that not prove that the soul was real? And in this case, was there not an afterlife too? Such a confirmation of something so intangible and spiritual was frightening, more so for the truth that she would never access it. She would exist forever, unable to die. Even when her flesh was destroyed she would simply be awaiting a time when blood splashed her remains and started the process of recovery. But where would she dwell during this period? Would she just cease to be? Would it be like going in for surgery; one minute she closed her eyes, the next she opens them as though no time had elapsed? Or would she dwell in limbo, aware, deprived of form, a ghost?

For hours she was fed through the opposing trials of the belt, each one ferrying her to and from orgasm with regular and unwavering devotion. Hanging in her bondage, it seemed like an eternity before her teacher strode back in. Shaking in turmoil as the belt built her towards another dose of shocks, she prayed that the woman would release her before the punitive session started again.

The woman was still in her red attire, and this time she held a crop and the leash once more, and the leash was not left idle. A girl of Japanese heritage, her dark hair hanging about her as a sable curtain, was being led forth into the room. She was like a miniature female, her curves soft and inviting, her breasts barely a handful but succulent to the eyes, and around her was a cloak of submissiveness, inviting others to bind her and use her for their pleasure.

Their tutor let the door close and then removed the gag from Kira's lips, drawing the wet ball free.

'Has my slave been learning her lessons?' she quizzed, cupping Kira's chin and lifting, making her neck ache as she strained to behold her tormentor.

'Yes, Lady Strafe,' she replied, recalling the title she was supposed to use for any of loftier stature than herself.

'I can see those hungry eyes looking over this nubile little flower. I bet you would love to taste her, wouldn't you?'

'Yes, Lady Strafe,' she replied eagerly, squirming against the rubber as the girl caught her licentious stare in the mirrors, the chastity belt bringing her ever closer to another session of abuse.

'Would you like to give her some compensation before she starts her sentence?' offered the woman, pulling out the cable attached to Kira's loins, making her sigh with relief as the belt continued, filling her with prurient lust, but promising no more of the baleful shocks.

'Yes, Lady Strafe, yes I would,' she whimpered, her toes jiggling in their bonds as the automated masturbation continued unabated.

'There will be no relief for you, though,' revealed the woman, drawing in the leash to bring the girl closer. 'This is merely an act of generosity on my part.'

Kira looked up across her supple frame, the slave girl looking down at her with expectation but also worry, for she seemed to sense that she would soon be bound in the configuration Kira now displayed.

'Well, get going then, slave,' the woman grumbled, and swatted the crop first across the girl's rear to make her yelp, and then down onto Kira's.

The slave moved forward and presented herself to Kira's features. Slipping a hand under Kira's chin, she helped the bound captive keep her head up, and allow her tongue a chance to find its quarry.

Bathed in the glow of the belt, Kira eagerly started to lap, reaching in and adoring the girl's clitoris, teasing it with small circles of motion and then flicking at it, sometimes sucking to heighten the sensations, and then returning to applying slobbering laps upon it. On occasion she simply launched her tongue as deep as it would go, to make the girl stiffen and her small hands grip more sternly to Kira's face.

All the while their overseer watched casually, occasionally throwing a swipe of her crop into the buttocks of either girl. Just as she was chastised by the riding implement, so too was Kira punished by her belt, the arousal of this deed, of servicing another woman under the merciless gaze of their gorgeous tyrant, it made the belt carry her all too swiftly to the brink before deserting her.

With such intense eroticism played before her, the device could only give her the most short-lived excursions into pleasure, her state of titillation being such that she was only a short jaunt from the point where she was deemed too close to relief to warrant more attention.

As the cunnilingus continued and Kira made the latex prison groan to hold her as she squirmed, their tormentor spoke to her, continuing with her education as was relevant.

'She's a delicate little thing, destined to replace you here. She'll suffer terribly too, because she's only a ghoul. That means her vampire owners feed her their blood. It makes her tough, resilient, and stops her ageing, but she can perish just as easily as any other mortal. If she serves well, if she pleases them, they might give her the Malefic Kiss, but then again, they might not. She's at least a century old, so if they withdraw their sustenance she'll age overnight.' Her words were followed by the swift sharp crack of the crop crossing the backs of the girl's thighs, making her stiffen and then sag slightly.

'She's still warm, she still lives, and that means she will be sweltering in this rubber prison,' she revealed, and gave Kira a harsh lick of the implement. 'Her body will ache, her senses swim. You should count yourself fortunate you are not in her position.

'But that is the fate her masters have decreed,' she stated, twirling the weapon around her fingers. 'The queen is entertaining one of the Japanese vampire clans, and so this poor little creature has been handed over to our care for the duration.'

The girl started to gasp and moan, her legs jerking to attention, her head lolling back. Soft choked cries started to slip her lips as Kira kept her rhythm steady and precise, bringing the slave to the point Kira was forever being thrown to but never beyond.

'Ah, here we go,' purred the woman, watching the show with glee. 'This is my favourite bit.'

With a series of stifled cries the girl started to shake and shiver, the pleasure rippling through her, making her fight to stay still, the effects almost too much for her to endure.

Her sounds of joy started to subside and she started to go lax upon Kira's tongue before withdrawing, clutching her tender stomach and looking to Kira with the most profound gratitude.

'You did well, slave,' said the woman, patting Kira's head and then starting the process of removing her from the bonds.

The girl just stood and watched, recovering from her session, leaving Kira envious that she herself could not taste of such forbidden passions.

The last of her latex prison was removed, and with equal rough attention, their ruler began to force the slender frame of the girl into it. She whimpered softly, the faint mewls a delicate sound as she was bound and strung up, her naked loins hanging in the air.

But instead of attaching the chain to her jacket, the woman instead forced a black bulb into her rear, making the girl sob with distress from its introduction, and with wide eyes she fixed her stare to Kira. Did she want help? Salvation? Or was she just envious of Kira for her freedom or her full vampire status?

The sac was crammed in and a nozzle applied. Their teacher starting to inflate the orb, expanding it until it refused to be easily dislodged, its diameter more than her sphincter could comfortably inflict on itself.

As Kira could have foreseen, the chain was snapped to the base of the plug, holding her up, making any act of wilting churn her rear with new mayhem.

'There, all done,' she said, and transferred the leash from the girl to Kira before leading her out. 'Now come with me, slave. We have a new lesson for you.'

The hall remained unchanged, and Kira was led across it to a door on the opposite side. Once more her identification was scanned in to mark her as its resident, but she was not alone; two others were already here, their existence marked by two other symbols on the LCD.

The heavy door started to shuffle aside, letting pitiful groans of travail seep forth with the warm scent of burning.

The long room bore three engines of restraint. The padded slabs were set atop cupboards to elevate them, the soft tables arming their base with unknown devices for the additional torment of the prisoner riding it. About the edge were sturdy ringlets, and these were used to grasp at the two other people already in residence here.

Both were fastened down in the same manner; their wrist cuffs were lifted to the uppermost corners after their arms were crossed, causing their limbs to grip their heads. Their ankle shackles were snapped to each end of the table, splaying their legs a little way apart. Both slaves had their jaws stretched wide into an impossible frozen scream by the application of a ring gag, the leather hoop flinging out slender straps that sealed around the back of their head to prevent them spitting out the brutal implement of silence. Into this enforced portal to their maw, a candle of exact fit had been slotted, making the slaves fight to keep still lest they spill the molten pool above their lips.

Another candle had been fastened between their legs, pressing against their crotch, again promising harsh chastisement should their squirming agitate the hot reservoir that loitered within the crater of the wick.

A third much larger midnight candle had been fitted with a chain and a clip halfway down its length, the links suspending the waxen rod over their bodies. The base of the candle had a hook screwed into it, upon which weights had been laced to lift the head of the candle, easing the rate at which it dripped down onto the hapless prisoner.

The candles continued to burn sedately, the wicks the only light in this entire room, making it swarm with consuming depths all about the floor, the six twinkling stars doing little to provide decent illumination. The steady fall of drops almost had the precision of a metronome, each landing making the slave below shake and struggle, the results offering more of their anatomy up to the mordant drizzle. It was clearly impossible to stay still, for panicked response occurred whenever the candles of loin or mouth overflowed their slim banks, sending a burning trickle down the sides and onto the skin of the oppressed slave.

The nearest table had a tall amazon woman, her body wiry, her blonde hair cropped short to a carpet of stubble. Her nipples, clit, and nose had been pierced, as had her ears, all the hoops fitted in her flesh being thick and dense, without visible seam, making Kira suspect that they were locked to her and could not be removed. Cords snaked off the edge of the table, holding to her nipple rings so that they might dangle a weight in the air, stretching at the points, making any struggle add punishment. The same method of racking was employed for her ears, the cords pulling at the delicate lobes, serving further to keep her head down and subdued.

Already her belly and ribs were coated with numerous frozen splashes, the waxen splatters clutching to her and occasionally cracking as her belly rose and fell with sobbing gasps. The other candles had sent numerous testing trails down the sides, reaching relentlessly towards her skin, making it only a matter of time before she was afflicted, no matter how still she kept herself.

The other slave was male. Young and slender of limb, his hairless body shuddered under the continuing burden of duress placed upon it. He had clearly been here for some time. His mop of thin white hair was damp from sweat, his body laced with glistening beads of perspiration that winked in the candlelight like gems. The candle in his maw had painted his cheeks, jaw and chin with a layer of wax, and his chest and belly were encrusted with a dense coating of accumulated rain. His penis had been attached to the length of the candle with cord, the organ standing upright against it, hugged to it by garrotting crosses of leather thonging. His shaft was similarly painted with the waxen sheet, the falling lines having rolled along it and enveloped it before spattering his parted testicles and loins. Obviously a ghoul, he was suffering more than the girl, whose hint of pronounced incisors betrayed her full vampire status.

'Get up on the table, slave,' commanded the woman, drawing Kira to the surface and flicking her hand to the crotch candle of the woman, sending a sudden splash across her inner thighs. The woman squawked, shaking the candles more, bringing several drips to her cheeks and more to the lips of her sex as they lay parted and shivering against the candle. The trainer chuckled and continued to push Kira to her fate.

Stepping up, Kira crawled onto the raised flat surface, the leather giving slightly under her hands and knees as she turned over and settled into place.

The woman took hold of her hands and raised them, crossing the slender appendages before offering them to the locks at the head of Kira's tormenting bed.

With her wrist cuffs secured, she lay resigned as her legs were drawn apart and caught by the anchors at the end, sealing her to the bed and stopping any hope of getting free.

The woman reached under, opened a drawer and removed a ring gag, presenting the instrument to Kira's lips.

'Open wide, slave,' she ordered, and smiled knowingly as Kira closed her eyes and stretched her jaws to accept it.

The buckle was pulled tight, stopping up her maw and then the candle was slotted in, the heavy shaft resting deep in her throat, her tongue too weak to expel it. Licking around she traced its circumference as best she could, opening her eyes and looking up the tall black tower sprouting from her lips like some monstrous cylindrical tongue of bleak coloured wax.

'I can see why the queen was so intrigued by you,' the woman purred, walking back down the length of the table, tracing her hand down Kira's naked body, letting her fingers drift through her cleavage and then across her belly and over the chastity belt.

'Such a terrible fate,' she commented, as she let her hand wander upon the device. 'I've had this myself a few times. Nothing makes you more eager to please than lengthy abstinence. But we have other matters to occupy us here, slave, such as where to put this other candle. These hungry loins have been denied, so we'll have to improvise,' she added, removing another pair of large candles and some thin latex straps.

With casual roughness, the woman started to strap the candles along the soles of Kira's feet, forcing her to keep them pointed up and to attention lest the candles dip. To stop her from tilting them the wrong way and sparing herself the wax, leather thongs snagged her big toes, the grip reaching back along her body and connecting to the straps of her gag. Thus with any tug of her feet towards the floor, she might spare her feet, but she was sure to punish her chin and neck.

With wide imploring eyes Kira studied the woman as her latex skin seemed to ripple in the gloom, her features marked with a sneer of amusement. Taking a Zippo, she flicked her hand and opened the metal shell, and with a second flick a flame jumped into radiant life, a few sparks from its ignition dancing in the small fire.

Kira saw the shadows about her retreat as the wicks lifted their flame high, bathing her in an amber glow, a soft warmth touching her chill flesh while the smell of petrol became a hint to her nose.

'Now we shall educate you as to the history of our sublime ruler,' said the woman with stern tones, making herself heard by all the occupants. Kira's eyes were locked to the candle above her, dwelling overhead like a cruel comet, ready to afflict her.

'Her majesty came with the Romans to this place. The Roman Empire was a place where vampire-kind held many high positions of respect and authority, controlling mortal lives much more openly in that decadent time,' said the trainer, and Kira looked aghast as she strode past bearing a leather strap, the dark hide decorated with swirling patterns of stitching.

'Her majesty is a dedicated follower of the arts of hedonism and sensual fulfilment. When the politics and bickering of the empire started to become too great, she migrated to the outer colonies with her house.' There was a brutal slap of leather to skin and the woman beside Kira yowled into her gag. Kira accidentally turned her head slightly to see, and when a trickle of liquefied darkness slipped the edge and started running down the candle she jerked her head upright and snorted as best she could to try and dry it before it reached her. The weaving drool slowed and stopped, darkening as it hardened back to a solid state. But it was only a matter of time before she was unable to stop the wax.

'It was a shrewd move, because many great vampire houses were destroyed or crippled in the fall of Rome, and the subsequent purging led by Christian vampire hunters in the aftermath.'

Kira gave a snort of fright as she saw the first drips falling from the overhead candle. Strangely insubstantial impacts fell onto her abdomen, the moment of indecision being replaced by a hot stab of sensation into her skin. Releasing a croak of distress, Kira started to wriggle and writhe, trying to keep her head still while seeking to shift her belly out from under the volcanic drizzle. But no matter which way she shifted she could not escape, and only offered more untouched skin to the steady drip of the candle. Tears started to flow once more as she shook and growled, trying to endure the mayhem, the candle continuing without pause to punish her.

'Part of the original founding of the city, her majesty was involved in all matters pertaining to it. Her links to every aspect of its enterprises and wealth made sure that no matter what mortal agency currently claimed ownership, she was the true ruler of the domain,' continued their tormentor, and Kira jolted to attention as the strap landed on her thigh, filling it with prickly feeling. The spry jump of response made splashes fall onto her feet and cheek, further elevating her ordeal. Fighting to keep still as the rhythmic pound of hot drops fell onto her belly, she clawed her toes to the candles, scratching at the wax.

'As the British Empire grew, her power continued to expand. The other lands of the vampire houses had suffered great setbacks such as the Inquisition, the French Revolution, and the civil war in the Americas. These were times when the eradication of vampire-kind rose to unprecedented levels,' she went on, and applied her strap to the male, his cry suddenly repeating as his movement brought an additional second wave of castigation.

Kira screwed her eyes shut, concentrating, filling her mind's eye with warm fantasies, trying to picture herself at the mercy of Cassandra, of being abused by her like this. It was easier to endure when she dedicated herself to finding pleasure, in believing that the sharp sensation of the wax was not a blight, but a delight.

'But with such strife abroad, other great houses wanted to take shares of the city, to relocate here and partake of the safety and security afforded by it. Lacking the martial strength to defeat a take over, her majesty agreed to the dividing of the city, with her and the other heads of the vampire houses forming a council that presided over all matters.'

Kira readied to feel its hot caress, giving small flicks of response to the wax that continued to fall on her, save that now she was finding relish in her abuse, in the searing touch of each wandering rivulet that stained her.

'Recently, however, the great houses have been subjected to attack by an as yet unknown foe. We have remained untouched, but most of the other houses have already fallen, their survivors in hiding amongst the vampire citizenry of the city,' announced the woman, and Kira croaked as the strap swung down and caught her inner thigh, punishing this most tender of regions. The leg jolted automatically, shaking the candle attached to its extremity, flinging a cascade of wax across her shin to eclipse her ability to enjoy the deed. With a sob, she shook and rode through the storm of her harrowing, letting it drift away until she could once more start to delight in the waxen rain.

'Taking advantage of this event, the queen consolidated her power, and with the assistance of several allies has retaken the city and fortified her hold on it to an extent where it cannot be so easily lost again.' The male was given a taste of the strap, the heels of the woman sounding as she paced back and forth, adding new torment to her slaves as she went.

'The queen controls every major institution of the land. She has total sway over constabulary and the judicial system, her power ranging from the most respected members of parliament and House of Lords, down to reigns over organised crime.

'None know what we are, and few even know who she is, but through various facades the queen is undisputed sovereign over the city,' stated the trainer, and the woman released her sorrow as she was abused again.

'At present a time of prophecy is upon us, an age where the forces of darkness are supposed to ascend to a new epoch of dominance,' she continued, and Kira tensed in anticipation. It was not a wasted precaution, and again, the strap fell between her legs to afflict the other inner thigh. 'Every quarter of power is bolstering their strength, readying for what might occur, each readying to grab as much power as possible if the opportunity comes.

'The queen's palace is a subterranean fortress, developed and constructed secretly from a main nuclear bunker beneath the city, and which incorporates several other long-forsaken underground structures,' revealed the woman, and made the male squeal with another heartless attack.

'Here we are safe, here we may live out undead lives to the full without any of the concerns and dangers that present themselves to ordinary vampire citizens of the surface world,' she stated, and abused the woman once more before walking towards Kira.

'That is all for this lesson. I shall leave you now to dwell on my words and suffer for her majesty's delectation.' She treated Kira to a stroke across her belly, one that made her jump and send wax across her feet and chin.

With no other word she turned and departed, leaving them to their long and trying ordeal. The door slammed shut, hiding their cries, leaving them all grizzling in apathy beneath their hovering sources of torment.

CHAPTER 9

Releasing the throttle, Cassandra let the bike drift to a slow crawl, and with the soft squeak of the brakes she came to halt. Dropping her booted foot to the kerb, she looked about her surroundings.

The city streets were so much different in the harsh glare of the day, the populace an entirely different herd than the one they preyed upon through the hours of darkness.

On the outside she appeared no different to hundreds of motorcycle messengers speeding to and fro - leather trousers, heavy boots, a closed biker's jacket, heavy gloves and a domed crash helmet with mirrored visor lowered into place.

But beneath she was sheathed within the tight opaque folds of a latex catsuit, the gloves stretching over her fingers, the high collar lifted up around her throat, coating her form, a dense shell to protect from even the slightest touch of the hated sun.

Beneath the helmet, sun block was smeared copiously across her skin and then concealed with ordinary cosmetic shades. Mirrored sunglasses crossed her eyes, and even through these two protecting layers the world was impossibly bright.

It was a different world to the safe presence of the night. The people were grim, preoccupied, strutting about possessed with their own bloated sense of self-importance. It was as though their suits were decrees that made them superior to all others, they marched with glum faces, locked without expression, steadfastly ignoring the world around them.

Those without need of employment conducted their shopping excursion, biding their time and extracting their tenuous joy with the distractions before returning home to marital servility.

The only similarity to her world of night were the tourists, the bright-eyed visitors to this foreign land. Laden with cameras and guides, their fingers pointed out the remarkable or amusing, their behaviour indifferent to those about them, as though their citizenship of a distant land made them exempt from the modes of conduct of this city.

All of them were ignorant of the predator in their midst, and of the other beast that walked calmly towards an unmarked door beside a stationary shop.

The female lupine had changed much since last Cassandra had observed her actions. She was hunched, the weight of her burden pushing down on her, the quest to find her lost brother the only thing motivating her now. The city was a cruel lover to those not born to it, one who welcomed all in with its bright lights and promise of comfort, but who exacted a terrible toll on those who listened to its siren song.

The werewolf had been here too long, separated from her natural environment of the wilds, and it was taking its toll on her. She walked cautiously, with paranoia, suspicious of those about her, the hate of the mortals infectious to one such as she. The claustrophobic hold of the city had piqued her unease, even though she had accustomed to it.

Her attire was dishevelled and haphazard, her appearance the same - untended, forsaken as all effort was leeched from her.

Fumbling for a key, the woman opened the door and shuffled in, closing it and throwing the locks. Cassandra could almost hear the sigh of despairing relief as she restored her barricades to distance herself from the world without.

The lupine had struck a small haven to the north, killing the three vampires within as they slept before lounging in the park for the rest of the day, basking in the sun. Cassandra had watched her through binoculars as the woman wept for short periods, letting lose her pent up emotion, feeling isolated and alone, distanced from everything she knew. The time amidst the preened greenery had only helped to anger her more rather than soothe her.

The lupine was operating from this rented slum, grabbing the change in the pockets of her prey when she remembered to do so in order that she might feed the greed of its owner.

With a smile, Cassandra turned around and peeled into the traffic, weaving deftly through its choked ranks and heading back to the palace to report her findings. It would be a good excuse to get a private audience with the queen, and hopefully to engage in a little sensual recreation between them.

CHAPTER 10

Kira had been drifting in and out of a shade of sleep for what seemed like hours. Unable to truly enter slumber, the hot spikes of dripping wax conspired to keep her awake. She was dizzy and felt a little nauseous from the deprivation, her senses being affected, her thoughts running in circles and to odd places.

Her awareness of her surroundings came and went, sometimes being distinct, sometimes being so faint that she almost believed herself elsewhere.

How long had she been here now? The long periods of bondage were confusing her track of time. It might have been days, or even weeks, for how did she know how much sleep she actually required in her new life?

The hunger in her heart was growing again, nibbling at her a little to start with, promising to gather its full rabid force should she not sate it soon.

Her chest was now coated in a thick layer of wax, the barrier shielding her from most of the drips, but some still slid down her flanks, or when they splattered onto the accumulated layers they spat spots onto more distant regions. Her thighs and the underside of her breasts were flecked with tiny dark pearls from such landings.

Her chin and cheeks were streaked with black icicles, as were her feet, the wax forming into a spreading pool about her ankles the more was poured down them.

With a click and several compliant whines, the door slid back and their trainer entered at a calm strut, completely equable to the sobs and groans of the long punished slaves.

'It is time for you to be moved onto other lessons, slaves,' she reported, and proceeded immediately to Kira.

Extinguishing the candles, she removed them from her body but did not release her from the chair. Reaching beneath, she produced a wicked curved knife, the ornate hilt and guard moulded into skeletal designs.

Kira tensed as the lethal tool hovered over her chest and then slowly descended with threatening intent. In fear of being cut she remained frozen to attention, the edge picking at the scabs of wax, scraping them way as the razor edge brushed her skin but did no harm. With sloth, the woman gradually shaved away all the warm crust from her body, the worst parts being her flanks. Her skin was ticklish to the touch, making it harder to stay still and accept the stripping.

When her feet were attended she was squeaking with exertion, fighting to keep still as her toes and sensitive soles were brushed by the weapon, the ordeal easing slightly as the woman turned to her shins and calves.

Finally, after some tense moments her breasts were lightly scraped free of their token markings. The blade circled about her features, delicately removing the lines, the woman's face alive with enthusiasm at Kira's calamity.

The last of the wax was removed and some vigorous brushing across her body threw off the final lingering dregs, the passage of latex fingers across Kira's flesh making her shiver with an iniquitous glee. The woman beamed her amusement and continued awhile longer, pointlessly rubbing Kira's skin to watch the slave squirm and writhe, her body flexing and straining beneath her touch.

Her shackles were unlocked, and Kira lifted herself with stiff movements, her arms having grown used to the position and now unresponsive to anything different.

The leash was applied again, and with a soft pull she was steered off the table. Finally being freed of captivity, a few flakes drifted from her skin with her first uneasy strides, her legs like wet paper beneath her.

Escorted out, Kira was taken to her last destination to receive the final part of her tuition, and perhaps it was the most valuable and pertinent of lessons. It didn't matter that much about the history, because everything that existed here was only relevant to immediate gratification for all parties, thus the past had no meaning. Similarly, the facts of her vampire anatomy and the threats and means of its destruction were irrelevant, because for all intents and purposes this palace was impregnable. Filled with ancient vampires and ghouls, surely no force either natural or supernatural could penetrate such a bastion.

The laws and rules were all that mattered, and these were the keys through which she would gain her fulfilment. As a slave of quality and obedience she would strive to impress and soothe the angst of the seneschal. Her obsession with the queen was fading. It was still arousing to be under her control, to be a subject in the realm of such an ancient goddess, but she was also an influential vampire power. With politics and scheming occurring all about her, any involvement with the queen could be extremely dangerous. After all, why would someone of the queen's longevity even care for the fate of someone as young as she? Kira could be a pawn in some machiavellian intrigue, squandered perhaps on nothing of relevance, just because it was the queen's wish to do so. The queen now intimidated Kira, and instead, her desire was firmly located on the cruel and aloof seneschal.

Cassandra was the mistress of her dreams, the sadistic bitch that would take her and mould her like clay into any configuration she required, Kira's will being a superfluous commodity to this greater design. The woman would use and abuse her without pity or second thought.

The prospect of being dominated by someone who cared for her had been pleasing at first because she believed herself scared of any intense play, afraid of what she could and could not stand. But now she had been dragged through trials that previously she would have gone pale with fright at the thought of even seeing. Someone who loved or was fond of her could not orchestrate such deeds; she needed someone of far darker temperament and motivation, and Cassandra was ideal.

A new door accepted her identity and she was ushered in to serve again as a pain slave, to suffer solely for the whim of the queen.

The room was like a tomb, the inside bare save for a grave-like indentation in the middle of the floor. Beside it was a long bag of latex, like a sleeping bag.

The door whinnied shut and set its locks in place as the trainer wandered over and lifted the base of the sack, revealing an opening at the feet and the insides of the sheath.

'Get in, slave,' she ordered.

Kira looked at it with dismay, but dared not resist, so she moved forward and lowered onto all fours, her leash being removed as she started to slither head first into the close-fitting slot, utilising the meagre slack to get her body fully within. Her head pressed to the end, signalling the limits of the sack. No holes for any of her senses were to be found.

'Place your arms in the internal sleeves,' came the woman's next command, the words barely able to seep in through the dense layers of latex resting atop her.

Shuffling within the stifling interior, Kira found two slots for her limbs, and obeying, she moved them down into the depths and lay back, her entire body now swathed in the deep folds.

The thickness of the cocoon lay across her front, heavy and dense, smooth against her skin. The smell of the fabric spilled through her senses, consuming them, making her ache to be able to touch herself, to feel pleasure again and find new bliss in her capture. Any shuffle had her slide against the material, prickling her skin, making her wriggle just to continue the feeling of rubber upon her.

There was the sound of movement, and fixtures were snapped to the sides of the bag, leaving Kira to just lay still and wonder what was going to be done to her.

Without warning there came a gushing inrush of air through the walls of the sheath, the latex inflating from within at a rapid pace. Almost immediately her exit was denied as the sheath swelled first about her feet to seal her in, gripping softly to her and increasing its crush in leaps and bounds.

'The laws of the queen's palace are simple,' stated the woman, starting the education as Kira felt the structure swelling about her, pushing down on her skin and welling beneath her. 'If you perform as required, if you please those who make use of you, you will find your life filled with pleasure.

'However, unsatisfactory performance will lead to immediate correction and the assigning of a number of demerits. On regular occasions you will be required to work off these marks of your inappropriate behaviour,' continued the woman, Kira now being lifted up from the floor, the latex beneath her becoming more severely pressurised.

'You will be offered the choice of one of three manners in which to alleviate your debt. Each choice will place you in punishment bondage for a certain length of time. Should you choose the first, the bondage may be mild, removing one point per half-hour spent in it. Every time your sentence carries you to a new crime you will be given chastisement with a paddle, flogger, or similar weapon after it has been related to you. Thus you serve the penalty for each crime consecutively,' decreed the trainer, and Kira started to shuffle uneasily as the sense of claustrophobia became more intense. The latex prison was growing evermore firm upon her, and was now squeezing against her skin.

'For example, you may be suffering for an hour for failing to obey. After this hour you are scheduled for another forty-five minutes for lack of respect. At the end of the hour you will be disciplined, then informed that you are now suffering for not showing enough respect to your superiors. You will be left to endure for the forty-five minutes, and so on and so forth until all your felonies are expiated,' added the female, continuing the inflation, the rubber shell now exerting new force, swallowing up her ability to move.

'Should you choose the second method you will remove three demerits per thirty minutes, but the bondage will be considerably more harsh and the discipline you receive will come from a crop or cat,' came the next part of her instruction. Kira was now concentrating zealously to the words as a means to distract from the rising grip about her. It was like being swallowed up by some consuming void, her body removed from her, replaced by the feel of latex imprisonment.

'The third method will remove five demerits per half-hour, and will result in severe bondage, and very likely modes of suspension. Plus, the chastisement you receive will be from a cane, dressage whip, or bullwhip.'

Kira started to panic, the latex now like iron under the extreme pressure contained within its walls. The face plate was pushing across her features, stopping her from stealing breath, depriving her of any hope of voicing her distress as the soft words of her tormentor continued to drift in through the thick material.

'There are numerous castes in the palace of the queen, each of them run by a head slave who answers to the seneschal, who in turn answers to the queen herself. You will come to know many of these castes during your time here, and they are as follows...' The process of inflation eased as the sack reached its maximum tolerances, the entire structure pressing inward from all directions, giving Kira a feeling of isolation that welled around the deprivation.

'The lowest caste is that of the Feed Banks, where mortals and vampires are held in bondage and regularly milked of their blood, like cattle. This is the manner in which all nutrition for the guests and populace is handled. The blood of vampire-kind feeds the ghouls. The blood of mortals sustains us and negates the need for messy and damaging biting, while also dismissing the need to stalk mortals in the dangerous open when we could better spend our time indulging ourselves.'

Suddenly the dildos were working on her again, teasing her clitoris with delicate mechanised kisses. The last of Kira's air was lost as a sobbing gasp of response, the breath filtering through her bleak cell and escaping.

'Then there is the lot of furniture and function slaves. These serve as seats, tables, shoe polishers, lights, toilets, bidets, doormats, any number of inanimate objects, and do so until they are granted reprieve and moved to another task. Of course, it has its rewards, for such slaves watch and learn all the various pursuits that occur here, they get to observe firsthand the most debauched delights and wicked passions. This of course adds to their frustration, for they cannot indulge, only observe until they are freed of this caste.'

Kira started to calm herself, forcing herself to relish this tomb, to find pleasure in its firm hold. The action was eased by the work of the belt as it hummed within her, filling her loins with warmth and sensation.

'Pain slaves such as you are here to suffer because the queen deems it so. You are exempt from the demerit system simply because you are punished constantly. Particularly disobedient and troublesome slaves are assigned here, as well as slaves who have been assigned on a whim. Sometimes, novices like yourself are placed here for a quick training and breaking of their spirit,' the woman revealed, explaining why Kira had been sentenced to this fate. Cassandra wanted the process of Kira's indoctrination greatly expedited, turning her quickly into a fawning degraded slave, unusable for anything else save sensual pursuits.

'The caste of pet has slaves placed in the bestial configuration of a dog, cat, or pony, through to the more obscure variations such as fish, cow, worm, and other lowly forms. The servant caste are our waiters and waitresses, our cleaners and handmaids; they perform the more ordinary tasks expected of a servile lot. They will also perform and entertain, service and sate any other sexual or fetishistic needs their owners may have,' she stated, making Kira wonder what it must be like to serve in this palace, to wander and attend, clad in a tight uniform to emphasise one's servility. It was a caste she would like to try, and images of waiting on Cassandra and having her take her servant whenever the motivation promoted her seeped through her thoughts. To be there when she awoke, thrown onto the bed and made to perform; it was a delicious concept. But to gift such a daydream with any credibility, she would first have to prove to Cassandra that she had no intention of trying to steal her position or the attention of the queen.

'The last caste for slaves is that of harem slaves. They are kept in private modules that house nine slaves each, one of whom is their personal monitor slave. This one is responsible for keeping them trained and obedient, and if they fail to do so they shall lose their position to another. The monitor slaves answer to a head slave who supervises the entire group. Harem slaves entertain the guests and denizens of the queen's palace in any way demanded of them. They are sometimes sold off to other vampire houses, or to any who wish them. Some multi-billionaires who know of our existence leap at the chance to purchase a vampire slave, for to have such a creature of beauty and power, and also be able to drink of their blood to gain eternal longevity is an unsurpassed offer.'

Kira's eyes were wide with excitement, her body slithering against the oppressive cocoon. To be a sex slave, to have these preternatural beasts using her as there slut, to be made to please them, and punished when she did not... it titillated her sense of longing to new levels. She could get to see everything, experience every vice and deviance from the guests of the palace, and then perhaps, to be sold to someone, to become their personal and most prized possession for all time, kept in luxury and subjected to their whims. Again, against all reason, she treated herself to dark fantasies of Cassandra purchasing her, perhaps to keep her from the queen. It was not at all likely, but with the belt tickling her insides it did not matter; she could concoct the most unlikely scenarios and imagine she were in them right now.

'The queen has a royal harem module, where the most valuable and prized of her slaves are kept. This module is kept even from the seneschal and is the queen's private domain where none may tread save her and those kept there. Harem slave is perhaps the most sought after caste to be in, and of this the royal harem is the highest rank a slave can enjoy without the privilege of becoming a monitor slave, a head slave, or even seneschal.'

Kira wondered what manner of slaves dwelt within. Such specimens had to be the most beautiful, the most skilled - creatures of unsurpassed and inhuman allure. To gain entry into that place, to be one of the queen's personal harem, would be an honour above all others. To be recognised as so precious that she needed to be locked away from all outsiders and coddled in that vaulted locale. It was tempting to dream of gaining admittance, save that should she attain such a height she would lose her beloved Cassandra forever, and her obsession with the regal vampiress was becoming too fanatic to brook such an outcome, even in the realms of fantasy.

The belt cut out as usual when she was delivered to the brink, and she flung herself to the task of breaking free as she felt orgasm slipping away once more. How much longer would they do this to her? How many more times would she be served up to this ordeal of being teased and then deprived? It wasn't fair; they had won her over. She was entranced with no mere carnal act; she wanted the more illicit aspects, the depravity, the taboo deeds.

They had systematically fanned her flames of lust, making them rage within her, and through this training had turned her ordinary lusts to ones of a far more evolved nature.

No more sound was reaching her from without, so she guessed she had been deserted to assimilate her lessons.

The palace was an unholy city unto itself, with citizens and numerous tiers of slavery for all, with the queen as presiding lady over everything and everyone.

It was amazing to think that all the times she had walked the surface world, lost to her own banal distractions, far beneath her feet and beneath the feet of every other ignorant mortal there was another world, an entire land devoted to sensual excess.

Vampires, werewolves, wizards, all the things of myth and superstition existed. Secluded from view, hiding under a cloak of fiction, their existence was believed so incredulous and unlikely that none even considered the possibility that such forces were real. And now she was part of them, drawn in by one of the most powerful vampire rulers.

Lost in her own world, thinking and stoking her prurient lust with notions of what she might be forced to do, all the things she would be made to do to others and have done to her, she started to slip into a hazy half sleep. Slipping to and fro within the somnolent folds, Kira's wishes started to manifest about her. Without any senses granted save frenzied and fact fuelled imagination, Kira began to think of herself placed amidst her dreams. Her mind wandered, finding increasing difficulty determining what was conjuration and what was not, for the real world offered so little at present that her thoughts were far more clear and appealing. By stealing away her senses, they had left her surrendered to imagination.

She felt herself under another's heels, being impaled by a pounding male sex, tied down, suspended, used as furniture, as a pet. All she had heard about wafted through her ravenous thoughts.

The hunger for blood started to arise around her projected scenarios, making her lust for the quaffing of life. She wanted to be fed her sustenance, to partake of a lover's vitality during intercourse, to relish her new role as a predator, a killer, a thief.

It seemed like years before something happened to contradict her realms of nothingness, and it took a long while for her to actually notice, so lost was she within the worlds within her mind.

The bag deflated for lengthy minutes, the release of its hold leaving her slack within it, too used to one enforced position to be able to find any other. It was like her body had forgotten how to move and needed time to dredge in its old memories to bring out the recall.

The head of the garment was taken and lifted up, causing her to spill from within it, reborn into reality from a rubber womb. Had she possessed even the vaguest shred of body heat she would have been soaked with sweat, drawn through a long and sweltering ordeal within the consuming folds.

Spilling onto the floor she flopped into a tangled and loose heap, unable to affect her own movement, her eyes screwed tightly shut against the meagre light of the chamber.

'I trust you have studied hard, slave?' came a female voice, and it took a moment for Kira to gain enough awareness that these really were her true surroundings. Then she recognised that Cassandra was talking to her, and this was not yet another hallucination plaguing her hunger for sexual release.

'Yes, seneschal,' she croaked, having trouble straining the words out.

'You will be glad to know that your time as a pain slave is at an end. It's time to place you in a caste more appropriate to my needs. I think you'll like being my pet, don't you?' she said with a sharp edge to her voice, almost like mocking, as though she expected Kira to resent such a fate.

'I will, seneschal, I will... I missed you so,' she managed to say weakly, her words skipping out as she thought them. The need to feel something real was too pressing to deny, and despite the lethargy in her limbs she pushed herself into fighting to move. She could not see, she had to at least feel that the woman was actually here. Guessing at where she was, she squirmed over and nuzzled her cheek to Cassandra's boot. It felt good to have the latex footwear against her face, to know that her owner was real and here.

There was a shocked pause, as though the seneschal had been caught off guard by Kira's response, then, instant fire swept through her rear, making Kira fling herself aside.

'I gave you no permission to touch me, slave!' hissed the woman, an incensed tone spilling through her clenched teeth.

'I... I'm sorry, seneschal,' whimpered Kira from her lowly position, relishing the throb of the weal, for it was the first real sensation she had felt in a long time.

'Sorry? You'll really learn sorrow, slave!' A heel settled into her body, pinning her down. 'As my pet you will not speak, and you will do exactly as I command. I'll train you to perform, to obey my orders, to erase your very sentience, wipe it from your mind and leave you as a genuine beast. But that can wait, first we have to get you into your uniform,' and a hand reached down, snapping a leash to Kira's collar.

'Follow me on all fours, slave,' she said with firm tones, tugging on the chain links to have Kira rise and stumble with reckless gait. The world was still a dazzling sheet of indistinct patterns and motions before her, her eyes still readjusting, her faith being placed totally in the guidance of the seneschal. Her legs and arms were stiff, barely able to meet the demands of the slow trek, but with effort and the occasional lick of the brutal cane to her cheeks, she made the journey.

A door closed and she found herself in a new room, blinking, her vision finally starting to bring clarity out of the chaos. The seneschal stood before her, the elegant curves of the female raising Kira's hunger to find pleasure. The woman was more beautiful than she ever remembered, her starved eyes feasting on the latex and mesh bound curves of the stern vampiress.

A pang of cramp tightened her arms, the myalgia spreading out with barbed tendrils from her heart as it sought an end to its blood thirst. The seneschal saw the advancing stages of hunger and merely aired a soft titter.

'Not yet, my pet, we have to get you dressed first,' she stated, her arms crossed, the cane jutting out from her tight fist, her legs apart to keep an arrogant facade.

Cuddled into a ball, holding herself tightly as she continued to endure the growing pain, Kira let her eyes wander the scene.

It was a large room, furnished expensively in the geometric shapes and striking hues of the styles produced in the eighties. A raised area accessed by zigzagging steps lifted away from the plush and deep carpet of pinks and blues. Painted with a contrasting zigzag black and white pattern, the stage bore a diamond shaped glass table, with four high-backed chairs about it.

A number of large plastic bowls were held aloft by a fluted foot on each, the interior filled with crazy patterned cushions, making the nest-like armchairs places in which to curl and find comfort. They were sporadically placed about a large television, the area beneath it being a glass opaque cabinet filled with other technological entertainment systems.

Two doors found exit from the room, and clustered patterns of acute shapes surrounded the lights on the walls, staining the emanations a variety of shades as they spilled through.

The seneschal clapped her hands thrice, causing the door on the left to open and two strong-limbed men to emerge. Tall, with solid banks of athletic muscles, their faces were hidden within tight rubber hoods, the dense helmet only broken by the two small eyeholes that served to allow them sight. Their maws were stretched, and no breathing vents existed, testifying that these were vampires as well.

Fitted with collars, they also wore firm stainless steel chastity belts of the type that brought Kira so much distress.

Strolling forward, they bowed before their owner until they reached their knees, whereupon they kissed her toes and paused to await further instructions.

'Fit her with the puppy outfit, slaves,' she decreed, reaching down to stroke their smoothed midnight heads.

They scampered away, returning through the door and emerging a few minutes later with piles of black folds between them. The time of their absence was spent with the seneschal merely watching Kira with a vacant intensity, hiding what was going on in her mind from the studied slave girl.

'Get her into it, slaves, and afterwards I might let you find some relief,' she crooned, making the two slaves straighten with sudden shock at the words, their desperate need to expel their frustrations one that had them applying themselves to the task with verve.

The hands of the males were upon Kira, smoothing across her skin, relishing the feel of her supple young body. She could almost hear the sound of their erections straining against the internal slot of the belts. She gave a little resistance, just to have it crushed as their strong arms leant more brawn to the task and started to feed her into the uniform.

A halter neck leotard of latex was drawn onto her, the front having had two round sections removed to let her breasts spill free. Buckled straps about the base were tightened with firm pulls to make the flesh swell, her nipples growing hard, her breasts throbbing.

The zip along her back rose up and then grabbed the zip of the hood that was pulled down over her features. With two pointed moulded ears, it offered a mirrored visor across her eyes, and a small slot for her lips to emerge.

Stockings and gloves were dragged up her limbs, the tight dense sleeves fitted with moulded paws at her hands and knees with slits that permitted the rings of manacles and fetters to be pulled through.

One of the men grabbed her calves and bent them up against her thighs, using the incorporated straps of the hose to connect them, keeping her legs folded and stopping her from straightening them. Buckled suspenders dropped from her shoulder blades and hips to grab the rubber garments on her extremities, stopping her from sloughing off the opaque shell and finding freedom. Trapped on all fours, her fingers were lost within the sculpted mittens, and with her legs bent up and her feet pressing to her buttocks, she had no hope of getting up from this lowly pose.

A tail was slotted in at the base of her spine, the fixture allowing it to spring up and wiggle with the motions of her hips.

Reduced to the visage and limitations of a quadruped pet, she looked to her owner with tears in her eyes, hoping there would be a reprieve from her hungers.

The seneschal smiled broadly at Kira's hidden gaze and pulled on her leash, drawing her away. Kira shuffled along, scampering as the suit demanded before nuzzling to the legs of her owner. Looking up, she stared across the glorious curves of the seneschal, burning with desire for her.

'No, my pet, I have a different show for you,' she stated softly, petting Kira's head, running her hand down it to make rubber squeak against rubber.

'Come here, slaves,' she ordered, making the men skip over to her, whereupon she produced a small circular key. Slipping it into their chastity belts, a turn made the crotch band spring out, their own tightly bound flesh causing it to leap from their tracts, dragging out the long thick dildos sheathed in their rears.

The males caught their imprisoning strips and set them aside, settling down onto their knees.

'Perform for me, slaves, but do not dare finish without permission!' she warned with grave tones, and with no further need of convincing their hands leapt around and clapped to their flesh, their shafts already rising to attention with their stifled libido.

Taking their time, relishing the feel of their masturbation, they watched the seneschal with piercing eyes, studying her curves, imagining all what they would adore doing to her. Their hands shuffled back and forth, drawing their orgasm until they were forced to stop and let it drift away, for no permission had been granted. After a short pause they would start again, stopping and commencing, depriving themselves, gaining snippets of pleasure but gathering fuel for their angst.

'That's it, slaves, keep going, but don't finish,' the seneschal ordered, glancing down to Kira as she stared hungrily at their sexes. Her mouth was watering at the thought of enclosing her lips about their raging lengths, to gobble them up and suck free their seed. But she could gain nothing for herself save the satisfaction of providing pleasure to others as frustrated as she.

'Now stop.'

The males reluctantly paused, clearly weighing up the choice of quickly finishing off their deed, or remaining obedient. After a moments questioning and the facing of the frowning glare of the seneschal, they stopped, their members raised and flushed with excitement.

'Now, my pet, go and finish them off, or did you think me blind to your desire?' she quipped, and applied a swift hack of the cane to Kira's rear.

Launching forward with a squeak of pain, she scuttled out of weapons range and dropped before one of the males. Her hidden eyes met his blank gaze, and she could see the burning need to have her do this written plainly in the sparkling pupils.

With a content smile she lowered her face gently into his loins, parting her lips and letting her mouth engulf him. Closing herself to the shaft she sucked in and let her tongue taste of the hints of semen his masturbation had released. Her eyes closed dreamily at the feel of being used such, of being made to service others as she herself was denied.

Kira's head started to rise and fall, hauling at the skin, making it ride the flesh, drawing out the pleasure of the male. To further facilitate her task the tip of her tongue danced on the head of his penis, this most sensitive spot bringing out subtle spasms from her partner.

His hands started to furl into tight fists, the veins and tendons rising as he strained to hold back, to let himself gather more of her delightful pleasures before he prematurely ended the fellatio. With a spiteful grin Kira tightened her hold and hauled more forcefully, making him compliant to her demands.

The slave stiffened and wriggled in his kneeling position, torn by intense pleasure as Kira felt cool semen fill her mouth. The viscous spurt rolled upon her tongue and without care she swallowed, ensuring she milked him of all he had to give.

When she could pull free nothing more, she cleaned his shaft with a deft tongue before she finally withdrew.

The seneschal looked down, meeting Kira's adoring gaze before checking the results of her pet's adoration.

'Well done, my sweet pet. Now the other one,' she demanded, indicating the expectant second slave with a jab of her bamboo wand. The male flicked a glance to Kira as she moved, her latex uniform issuing sharp squeals as her limbs brushed each other.

His length was already rigid and proud to her eyes, aroused to a point of derangement by the sight of Kira's oral attention on his comrade. The slave stiffened with pleasure as she swallowed up his length, performing as before, sucking firmly, exacting her demands. As she worked she let her forearms stray inward and skip across her teats. The flashes of delectation from the strangled orbs had her attending her deed with even more fervour.

'Stop that!' snapped the seneschal, delivering the cane across Kira's buttocks with meteoric force. 'Dirty little pup!' Kira cried out around the shaft, resonating it with her scream, keeping her lips tightly sealed to it so that it gagged her response. New tears welled in her eyes as the first meagre barrage of shock gave way to the full ferocity of the cane's most potent chapter of punishment.

Her rate was stopped, and slowly started to recover as the hot flashes began to subside. Returning to the oral act she kept her arms out, so as not to irk her owner.

The sight of having Kira punished before his very eyes, her nubile form squirming in the tight folds of the latex skin, pushed the slave over into orgasm, and a chill wash of salty issue was splashed over her palate. Again Kira gulped it down, shaking with rapture as it clung to the walls of her throat. With detail she cleaned him, and then withdrew.

'Good girl, a fine performance,' crooned the seneschal, and pulled back with the lead, reeling Kira in.

'Put your belts back on and get back to your duties, I want everything done by the time I finish this week's inspection or I'll give you fifty demerits each,' she warned.

The slaves nodded and snagged their lost chastity belts, their shafts already wilting after the sating of their desire. Aiming them back into position, they threaded the dildos into their opened rears and then with a sudden haul, slammed the locks back into position, sealing them in once more. With their sexual organs again placed under the control and whims of the seneschal, the slaves scuttled forward, kissed her feet and them jumped to their bare soles. Jogging away they vanished through the door, their step considerably more spry since Kira's easing of their distracting tensions.

'First, let's get you fed,' said the seneschal, drawing Kira over to the other door. 'I want you on your best behaviour during my tour. Come with me, puppy.'

Through the portal was a short corridor with several doors laid in its walls. The first brought them into a kitchen where the refrigerator was opened, revealing row upon row of blood bags, the tags for transfusion purposes still upon them.

Removing a bag, the seneschal took a bowl from a cupboard and poured the contents into it. The sweet essence sloshed to and fro, shimmering and making Kira's incisors emerge. Her eyes were wide, her limbs shaking with expectation.

Setting the bowl before her, the seneschal stepped back and watched as Kira plunged her lips into it. With a lapping tongue she drew gulps of the succulent fluids, the chill in it a negligible taint against her ravenous hunger. Her sight flashed with spots as she fed from the vitality of the anonymous donor, stealing from their very essence by her leech-like feeding. In moments she had emptied the reservoir and quickly lapped at the sides, not even leaving a smear behind as she took all she could, uncertain as to when she would be fed again.

'Now my pet, we have to go and make a check of the queen's realm, to look in on a few regions at random' revealed the woman, settling into a crouch before Kira, the latex purr of her descent making Kira swoon. A hand came forth and cupped her chin, bringing her eyes up to meet those of her owner. 'Then there will be a meeting with the head slaves, after which we shall attend to the matter of training you more thoroughly, erasing all that you are, turning you into a humble beast. I'm going to take your mind from you, little pet, and there's nothing you can do to stop it.'

Kira pondered the matter in a heartbeat and was captivated. The threat that was meant to intimidate and horrify was a pleasure to her. She would willingly surrender to such training, to being stripped of her humanity so that she was nothing more than a hound at the heels of her gorgeous owner. Fully trained and obedient, that was her goal, and by reaching it she would impress the seneschal.

'So while you see all the sights this world has to offer, think well, as it will not be long before I've taken such a power as thought from you,' Cassandra purred, and then arose, pulling on the leash to have Kira scuttle in her wake.

CHAPTER 11

Sitting at the heels of his owner, Thanos watched in a forlorn mood as the procession of the oriental vampires and their entourage emerged into view.

Strolling with calm grace and regal majesty, the representatives of Tsuki-Yomi were led by the infamous Amatsu Mika Hoshi. The Dread Star of Heaven was ancient despite his youthful appearance, a creature of immense power that was at least fifteen hundred years old, probably more. A force in the Shinto religion that preceded Buddhism and the other faiths, he had been a lurking presence throughout Japan's long history.

Thanos had heard tales of the vampire ninja he used to eradicate his enemies and opposition, warriors trained for centuries in the subtle arts of quiet death.

The man was almost hidden from view beneath his ornate armour, the ceremonial dress and weapons worn for this occasion with the queen.

Behind him strolled warlords in similar archaic extravagance, followed by their wives and concubines, and servants and human pets. The clan was akin to the house of his mistress, a place of carnal pursuits and subtle politics of sensual hedonism. Pleasures of the flesh and spirit were the guiding force behind their actions, the vampire nobles living lives of unbridled luxury with a vast slave contingent of willing or forcibly trained men and women.

Thanos was concerned because of this, for he had heard Dana talking with Cassandra a few nights back, and the queen had informed her of the old custom they still honoured. While the clan was her guest, she would lend them one of her most prized slaves, and they would do the same for her. Thanos had an apprehensive insight that he was going to be the olive branch to commence the negotiations. Lupines had never managed to reach Japan, the island was too close knit, its vampires too deeply entrenched with numerous forces of the Wyrm and its demons assisting them. Every attempt to lead a crusade against the islands had never been anything other than total disaster.

Since Dana had captured him and exploited his submission to train him as hers, he had successfully remained her faithful pet. He had willingly gone forth to smash the rival vampire houses, capturing some of their leaders for the queen to take revenge on.

He still adored her, still worshipped her, and at such times when she tormented him and abused him for her dark joy he was happiest. Even Cassandra, who had been a jealous bane on his life since his arrival had not turned up to inflict her tortures on him for a long time now, finding other diversions instead.

Life was progressing in new directions, and it was starting to seem that soon he would be a neglected hound. With such thoughts brought forward, he almost welcomed being handed over to the clan, to serve more attentive owners, and maybe, just maybe, seeing him taken by others would rekindle the queen's old enthusiasm for her toy.

CHAPTER 12

The main door opened from what had to be Cassandra's private apartments, and Kira was delivered once again to the winding corridors without.

On her hands and knees she trailed lovingly in the wake of the seneschal, watching her world pass by. This was her home now.

A set of doors glided apart, offering the diamond plate interior of a large lift to her gaze. Shuffling in, the seneschal tapped the lowest of the three buttons and the doors were sliding shut once more.

With a soft lurch of motion they started to descend, the smooth ride ending with a clunk as the veil of metal parted to reveal a new area in the deepest bowels of the palace.

A short corridor led to a box room that was clearly a guard post. The portal to enter it was filled with dense bars and a locked gate. Another lay directly beyond, and to the right a vault-like door lay open, letting sounds of merriment spill out onto the air.

In the room, manning a wooden desk, was a dark-skinned woman of stern physique. A short bob of dreadlocks fell about her alluring features, her eyebrows thin and perked to grant a perpetual quizzical expression.

Clad in a sleeveless leather jacket, the garment lay open to expose a leather strapless bra, the seamed cups embracing her smooth and ample breasts. The physique of her arms and torso were brazenly exposed to intimidate, her very demeanour one that brooked no dissension to her will.

Black lycra leggings rolled with her curvaceous legs before slipping into heavy knee high boots, the fronts armed with opaque shin-guards and numerous buckles.

Crouching at her side was a man condemned to the same cast as Kira, his body squeezed into the confines of the puppy uniform, save that his bared nipples were pierced and weighted. The hound sat equably at the heels of his mistress, kept on a short leash while the woman perused details on an expensive laptop before her.

The seneschal approached the bars and stopped, catching the eye of the guard.

'Greetings, seneschal,' she said, with a hint of foreign accent.

'I'm here for an inspection. Is head slave Gherth about?' Cassandra asked.

'No, seneschal, she is out recruiting again,' replied the woman, thumbing a switch under the desk. The lock gave a startled buzz and dragged back, allowing the seneschal to meander through and throw it shut in her wake.

'Are the reserves low or something, then?' Cassandra continued, stopping before the hound and petting its head while speaking to the guard. Through the door, Kira could see another four of these guards, men and women, their fangs bared as they drank from glasses of rich red life.

About their feet scampered demeaned slaves. Bound in confining uniforms, some were clearly pets that they teased and made perform for their amusement, while others had hoods whose crown bore a platter and which carried bottles, glasses and myriad small implements of abuse and torment.

The men and women used clamps and pegs to snag the skin of their victims, employing pinwheels and other devious instruments to make the slaves about them suffer while they toiled to please their betters.

Turning from this spiteful scene, the next barred gateway was opened, and Kira followed her owner within, casting a brief look across the fully trained pup by the desk. Was there any thought within that hood or had it all been expelled? Did the training actually reduce sentience to a primitive level? Or did it merely condition one to behave in such a manner, leaving normal thoughts to roll around and find satisfaction in the lot forced upon it, unable to slip free because of the indoctrination?

Walking the slender corridors beyond, Kira was horrified by what she saw as she was led through, the casual gaze of the seneschal skipping across the sights and merely making sure all was as it should be, untroubled by the nightmare of what this place represented.

Each wall was fully laden with small alcoves, each placed close to each other to optimise on space. In almost every single one was a contained being. Men and women, held to the interior wall by a plexus of metal bonds, stout tubes emerging about them and burrowing into their orifices. Pipes into their stretched maws ensured they were kept fed, and others about their loins carried away waste. They were completely unable to do anything save simply continue existing.

They could have been mistaken for the dead but for the display board on the wall, the monitoring sensors fed by wires attached to the bodies and keeping track of their vital signs.

Also, shuddering influence assailed their bodies on occasion, the metallic bonds serving to pour voltage nips into them, to keep their muscles from wasting, eliminating bedsores that might start to spring up from such unrelenting captivity.

Beside their necks and arms, on each side, was an intricate engineered construct, the device a detailed sculpture of pipes and mechanised parts the purpose of which she could easily guess. The osmotic syringes would stab to their prey and siphon out the precious fluids, never breaking the skin, ensuring a long and terrible life in the arms of such strict capture.

Other alcoves held creatures such as she, served up as cattle to the appetites of others. The vampires were bound with far thicker restraints, and their monitoring devices gave up a far less distinct pulse. Locked in place, they could only watch the seneschal and her hound pass.

Mortal life was steadily introduced down their throats and the far more valuable vampiric sustenance was then harvested, serving to feed the army of ghouls that dwelt in the palace. These were the worst sights to see, for Kira knew that without the hampering of age or failing of body, such farmed immortals could well be held so for eternity.

Wandering the many halls of such distressing slavery, the seneschal checked that all was progressing as was prescribed, the dreadful silence in the air only beaten back by the shuffle of Kira's feet and the brittle clack of the seneschal's heels.

Suddenly the woman paused. Turning, she moved into an alcove and with one hand, captured the occupant's nipple. The man winced, regarding her with utter rancour, straining against the bonds.

'Still got some fight in you, eh?' she mused softly, regarding the captive from beneath a lowered brow. 'Well, a few decades of this will cure you of that. How does it feel to be feeding the house that ruined you?'

'Foolish arrogant upstart,' she scowled, turning the nipple and then letting go. 'You have paid the price for your insurrection. I hope the memories of your meagre leadership and limited rule of the city above are strong ones, as you'll find they are the only comfort you'll find here.

'Your time is over! Her majesty has taken back what is hers, and will now bleed you until time itself perishes,' promised the seneschal, before airing a sadistic laugh and leaving the slave to his fate.

As Kira walked on all fours she wondered who the man was. Clearly he was a former enemy of the queen. Was he one of the council that had been established, perhaps a chairperson of it, someone who led the city and represented the vampire houses? If so, she could understand why such a sentence had been imposed, for it meant he had been one of those who helped steal the city away from the queen, and because of this, Kira could feel little pity for the vampire.

Leaving the ranks of the feed banks, Kira was taken back to the lift and restored to the area of the queen's domain.

Once more entering into the maze of corridors, the woman took her back to the main lift, passing through the now deserted throne room of the queen. It had seemed like an eternity since last she'd seen these hallowed halls, and it was still as breathtaking a sight as she recalled.

The elevator restored her to the upper reaches, and through the splendid halls she was taken. The levels above the training and storage grounds of the queen were replete with life, with servants bustling to and fro, pets being walked, guests strolling with an entourage of comrades and slaves to attend them. It was almost intimidating, for in her time of training she had grown used to being alone or attended by a small number. Sudden immersion in such numbers made her distinctly nervous. Kira kept close to her owner's heels as they walked, wondering where she was being taken, but too devoted to impressing her owner to risk daring speech.

A stretch of corridor was blocked by two burly male vampires, their teeth exposed in sneering snarls, their hair cropped to little more than stubble. Round-eyed welding goggles hid their gaze, no doubt to protect from any intense light that might otherwise be used to disable the gloom accustomed vampire sentries.

They wore leather trousers, the knees and shins fitted with black armoured sections that fell into weighty and steel-plated boots. A heavy silver knife was buckled to each outer side, and the close-fitting trousers arose to a studded utility belt. Pouches spiralled around it, along with eight fitted holsters which bore lethal barbed stakes of reinforced plastic far tougher and more durable than any wooden version, their wicked teeth serving to lodge them in position. Along with these weapons to end un-life, an MP5 lay in a waist holster, the sub-machine gun fitted with laser sight. The slender banana clip was overlong - extended and modified to hold greater numbers of rounds. Three more spare magazines lay on their waists in quick release pouches.

Dense flak vests added to their robust stature, the garments rising to protect their throats and almost hide their collars. Their muscular arms were left free save for spiralling tattoos down the right arm and the symbol of the queen on the left, with heavy leather gloves encompassing their hands.

Across their backs were crossed swords, the slender silver falchions equipped with heavy shearing guards.

The sentries bowed deeply as the seneschal approached, offering their fealty and genuine respect to her. They were not performing such obeisance out of habit or order; it appeared that they were actually in real awe of Cassandra. Was it because of authority, or strength? Could it be that these mountains of trained muscle knew they were no match for the seneschal? Was she really that formidable?

Kira felt them staring at her as she scuttled past, her sudden fright making her move even closer to her trainer. The warriors were terrifying, their faces gaunt and grim, hardened by murder and killing. If these were examples of the queen's defences, surely nothing could harm this domain. It was reassuring to know they were there, but they were still intimidating to behold.

The passage beyond the defences was a dead end, both sides lined with heavy vault doors of polished silver.

Her owner placed a hand to the first, the door giving its customary response of grinding clunks and started to slither back, revealing the interior.

A short passage led into a round hall, the black marble of the chamber polished to a sheen that emphasised the slender weaving streaks of deep pouring through it.

Nine separate doors were equally spaced throughout, the one directly opposite the entrance being silver, the others all a striking and unblemished white.

Beside each of the doors was a heavy metal ring, riveted into the fabric of the wall. A long chain lay fixed to each, linking to the collar of a woman of great beauty, their naked forms crouched and humble.

'Seneschal?' asked a soft, heavily accented voice from behind, their approach unheard by Kira.

'Yes, Lord Amatsu Mika Hoshi?' replied the seneschal before she turned, discerning the identity immediately. Bowing slightly, she faced the guest as Kira shuffled in a circle to regard the new arrival.

The Asian male was young and slender, his smooth skin cloaked within folds of black satin. His hair flowed back into a long ponytail, the base fixed with an ornate jade clasp. Despite his innocent and equable exterior, there were depths behind his small smile, and an age and power in his eyes that testified to him being an exceedingly ancient vampire.

At his feet he had a diminutive Japanese girl. Un-tethered, she was clad in a comprehensive suit of black that reduced her to a feline appearance. A mask sprouted whiskers and pointed ears. Her eyes shone like diamonds within the darkness of the hood, and she watched Kira with a disturbed intensity. Shuffling on the spot, her tail twitched to and fro as she kept to her master's heels.

Kira ignored her and continued to regard the girl's owner, marvelling at his visage, his grace and poise. It was strangely captivating to watch him, as though even when he was idle there were a dozen things to behold and fixate on. She could watch him for hours, even if asleep, and never bore of him.

'I am seeking some new diversions, something special for a display I'm planning,' he reported, barely even noticing Kira and her stare.

'We have numerous fine harem slaves for you to choose from, lord. Would you like to see a selection?' responded the seneschal, offering the queen's wares to this visiting ambassador of the Orient.

'Lead on, seneschal,' he confirmed, and allowed himself to be shown into the room.

As Kira followed, watching him slink casually into the room, there was a sudden flurry of movement and sharp pain slammed across her cheek. Her back slammed to the wall, a harsh strike having caught her features and thrown her back.

Dropping into a loose sprawl, she shook off her giddiness and saw the cat lunging inward for the kill, a hiss of jealous rage spilling from her throat. Kira's study had irked the beast beyond tolerance, no doubt deeming one such as she inferior of being able to regard her master.

Without thought Kira acted like lightning, her body employing a speed it could never before have borne. In a split second she was restored to a crouch, and before the girl's rage-inspired dive even reached her, Kira launched forward, the stone beneath her feet cracking from the sheer power in her kick. The binding latex of her uniform snapped like tissue paper, setting her free to attack, a sudden red veil of pure berserker fury descending through her mind.

It seemed as though her enemy were trapped in slow motion, her senses raised to a new and intense peak. Effortlessly she swatted the girl's arms aside while both were still in the air and screaming towards each other, her strength treating the girl as straw. A moment later her fingers jerked out, shredding the latex mittens, bursting effortlessly free of their prison. Her hand clapped across the throat of the girl and as they passed each other in the air, Kira wrenched forward with a sanguinary growl.

The incensed velocity of the girl was countered in an instant, Kira's dive a thing that tolerated no deviation. Snapping her to a halt Kira dropped her feet to the floor and continued her haul, throwing the girl back whence she came.

As a blur of movement the cat was delivered to the floor, bringing out a titanic splintering crash as her body shattered the marble floor and was driven a full foot into it.

Without pause she flung the girl back again. Her limp form piled into the wall, demolishing an area of it. As the girl's body was just starting to slip from the ragged crater it had been forced to excavate, Kira was already moving in, fangs freed and hungry for blood, her rage like a storm within her. But a hand grabbed the back of her neck and she was thrown against the opposite wall with jarring force, her rage oblivious to the pain. Another arm snagged her limbs and fought to contain them as she roared in fury, fighting the grapple upon her.

'I was not aware you had brood on offer?' quizzed the man, holding Kira to the wall, his small frame a monstrous deception, for he held Kira with little effort. Already she was calming, her efforts to subdue her rage helping to bring serenity and rational thought back to her.

'My apologies lord, we had not determined for sure that she was. A quad of fangs can sometimes manifest for a short while in new-born Nosferatu,' testified Cassandra, looking over the fallen vampiress, her body laying inert amidst a pile of rubble, the floor and wall a vast web of cracks that jerked from the impact area.

'I understand. But there is no need for apology, it was my poorly behaved property that instigated this affair. And the defeat of an eight-century slave at the hands of this new-born, only proves that she is brood.'

'What do you wish done with them, lord?' asked the seneschal.

'Take my pet to head slave Strafe. She is to be disciplined in the most stringent manner possible. She was warned that we were to adapt to different customs here, and her failure will be reprimanded accordingly. As for this little creature, I believe I have made my decision after all.' He shifted his grip slightly against Kira's anatomy. There was a pang of discomfort, and suddenly consciousness fled, an expert pinch to some valuable nexus stripping away her awareness.

CHAPTER 13

Arising through layers of coma, Kira let her senses gather to some measure of coherence before opening her eyes. She felt strange, her body aglow from within, as though it had been the lightning rod for some awesome burst of energy, and had kept a few residual traces lingering throughout its structure.

The slow lifting of her eyelids became considerably more hasty when she felt soft hands brush against her flesh. Sitting upright with a jerk of motion, the handmaidens about her flinched and shied back, their hands rising to protect them should she attack.

'Please, mistress, we mean no harm!' exclaimed one of them with fear in her voice.

Kira was laid upon a low altar in a small room. The plinth had a padded top, and was supported by rows of squat pillars shaped like leering gargoyles.

Candles lined the perimeter of the floor, casting cones of amber light up the dark walls. The rectangular room had a door in each of its smallest faces, and overhead the symbol of the queen dominated.

About her were six Asian girls, all clad solely in white thongs, their small ripe breasts on open display. Their long sable hair was tied back to cascade down their bare backs, the clasps flinging out short spines. They wore no make-up of any kind, their faces too exquisite to be tainted by such things. Any attempt to heighten their already perfect features would only mar them. The artist that created them had succeeded in attaining near perfection, so any attempt to continue the process would only spoil it.

Realisation struck and Kira's hand dropped to her waist to find the belt gone. Dropping her gaze, she found herself naked save for her collar and cuffs, even her body hair had still barely begun the process of emerging, her metabolism slowed to a veritable crawl, just like her heart.

Kira calmed herself and remained where she was, looking across her new flesh, having not had the opportunity for some time due to relentless latex bondage.

The handmaidens moved a little closer, approaching with caution as though she were a wild animal. But the entire affair was still well beyond Kira. How had she managed to do what she'd done? She had been impotent to act contrary to what her rage demanded. The fury had swallowed her whole, devoured her reason and left her only with the ultimate urge to bring carnage. Just what terrible force was in her body? The cat had not been killed by her attack, so she had to be a vampire of centuries spent honing her toughness, training diligently to attain such levels of inhuman hardiness. And yet, Kira had found her a trivial opponent, the girl's strength nothing compared to what she could unleash.

'May we continue, mistress?' asked one girl.

'What?' said Kira, being brought from her thoughts, her mind still filled with the image of the cat girl shattering the marble as though it were chalk.

'We are to prepare you for the show, mistress. May we continue?'

'Show?' asked Kira.

The recall of Lord Amatsu Mika Hoshi was hazy and indistinct, her awareness of her surroundings half-seen through the eyes of the maenad she had become. His words were barely noticed, and she was not sure she had heard accurately. Had she been given to him?

'Our master has chosen you for entertainment this night,' said the girl, seeming a little exasperated that Kira kept asking so many questions. Clearly they were used to the slaves of their master simply giving themselves over without word or hesitation. 'We are his servants and are here to prepare you for it.'

'I see,' she replied with trepidation, wondering what this show would entail.

The maids moved in as one unit, working together in practised unison. They brushed her hair, as another maid applied token appliances of cosmetics and some lipstick.

A white thong of satin was drawn up onto her and settled into place before a suspender belt was added, then snow-white fine denier stockings. It was strange to be dressed by others, the process slightly relaxing and very arousing. Kira wanted to exploit the opportunity to caress herself, to appease the hunger in her long starved loins, but she had a feeling she would need all her sexual appetites for the feast she was being served to.

White ankle boots were laced onto her feet, and as her collar and cuffs were polished to a dazzling sheen, one of the girls began to use rope at her back.

The weave worked from a hub in the middle of her spine, the central point reaching around her torso to run lines above and below her breasts, making them stand out a little more from the slight squeeze. The soft ropes grabbed her biceps with a wringing fist and pulled them in before her forearms were laid parallel to each other and the wrists caught together and held in an intricate pattern of knots and hoops.

Kira did not resist as she was bound. She could only clamp her legs together and dream of what was going to happen to her, surrendering herself to the feel of the velvety ropes slithering across her skin, capturing her limbs and embracing her torso.

With their charge readied for her performance, all but two of the girls moved back and remained on their knees, sitting erect and stiff. A pair of them arose and applied a lead to her collar.

'Come with us please, mistress,' said the bearer of the leash, and with a gentle pull began to walk with precise steps towards the door.

The other girl followed behind, taking a cane from beneath the slab and holding it as testament to prove Kira's slavery.

With wide eyes and a fluttering belly, Kira followed obediently, her fingers stroking her bound skin, her limbs trembling slightly with anticipation and anxiety.

The door opened and revealed a catwalk. The slim white path was lit from directed overhead spotlights, leaving everything but its surface hidden in nebulous depths.

Led down this glowing road, Kira was brought onto a large platform, the lights flashing on from every direction to bathe it in a warm radiance. The spotlights from without poured their gentle radiance onto the circular stage, denying Kira any clue as to what lay beyond. She could hear the faint rustle of movement, of cloth shuffling against skin, but had no idea who or how many were watching. Was the queen out there? Was Cassandra?

The catwalk lights winked out, leaving her the sole point of attention. The girl with her leash gathered in the slack and closed her other hand into Kira's hair. The delicate fingers reached in at the root and enclosed to hold a large bunch.

Using this anchor Kira was drawn down to her knees, held captive by leash and hair. Her eyes closed a little as she complied, a glorious sense of exhibitionist iniquity roaring through her. She knew she was on display, but it was a display tempered by anonymity. Like facing a television camera, she could tell herself that one person watched her, or that hundreds of people were arrayed about her. It was her choice what she found easier to believe.

The other girl spread Kira's knees a little more, so that she knelt upright, her rear presented to the crowd.

The hold in her hair pulled a little, making her crane her head back, her mouth opening slightly with a sigh of delight at being manipulated thus. With a gradual acceleration the stage started to revolve, turning slowly, presenting her from every direction.

Staring into the bright lights, she wondered what the others must be thinking or doing. Was she arousing them? Were they growing stiff or wet with desire for her as she was shown to them in such an enforced manner?

The handmaidens released her, taking away the leash and bowing deeply before retreating into the shadows, leaving her alone in the light.

Long minutes passed where she had to fight to keep still, the temptation to move or get up pressing to her. The sense of jeopardy also had her wanting to flee, but her hunger for experience kept her firmly in place.

Shuffles and creaks of rubber emerged from the perimeter and she saw hints of silhouettes, the lights catching refractions on polished forms. Emerging from every direction came six forms, and Kira gasped as she saw them. The Asian women had stern uncompromising faces, moulded into one severe expression that had hardened like iron and would never change. Their eyes were rimmed with dark shades, their lips painted a similar deep hue, adding greatly to their glower. White and black latex poured down their heads in the form of nuns' habits, the rest of their bodies hidden beneath a curtain of the fabric, the vast cloaks completely enveloping them.

The one directly before her held the silver chain that connected two clover clamps. The devices were affixed to the nipples of a young Caucasian male. He was of average height, with a physique that was wrought from battle; hard like a diamond and swift like the wind. She could confirm such suspicions with hints of old scars on his form. His skin was slightly tanned and weathered, but hidden from the sun for long enough to make it start to pale. Already he had been subjected to punishment, numerous crucifix shaped weals painted across his thighs and rear, the custom-made weapon leaving a strange shape in its wake.

His dark hair was short, and his attractive face was kept rigid, hiding his desire for her and his relish for his treatment. In his eyes she could see the truth his features sought to hide. The pupils were wide, soaking up her form and that of the latex nun holding him hostage.

When Kira spied his collar she realised who it was. The collar was the same segmented implement she had seen on the lupine at the queen's feet. The collar had shrunk with his transmogrification to a human visage, but it was definitely the same one. Even his hair was the same colour as the pelt of the monster she had seen. It was hard to believe that these were one and the same, and Kira wondered what it would be like to witness him change, hoping she would soon have opportunity to see.

He was bound with rope as she was, save that a crotch rope ran down to grab a cock ring, the steel hoop squeezing his testicles and shaft, preventing him from wilting as he remained swollen to the eye. The sight of him erect thus had Kira dreaming for the feel of him thrusting into her, to make her a carnal display for the amusement of the watching voyeurs. Was this to be the show? The mating of a brood vampire with the most ancient enemy of such a creature - a werewolf?

Kira continued entertaining the notion of having him penetrate her, and then she added the fantasy of him undertaking the transformation she wanted to observe, while within her. Having her partner become something new during the act of sex and becoming the creature she had seen humbled at the heels of the queen was a delicious concept.

Leading him before her, the nun drew down the lupine until he was kneeling as well, leaving the two of them staring into each other's eyes, separated by a short distance. Latex-gloved hands emerged from the veils of the two nuns that stood on either side of her and brought Kira back to her feet.

Rope was tied around her mid-thigh and then pulled out, the tight lengths easing her legs apart into a lewd split where her ankle boots wobbled to keep her supported. Her balance was hard to maintain without her arms to steady her, but still she tried to keep calm. The ropes were fastened to moorings in the shadows beyond the lights.

One of the nuns emerged before her, standing still, fixing Kira with a lifeless stare. Then, with dramatic extravagance, she threw open her cloak to reveal what lay beneath, making Kira's eyes widen in shocked astonishment.

The folds of black rubber ruffled in the light and fell behind her shoulders, trailing down her black and leaving her free of its encumbrance. The woman was compressed within a halter neck leotard of rubber, the high thigh reaching over her hips and plunging as a narrow slit down the front, barely concealing her.

The white collar expanded to her throat, reaching to the shoulder and falling as a diamond to point between her enclosed breasts.

A single wide suspender dropped down to grab the black band of fishnet stockings, the hose clinging to her legs before losing themselves beneath knee high patent boots with stiletto heels and laced fronts.

Opera gloves encased her arms, and about her waist hung a cross of belts fitted with custom holsters and pouches to contain the wares of this stark pseudo-priestess.

Clamps, pegs, cord, a short strap, and a vicious crop with crucifix head were the only visible items, those on the rear of the belt hidden from view by the cloak. With the crop exposed Kira could see now where the lupine had gained his welts.

Looking to her sides, the nuns located there similarly cast back their obscuring curtains of latex to reveal identical costumes, all armed similarly but with their own variations. All carried the crucifix crop, however.

One nun remained behind her, hidden from view, while the other two stepped back, keeping their cloaks about them and watching impassively as their fellows conducted the rites of dominance.

Reaching behind her, the nun before Kira removed a pair of what looked like chopsticks. Holding them up into the light she presented them to the spectators and moved forward, hiding the lupine from Kira's gaze.

Staring at the wooden struts, Kira was startled when the woman grabbed her jaws, sinking her fingers and thumb into her cheeks, forcing her to open her lips.

With the other hand the nun held the devices as one would for eating, and reached in. Fishing around in Kira's mouth as though it were a plate, she caught the end of her tongue. Kira winced at the bite placed upon her, but could do nothing as the woman drew her out, extending her tongue as far as it would go, making the organ ache from being racked so forcefully. Releasing Kira's face she instead took hold of the wet appendage, keeping it extended as she laid one chopstick on top, and one beneath.

The nuns at the side moved in immediately and wrapped cord around the two ends, turning the struts into a wicked vice that squeezed the base of Kira's tongue. She moaned and wriggled against the ropes, the wooden sticks pressing to the corners of her mouth, preventing retreat.

The nuns withdrew, leaving Kira plagued by this most cruel of gags. Shaking her head she tried to get it off, but could do nothing to prevent its effects on her, and a keen ache started to build within it as circulation was hampered and sensation tormented.

Again the nun reached into the depths of her costume, this time bringing out a purple vibrator that she held aloft as she flicked the switch on its base. The rigid plastic finger started to thrum, and the nun brought it forward like a blade, to touch its tip to one of Kira's breasts. With soft stroking motions she circled the tender bud, making it rise and stand proud to accept more of the delicious tickles.

Once one teat had been attended, the other was similarly teased and made to stand for attention.

With her work complete, the nun slotted the toy into Kira's thong, the tight garment pressing it along the length of her sex. Gurgling from the discomfort of the gag, Kira shook from the glorious effects, her torso bending forward a little as she squirmed upon the device pressed to her.

The nun walked aside, the group rotating one place to deliver a new individual to Kira's eyes.

This one presented a pair of clamps to the air, holding the two pincers up, their chain links swinging a weight beneath them, the leaden ball spitting out an array of long slender pins.

One at a time she had the baleful jaws swing in and grab one of her presented nipples, squeezing it within its plastic-coated jaws, making her shudder and try and pull away from what had been affixed to her.

The nun released the devices, letting them hang, the weights adding to her distress as they pulled at the morsels, installing more havoc. The weights brushed her stomach, making Kira air a pip of shock and restore her slight stoop, the prickly kisses of the pin-laden ball demanding it.

A cold throb started to rise in the flesh, sending resonant echoes through her breasts, the depth and intensity growing slowly, making it harder to accept them. But with this duress was also the soothing effects of the vibrator, letting her sense of submission find a welcome source of fare from this erotic torture.

Her current angel of pain was one dedicated to compression, for after installing the clamps she started to reach to her sides, where looped strings bore fastened banks of black pegs. The gloss clothespins were painted with delicate silver symbols in the same arcane script that adorned the collars of slaves, and lifting a pair into the air, she snapped their wooden teeth for the amusement of the crowd.

Kira shied back as they were wafted before her, drawing patterns in the air, preventing her from judging where they were to be placed. Her motion made the pins scratch her stomach again, and cursing her memory she stooped immediately.

The hands reached down and the pegs snagged a meal from her inner thighs. Kira croaked and stiffened, making the weights bounce and afflict her nipples further.

Unable to close her legs and get them off, she had no choice but to endure, and again she concentrated her efforts on enjoying this, on submitting to her own dark desire for such torment.

A new pair were delivered into the light and began their descending dance, the nun working like a snake charmer, distracting Kira with the performance before clamping the implements to the underside of her breasts.

Another pair joined those on her inner thighs, the nun concentrating on this region until a row of seven descended in a neat line down each side.

Whimpering, Kira was dizzy from the sensations being heaped upon her. It was a struggle to stay upright, her sorrow rendering her giddy. But it also felt so good, a terrible contradiction of sensations that left her confused as to how she should accurately react. With her thighs attended, her hips caught a flock of pegs, these being surprisingly mordant in their gnawing companionship to her skin, and any wriggles she made to try and get them off only had the spiked weight pecking at her belly.

Tears began rolling down her face and she croaked pleas for mercy as the nun started to concentrate more fully on her breasts, applying a full dozen to each, reducing them to a porcupine of dark wood.

With her supplies exhausted the nun withdrew, walking around with the others behind Kira, leaving her on full display as the stage continued to turn and show her suffering to all.

Shaking, she sobbed and pulled against her restraints, her struggles proving to be the real source of entertainment. Looking down she beheld the lupine, staring up at her, his eyes like stars as he beheld her woe.

The sound of heels on a measured pace sounded, and a pair of exposed nuns stepped to either side of the lupine. One woman drew her cloak aside and over one arm as she stepped astride his head, placing it between her thighs as she faced his rear. Kira saw his utter relish in being held like this, trapped between the legs of the woman.

The woman's belts of equipment were selections of needles and pins, this nun being one devoted to more severe pursuits and Kira was glad she was not being attended by her. But even so, she could not help but feel her lust rising at the sight of the nun.

The leotard plunged as a slender buckled strap between her pale cheeks, bisecting the pert mounds as it traversed her loins. Between the naked thighs and the stockings was the trapped head of the male, his features suddenly tightening with forced stoicism as a thwack sounded out, the second nun having started applying her crucifix crop to his rear. With steady strokes she cast the weapon back, the strut humming into the shadows before whistling back and sounding with a sharp note against the target.

Again and again he was struck, his suffering staining his countenance as he whimpered and shuffled against the imprisoning legs. It was a wonderful distraction from Kira's own ordeal, one that had her entranced while it was occurring.

Her wondering as to what he was going through was suddenly and graphically revealed to her when there was a soft song of speeding passage from behind her and a pair of crosses landed on both her buttocks. Caught by surprise Kira let out a cry, and then danced against her bondage, trying to roll through the burning flickers they'd left behind.

A moment later a single crop struck, and then the other, the two nuns alternating in her chastisement, applying it with a fixed rate, never wavering from their pace, no matter how much she shrieked and struggled.

Tears were rolling freely down the features of both slaves as they were mercilessly punished for the hunger of the crowds, the savaging of her rear stopping Kira from gaining the release the vibrator promised.

With her reduced to a sobbing wreck the beating stopped, and she almost swooned in the ropes, choking back a sudden flare of utmost satisfaction. To have been pushed beyond tolerance, and to have exceeded it and been punished so thoroughly was utterly liberating.

So disorientated and confused were her scrambled senses that she barely noticed the loss of the vibrator. But as the second nun started to recover the pegs her awareness returned suddenly, each flight releasing a sudden shock of stabbing havoc through the pinches as sensation galloped back in and told tales of the trauma it found. Wincing and croaking her petitions for clemency against such travail, Kira spasmed in her bondage, fighting the ropes in a bid to alleviate her stress. But even if she were free, what could she do? She would have to remove the pegs to get rid of their insufferable curse upon her, and to be free of them meant she had to accept their parting gift of suffering.

Torn by the calamity, Kira was weeping freely when the last came away, and then the nipple clamps were taken hold of. The nun looked into her eyes, pulling gently on the chain to increase their effects, teasing her as Kira tried to brace for what she knew would be the worst of the extractions.

The clamps came away together, and a second later Kira screeched into the air, her breasts exploding with effulgent pangs. She tried to break free, to grab them and comfort the punished flesh, but she was still bound too effectively and could do nothing save feel the effects slowly dwindle back to a bruised throbbing.

The gag was opened and taken away, leaving her tongue slack and lifeless in her mouth, seemingly unconscious after its capture.

The nun capturing the lupine stepped aside, releasing him, letting him sag to the floor in a heap, exhausted by his scourging.

The other nuns also withdrew into the shadows, leaving the monitoring pair to throw open their cloaks and come forward. Both lupine and vampiress were startled to see that they bore no other armaments save a black replica phallus that spouted from their loins, merging with the fabric of the garment. They strolled forward, stepping behind each slave and taking hold of collar and phallus. The male was pushed forward, driven by a prodding penis until his face reach Kira's belly.

The nun behind Kira locked a hand into the rear of the thong and yanked. The fabrics snapped easily, pulling Kira back and onto the tip. As she fell back from the coarse stripping she mounted herself onto the waiting pole. Arching her back she released a howl as it opened her long starved rear and sheathed itself deep into her tracts, the motion of its passage almost making her faint from sheer ecstasy.

The pleasure was taken to a new zenith as the face of the other slave was buried into her freed sex, his lips kissing before his tongue reached into her and started to lap. An icy groan spilled from her throat, shaking unsteadily as the nun held her close, pushing back and forth, grinding the phallus deep.

Latex-gloved hands reached around and held her stomach and caressed her breasts, the cool digits tracing routes across the flushed skin, teasing the bruises and sites of previous torment.

Cupping Kira's chin, the woman drew her back to lay against her collarbone. Her rear was being opened by deep plunges from root to tip, her tracts dragging along the length, filling her with hot bliss.

The tongue of the male attended her with skill, circling and lapping, flitting and sucking at her clitoris, occasionally driving deep to offer a shade of penetration. All the while his body moved back and forth with the relentless plunge of his anal attacker, the woman riding him, holding his hips for an anchor.

'Change,' whispered the woman, as he was pushing into Kira's depths as far as he could.

There were some resonant crunches, like bones snapping within flesh, and the moist creeping chuckle of migrating meat. Kira jolted her head up, defying the hold of the nun behind her to see what was happening. As a penalty the woman jabbed deep and twisted, making Kira cry out, but still she kept to her pose; she had to see.

The male swelled, snapping the ropes as he grew into the abomination she had seen previously. His features spilled forth as a fierce light lit up within his eyes. Dense fur erupted from his skin, covering him instantly as the nun was forced back a little way, his body growing larger, his limbs arming themselves with rippling banks of muscle.

When his tongue accepted the canine change Kira threw her head up, her neck straining towards the ceiling as she released a keening holler of response. His tongue drilled into her, reaching deeper than any mortal specimen, rivalling the most well-endowed manhood, its base opening her, its roughness scraping against her clitoris to have her yell with a mix of pleasure and pain.

The results were increased as his fangs nipped at her inner thighs when he meandered aside to lap at the tender regions. The light scratches made her sing her turmoil, the feel of their caustic nature to her flesh making them throb, her body protesting at its inability to heal the cuts with its ordinary unnatural celerity.

Controlled by paroxysms the nun held Kira tight, keeping her upright as her muscles pushed the ropes to their very limits. Her legs yanked at the bonds, her arms flexed against the entrapment, her rear still being filled by pleasing jabs.

She could not handle the sensations, they were too much for her, they were even harder to sustain than the beating and the pegs. Fighting fervently to get free, her scream rose through infinite reaches as orgasm arrived. The long deprivation heightened it further, and as the lupine poured his tongue into her every muscle was taut, every tendon raised against her skin, every vein thumping with her dwindled beat. flare of

The nun stabbed deep, filling Kira even more acutely before retreating to expose an exhausted wreck.

Sagging against the rope and the hold of the nun, the male was drawn back, the woman removing herself from his rear and standing up, leaving both slaves quivering.

The nuns threw their cloaks back into place and moved into the shadows with their brethren, the shadows devouring them all, engulfing their dark clothing, leaving only the hints of their pale skin before these too were lost into the depths.

The stage slowed and stopped, ending the carousel of depravity and letting the catwalk again be revealed by intense beams.

Four of the handmaidens appeared, entering the glow, their naked flesh gleaming in the light like milk. They sauntered over and opened Kira's thigh bonds. She staggered a step and almost fell to her knees, caught unawares as to just how dependent she had been on them for support.

The servants snapped leads to the collars of the slaves, and with a monitoring servant lingering behind with a cane, they were escorted back along the path and into the waiting area.

Once within the solitude of the chamber the girls removed Kira's ropes, folded them neatly and set them beneath the table. Without word or explanation they left, leaving the drained pair to slump on the floor.

Regarding her legs, Kira saw the small scratches the werewolf had imparted with his kisses. The skin was healing as though she was mortal, unable to level its regenerative powers against the bite of the arcane beast. As she traced the lines a warm heat ran through Kira's spine and she turned and regarded the lupine. The beast was crouched low, his incandescent eyes locked to her form, burning with lust. But instead of fear, only the most powerful excitement rolled around her mind and belly, churning her throat, making her pant with unneeded breaths, her cold heart quickening to a new and fervid pace.

The lupine tensed, his fur undulating upon the waves of rippling muscles. His tongue spilled out and licked his lips, revealing massive fangs as he gathered his legs beneath him, readying to pounce.

Kira kept her ground, adopting a similar prepared stance, clawing the floor.

With a snarling hiss she revealed quadruple fangs, her painted lips curling back to reveal them in full as her eyes lit up with an inner light, the crimson fires throbbing deep within, a manifestation of her temperament.

With a subdued roar the werewolf charged towards her, his erection plain, the teasing wrought from his abuse and the tasting of her having stoked his hunger for more substantial fulfilment.

His speed was uncanny and rivalled her own. Connecting with her midsection he tore her from her feet and carried her in the air before slamming her to the wall. Kira's back cracked the stone, driving defunct air from her lungs but stunning her a little. Held to the surface she felt him establishing a more severe hold through which he could attain his goal.

Dropping an elbow she caught him between the shoulder blades, the severe impact driving him down a little. The strike would have severed a mortal spine with ease, but to the lupine it was little more than a stern punch.

Releasing his hold he span and flung claws at her head. Kira ducked with a ferocious grin, letting a scintillating spray flash above her as his talons tore deep grooves in the stone, spitting out glowing motes under their passage.

A drum tone was sounded as her fist slammed into his stomach, the muscle like sandbags beneath his skin. With a startled rasp of exhalation he threw up his right leg and swept it aside, the speeding kick catching her across the side of the face. Her gaze jerked aside as she felt heat in her cheek from the strike, but unfazed she merely lurched forward, fangs leading the way to try and take a chunk from her assailant. With a shuffle of movement her head was caught in burly arms, the headlock stopping her dead and leaving her pinned.

Immediately she back-flipped, arching her legs up, contorting herself in a way that should have snapped her backbone. But the blood in her veins had made her body something beyond mortal, beyond vampire, and with a savage impact her heels cracked against the lupine's jaw, spinning his head aside. With a growl of wrath he spat the blood from his lips and cast her aside, sending her careering recklessly, fighting to keep her equilibrium as the velocity he imparted faded from her tumbling form. With a premature strike she met the other wall, her head leading her passage to bring a flash of white before she toppled back and landed on her rump.

The sound of clawed feet pounding the floor reached her ringing ears, and operating by sound alone she whirled from her lowly position. A pirouette on one heel let the other leg lance out and strip the beast's feet from beneath him. Before he fell she launched herself up, letting a wicked swipe of her fist lead her ascent. The crack of knuckles against jaw buffeted her ears and the furred mountain was sent reeling back. His feet scrabbled beneath him, trying to recover, but Kira's assault had been too much to cope with and he fell with a heavy thud, sprawling across the floor.

Kira dropped back to her feet after her brief flight and dove into a cartwheel, emerging from it into a dive, her hands reaching out, formed as claws to sink into him.

There was a swift spin and the beast twirled, flipping over and stopping her in the air by clamping a hand about her throat. Before she could react he thrust aside, casting her back into the wall once more. The creature sprang to his feet and stormed her before she could recover, her weary legs carrying her forward a few steps, her back pounding with the contusions heaped upon it.

Throwing himself into her stomach, she was thrown into the air by his hold and then dropped to the floor, the beast hurtling down and using her as a cushion to break his fall. The stone shattered into shards and nuggets beneath her, and Kira's mind dissolved into primitive reaction, both of them reduced to beasts.

Kicking and scratching she aired sibilant tones, her jaws wide, her face contorted with wicked choler, corrupted by unholy power. The lupine grabbed her wrists and pounded them to the floor. Pinned down, Kira felt his length touch her moist sex, prodding like a blind man's stick, seeking entry. Unwilling to give in so easily she fired her head up. Her brow met his snout, jerking his head back. Immediately she thrust her head back in after it had bounced from the assault. Her fangs caught skin and sank in, allowing her to steal a lap of his essence. It was like drinking liquid fire, a cocktail of the most volcanic emotions that seemed to enter her through osmosis, pouring through her soul and driving her onwards.

The lupine scowled at the bite and keeping hold of her, flung his right arm to meet his left, trapping Kira on her side as his legs hooked into hers and kept them subdued with his weight and strength. Kira let loose a series of serpentine hisses, trying to break free as he used his hips and legs to complete the manoeuvre, turning Kira over and placing her face down so she could not repeat her attack.

With rasping frenzy she squirmed beneath him, fighting his hold as he dug his feet into her inner thighs, pulling them apart and shuffling down.

Her sex was wet with arousal, the sanguinary blood rage heightening her libido to unprecedented levels, leaving her open to penetration. She felt his length rub against her portal and then slither in, drawing her open and rolling into her like a piston of elation. Kira froze, her mouth wide, releasing a groan of rhapsody that poured out in a prolonged note until he was pressed against the limits of what she could house.

Immediately she calmed, melting beneath him, her defeat acknowledged. Now she was free to relish his attention.

With steady drives he sank himself into her womb, making Kira buck with rapture, her long chastity finally broken by this most bizarre of lovers.

Gasping with pleasure she remained trapped beneath him, his body pressing down on her, the fur soft and tickling every portion of her that was exposed to it.

The creature offered up his wound to her, the thin lines of red that wove from it sparkling with life. Straining forward she could not bring her teeth to bear, but with a stretch her tongue could just skim the surface, letting her taste the untamed power of the lupine. The bliss of such a delicacy was a keen rival to their intercourse, the power of it making her feel invincible - like a goddess.

The rhythm of his stabbing shaft started to increase drastically as he approached climax, and Kira too could feel herself giving in to a matching release. Panting her affirmation she called for him to complete his task, begging for it as she sought to hold on, to deny herself until the moment she felt him fill her womb. It was nearly impossible.

The werewolf threw his head back and unleashed a canine howl that resonated the floor beneath her, shaking the air with its volume and depth. Kira bucked beneath his hold, his hands crushing her wrists in vice holds as she joined his inhuman bray, her mouth stretched impossibly wide, her fangs stained with her lover's blood, her screech adding a piercing treble to his pounding bass. Her world flashed with colour, her nervous system beset by a volcanic detonation of bliss.

The last spasmodic drives carried him through his climax, and the beast settled onto her, his limbs draining of power as though he had transferred it to her via his seed.

Slouched on the floor, both of them failed to move for long minutes, enervated and lost in the soothing afterglow of their insane passion. Held beneath him, Kira simply lay with her eyes closed, her womb squeezing to his shaft in fits of gratitude.

With a moan of effort he rolled aside, withdrawing from her. The lupine shed his wolf semblance, withdrawing the fur and fangs, the claws, dragging in the massive frame and retreating into the flesh of what appeared to be no more than an ordinary mortal. The four small holes at his neck were still prevalent, but the bleeding had stopped, as the beast was better equipped than she to heal such damage.

Kira shuddered, and thought of how the pegs and the crops had felt, their wonderful stinging kisses, their long abuse to her skin as she was tormented for the amusement of others.

'What's happening to me? I never used to be like this,' mewled Kira, wondering how such alien appetites had arisen so quickly. She had never before loved such subjugation, never even considered it. Now she relished it like nothing else. Even now the torture of the nuns was a memory to be placed in the treasury of her mind, polished and set on a shelf of most valued mementoes.

'Don't fret, I was just like you once,' replied the lupine, stroking her hair as he lay on his side, Kira still unmoved. 'In fact, we are probably more alike than you would think.'

'What do you mean?' she asked softly, smiling at the feel of his fingers running through the strands, her eyes closed to savour the feel of such comfort.

'We are both exceptions to those around us. We are more powerful, stronger, and that makes us prizes that others want to experience for themselves. You might say we are novelties in this domain.'

'Because of what they say I am? What is this brood stuff anyway? How come it happened to me? I didn't do anything special.'

'No one knows the exact cause. But I've heard tale of such things as I've sat at the heels of the queen. It's a random quirk. Some say a throwback to the first vampires, a shadow of their primal power.'

'So what caused it?' she asked, propping herself up on her elbows and turning to face him.

'Vampirism?'

Kira nodded, studying the contours of his face, committing it to memory as he laid back and looked to the ceiling, almost wistfully, as though serenely casting himself back to halcyon and half-forgotten days.

'The only legend they speak of here is one that begins with a demon lord of the Wyrm possessing one of its shaman. The rituals involved brought more than a mere inhabitation; it fused them, creating a hybrid creature. The blood of this beast was virulent and malevolent, and mortals who ingested it suffered instant Maleficence. The power in it has dwindled as it was passed down the ages, but if the demon essence meets mortal blood that is akin to that of the first primary host, then it creates a vampire such as was first forged. The other vampires about us have been created using blood passed down through hundreds of others, whereas you, because of your blood, are like one created by that very first ancestral beast.'

'You believe this?'

'Why not? I've fought the Wyrm and its shamans, I've fought the vampire, I've seen demons and their hosts. It is reasonable enough.'

'Don't you regret anything?' she asked, and there was a moment's pause before he frowned and then gave in to a secret smile.

'Not any more. I fought the seducing will of the queen at first, tried to resist because I was taught to do so by my kind. I had battled the machinations of the undead my entire life; it was my purpose. And to be held by them as a slave? Well, it took awhile to give up and surrender.'

'Were you always like this, or was it the queen who made you submissive?' she asked, laying her head on his chest, curling her legs up, the stockings torn by their battle and subsequent savage lovemaking. His hand rose to lay across her, holding her to him.

'I can't say. But when I was first in the city I started to feel new appetites welling within me. I resisted at first, told myself that the decadence of the city was trying to infect me, like a shamanistic charm. But then I started to indulge a little - then more. It was during a visit to a professional dominatrix that resulted in my capture. The queen nurtured my growing nature and let me live it, releasing me.'

'If you had a choice, would you do the same thing again?'

'I'm not sure. I think so. I love her,' he stated emphatically, no hint of questioning in his voice.

'But—'

'It's a paradox, I know, because I can never possess her. She is my ruler and I am her slave. But at her feet, as her pet, I am filled with a sense of pride. It's hard to explain, but I'm helpless to resist it. If I wasn't here, I think I'd be distraught and would end up trying to find a way to return. There's no going back.'

'You think I'll end up following the same path?' she asked, responding so quickly because it outraged her. The fervour in his admission of love had lit a jealous pyre in her mind. The male had won her admiration and craving to know him better. They were so similar, so perfect for each other, but to hear that he loved another made her furious. Her full sentence, if not interrupted, would have angrily accused if their recent deeds had meant nothing to him.

'It's up to you, Kira,' he said, 'but I can think of far worse things than being a slave here.'

'But isn't it sick?' she wondered, a lingering notion of morality still obstinately grating against her licentious hunger for everything this place had to offer. The stalwart relic also demanded that she flee, find a cure for herself, try and recover her life, go back to being normal.

'What's sick? Grinding away with base urges to fulfil a social obligation to pointlessly procreate? Tedious little love rituals and offerings, indoctrinated to be "romantic" by those who profit from their supply? Losing yourself in some banal tedious job that sucks your soul dry before casting you onto a dung heap to fester for a few years before you finally die? Old age and infirmity, a life surrounded by mortals, with their pettiness, their arrogance, their bigotry and hatred of anything different? Stifled by civilised life, kept quiet and in line, unable to break free and let yourself truly live? Dreaming of so much, but deprived of all—'

'Or eternal life in splendour, living a life of pure indulgence, surrendering to debauchery, exploring sensation,' she added gently, knowing that he spoke from what he had seen, and what she faced, not for himself. He was a werewolf. He lived with his tribe in the wilds, hidden and concealed, fighting their supernatural war without any mortal ever knowing about the grievous conflict raging about them. He had genuine purpose. He wasn't out to impress fellows or bosses, or to gain a career and wealth and renown. He struggled for a noble cause, to save what he believed in. It was a cause more worthy and more dedicated to than even the most hard-line activist she could conceive of. Yet he had given that up for this, to live for himself above all other considerations.

'It's not much of a choice is it, Kira?'

'I guess not,' she replied. If he had given up such a free and purposeful existence, then she should not even doubt shedding a life that would have been brief, pointless, and useless in order to become something far better, for all time. 'I just needed to convince myself I suppose, to throw off those last lingering second thoughts.'

The exit door opened, causing them both to jerk their heads up to see who it was.

'Well, well, well, isn't this cute?' derided Cassandra.

The vampiress was clad in the image of a police officer. An unmarked cap adorned her head, granting an extra ferocity to her sneer of contempt. A crisp deep blue shirt held her body with a matching tie, the sleeves hanging starched at her biceps. Short leather gloves were clasped about the hilt and shaft of a black crop, the slender stave being wrung in her grasp.

A waspie belt tightened her waist before giving way to a short rubber mini-skirt, stockings that followed the curves of her legs, and knee high plain boots of leather.

'Seneschal!' exclaimed Kira's partner with shock, both of them scrambling to their knees.

'So, have you been a bad pup, Thanos?' snapped the woman, stepping in with a bold stride, tapping the crop into her palm as her eyes fixed to both of them with animus.

'Seneschal, please, I didn't mean to, I couldn't help myself,' he offered, cowering slightly to try and appease her wrath and draw the blame from Kira.

At least now she had his name, a consideration that had not even occurred to her until this point.

'Really, slave? So little Kira here was an unwilling partner to your base advances, eh?'

'Yes, seneschal.'

'So why is there that piercing hickey on your throat?'

'She bit me, she fought back, seneschal. Look at the walls, I had to fight to take her.'

'You lying little shit! After all this time, after all the punishments I've given you, you still think you can trifle with me, maggot!'

'No, seneschal, it was a momentary slip, I lost myself when I was in my full form,' he protested.

'Don't give me your tired excuses,' she roared, her incensed attitude terrifying. The woman truly hated Thanos and was ready to apply any humiliation, any abuse to ease her choler. 'You have to be disciplined, Thanos! So say it! I want to hear your confession before I do!'

'Seneschal, I have been bad, I lied to you, I need to be punished.'

'Good. Now maybe this will teach you a more lingering lesson.'

Reversing the crop she thumbed the base, causing a startled cry to slip from Thanos. She grabbed his collar and he dropped back to the floor, kicking his legs as he roared, the metal crackling with arcs of lightning as he was shocked by the seneschal. The woman released the button, letting him go slack, panting on the floor, shaking a little. Walking over she gave Kira a capricious flick, the crop stinging her flank, making her fling herself aside with a hiss of pain, clapping a hand to the stern weal.

'Out of my way, slave,' she growled, and continued her route to place a leather boot onto the body of Thanos, digging the heel in to make him wince.

Kira had already tasted Cassandra's animus. The woman was going to shatter Kira for daring to have gained the queen's attention, but Thanos was a far more established threat, one she could not tear away from his owner. Instead, she could only make him suffer, and the sheer savagery of her demeanour made Kira fear what would happen to her should the queen actually renew interest in her. Could she cope with such unbridled loathing? Derision to a slave was one thing, it made her feel more servile and truly submissive, but surely such hatred would prompt only resentment and rebellion. But where Thanos had the compensation of being the queen's regular pet and plaything, she had nothing like it.

'Are you ready for more, slave?' the seneschal quizzed, a malevolent smile spread across her lips.

'Please... please, seneschal, no... no more,' he rasped, and had his words turned into a squeal of anguish as the woman repeated the shock, leaving her finger in place, making the collar flash with pulses of voltage as the serpentine tongues of energy licked at Thanos.

Stopping her lesson, she let him catch a few breaths, and then stroked the button before his gaze, making sure he could see it. Just as he was about to air words of clemency she applied her punishment again, tearing at him with the terrible blight of the collar, making him thrash and suffer terribly.

'Seneschal, it wasn't him - it was me!' yelled Kira, unable to see this injustice continue. She was partially to blame as well. She could not let him bear the whole ordeal himself.

The woman turned with a surprised look that quickly melted to one of contempt, but she did not release the control switch. 'Did you say something, slave?' she spat.

'Seneschal, please, I'm sorry, but it wasn't him, it was me, I seduced him!' she implored, hoping to end Thanos' abuse.

The woman pondered for a moment, keeping Thanos in purgatory as she thought on Kira's words. Kira knelt and flicked her stare from the lupine to the vampiress, praying that she stop.

Releasing the control the attack ended, letting Thanos collapse into a stolid ball, quivering, his body wracked with pain and drenched with an icy sweat.

'So, you wish to take the burden for yourself, eh, Kira?'

'Yes, seneschal, I have to tell you the truth.'

'How very noble.'

'Kira, don't,' rasped Thanos through shuddering lips, trying to stop her before it was too late, but she had no intention of letting him continue to suffer for what she herself had craved.

'Quiet you!' the seneschal snapped, and made him yowl with a momentary burst that sent the werewolf back into silent endurance and recovery. 'Now, what did you say?'

'It was all my fault, seneschal,' she stated with a quaking voice, knowing it would be a terrible ordeal, but one she would gladly face to preserve Thanos. It was the only manner she had in which to offer him a clue to her attraction for him. 'I'm sorry, please don't hurt him any more, it was my mistake, you should punish me instead.'

'You are willing to admit your folly and surrender to the consequences, slave?' Cassandra asked, walking towards Kira, making her shake with dread.

'Yes, seneschal,' she testified sheepishly, quailing under the woman's shadow.

'Then get on your belly, arms by your sides,' she commanded.

With frightened sloth, Kira obeyed, lying upon the floor. The woman stepped astride her and sat down, her rubber coated rear pressing into Kira's shoulder blades, her folded legs squeezing Kira's arms into her sides.

'If you make a single noise I'll go back to punishing Thanos, slave,' warned the seneschal, making Kira swallow with dread, wondering if she could hold out, if she could keep quiet and take this chastisement in silence.

'Kiss,' she demanded, offering the leather hoop of the crop to Kira's lips.

Placing a trembling peck to it, she laid her head down to the cool stone and stiffened in anticipation.

There was a deep thwack and Kira stiffened, her jaws clenched tight, her eyes screwed shut as the usual fires swept through her rear. The stroke had been impossibly harsh, more than she could cope with.

Another impact sounded, rippling the soft flesh, making her mouth drop open, her hands furling into fists as she fought to hold back her screams.

Another fell, and another, the sheer strength the woman was applying feeding the scream that was starting to well more distinctly in Kira's lungs. Biting her tongue she tried to distract herself with this different source of pain, but as a fifth fell it proved a useless tactic.

Tears welled in her eyes on the sixth, her body shaking with its fight to hold her throat in check. Her flesh was boiling with the need to fight to get away, to flee and preserve itself, the concept of taking this abuse to save another something only her mind could appreciate, making the two sources vie for control.

A sudden deluge ended with a twelfth stroke that had her lungs swelling with a shriek that was creeping insidiously up her throat, gathering in her larynx.

A thirteenth fell, causing Kira to kick her legs against the floor, the boots scraping the stone as her rear pounded with a lambent internal heat. Salty trails were trickling down her cheeks as she screeched in silence.

Another fell, bringing the scream to her mouth, escaping as a long exhale of air, refusing the final portion of effort that would manifest her sorrow and condemn Thanos.

Again the woman struck, Kira no longer aware of how many strokes she'd received. Further strokes swatted her rear, dropping like meteors, filling her rear with fiery bursts of agony.

The excruciating travail was too much, she couldn't hold it in, she had to scream, the need to wail an internal pressure that felt as though it would rupture her insides should she not release it.

A virulent sweep caught her inner thigh and a faint purl slipped her lips. The seneschal exploited it immediately, attacking the exact same spot with all her might. Kira's yowl tore through the air, matching her previous wail of bliss with one of harrowing. The moment she was broken the woman began a swift deluge, ripping into the soft buttocks of Kira as she bucked and wailed, fighting to get free.

When the woman stopped Kira was barely conscious, sobbing at her defeat, grizzling in apathy at her failure. For all that she had gained she might as well have screamed at the first stroke.

'So the truth has come out,' Cassandra said, placing a heel onto Kira's back, holding her down and tracing her striped rear with the tip of the weapon. 'I guess it was all Thanos' fault after all.'

'Seneschal... please... it was me, I swear,' she choked, barely able to speak, her flesh alive with havoc.

'You still cling to your fable?' she quizzed, pushing the heel in.

'It... it's the truth, seneschal,' Kira blabbed.

'Well, okay, I will give you a second chance to prove your words. It's a choice, Kira, a simple one. Either I fry Thanos for his wanton urges, or...' The seneschal looked down and met Kira's tearful eyes, her smirk of utter glee spread wide, showing how much she was relishing this subjugation of her two rivals for the queen's attention. 'You go back in the chastity belt.'

With those words Kira flinched as though slapped, the sentence imposed on her a most grievous one. She couldn't go back to the horrible frustration, she just couldn't. But Thanos would suffer far worse if she didn't.

Looking to the dazed male, she saw him lying slack, barely aware of his surroundings, torn by the electric scourge about his throat. She couldn't let him suffer such a fate for it. Chastity was a mild imposition compared to the vengeful abuse of the seneschal.

'I'll go back, seneschal,' Kira said.

'If that's your wish,' she grinned, removing her boot from Kira's body and stepping back, twirling the crop and lodging it under her arm. 'Now get up,' she commanded, and then continued with revealing the sentence Kira had earned for herself.

'Seeing as you have such a penchant for hounds, we'll get you back into your uniform and keep you away from any testy cats,' she grinned, walking to the door and beckoning for Kira to follow.

CHAPTER 14

Once again Kira was faced with the interior of the seneschal's private residence, her heart dripping with dismay that she was again to be starved of sexual release. The previous incarceration had been terrible, but how much sterner would it be on her now that she had gained this new inflated sense of appetite for debauchery? She would be aroused constantly by her punishment, her bondage, her slavery to this vicious goddess, and yet prevented from enacting a more physical reply to it. The thought was too terrible to dwell on.

'Come this way, slave, I've just had another idea,' she smirked, walking through the door Kira had used to be served into the kitchen. But this time she was led past the plain door to the storage place of stolen blood, and instead she was escorted forwards towards one of the further subterranean rooms.

The door slipped aside with a smooth swing and permitted them access, the lights arising through strengths to a dim glow. They revealed the interior and its contents first as subtle hints, then as more substantial outlines, and finally in a melancholy light that added to the ferocious image with ample shadow and hesitant illumination, as though even the light was afraid of the implements within.

'First we had better strip you of your demerits, eh, slave?' chuckled the seneschal, indicating the array of engines of torment and precision tools of suffering with a wave of her leather gloved hand.

Kira wilted at the sight as she beheld the stern rack, its leather restraints hanging loose and expectant, awaiting a captive to stretch with their mechanical winches.

A large and extremely stocky throne dwelt against one wall, the rigid structure armed with numerous buckled straps to pin down its occupant.

A tiny cage, its bars thick and flecked with small thorns to dissuade movement loitered to one side, promising the tenant a dwelling of cramped restriction.

The last of the diabolic furniture was what appeared to be a large and roughly constructed ladder. Made solely from thick beams, it was fastened at an incline to one wall, allowing body parts to be fed in and around, allowing for extreme restraint with the many coils of brightly coloured rope hanging on wall hooks beside it.

The walls also bore other items that dwelt patiently on hooks. Weapons of punishment: canes, crops, dressage whips, cats and tawses, all of them fashioned from dark leather and decorated with an obsessive detail.

As well as these devices of lambasting, there also hung the usual selection of clamps, toys, pinwheels and bondage paraphernalia, much of it defying Kira's shallow knowledge.

'Stand in the middle,' snapped the seneschal, the crop swinging around and clipping Kira's buttock, making her yelp and spring into the centre of the room, her heels sinking into the deep texture of the blue carpet.

Looking up, she saw heavy rings fastened to the ceiling, the metal hoops matched by similar ones against the foot of the walls all about her.

The seneschal removed two lengths of dense chain, each end armed with a thick padlock. Snapping these security devices to the rings of her cuffs, the other end was lifted and connected to the overhead rings, stretching her arms wide and preventing her from sagging from this erect pose.

'Now, slave, you have a choice to make. What level of punishment do you want?' asked the seneschal, stepping before Kira, one leg out to stretch the skirt tight. The crop lazily stroked up and down Kira's torso, tracing the outline of her breasts, the leather soft against her skin, a distinct contrast to the usual feelings she associated with it.

Kira considered her options quickly. Afraid to try the most extreme, she also did not want to spend a vast period of time hanging in suffering. So she opted to play it safe and select the medium method.

'I'd like the second way, seneschal,' she whispered with resignation, wondering if she would regret her decision once it was applied. But then again, that hardly mattered, for once some time had elapsed she would be looking back on it fondly. Even now, she was using the abuse of the nuns to remind her that she should try and find enjoyment from this session, that she would love it in retrospect and should try to transfer some of that relish to the deed as it was occurring.

'Three demerits per half-hour it is, slave,' confirmed the woman, and strode aside to fetch coarse rope.

The middle of the woven coils was flipped about her waist and the ends fed through the hoop at the centre. The excess was passed between her legs and drawn up, pressing to her loins. A swift knot was established to press into her clitoris, and the crotch rope was threaded under and over the rope digging into the base of her spine. Kira winced as her ankle was lifted up to her rear and the rest of the rope used to bind her right leg. Encircling the boot, Cassandra used the heel as an extra anchor to form a tight harness, stopping Kira from dropping the leg, and causing any strain or kick of the limb to chafe her sex with the minute shuffle of the crotch rope.

Standing on one leg, her hands pinned in the air, a blindfold was tied about Kira's eyes, plunging her into darkness, and she assumed she had been set in her bondage position. A sigh of relaxation spilled from her lips, glad that she was not being afflicted further.

When she felt the woman tying more rope around her other boot, creating a similar harness, Kira was straining to see through the tight blindfold, to try and spot what the woman was doing. Surely she wasn't going to be placed in suspension? That level of abuse was only for the most severe level of justice. What was she doing? Was she disobeying her own rules? Kira started to fret, worrying that she was going to be confined in the air, and she knew that such a fate would be a dreadful one. The cuffs she wore were inadequate for such a mission, and would dig into her as she dangled, kindling the most distressing pains.

Kira wanted to petition mercy, to ask what her owner was doing, maybe even just to remind her that this was not what she'd asked for. But she had to keep quiet, if she complained, if she showed disobedience, the position might be compounded with spiteful additions.

The rope was drawn out and threaded through one of the low rings on the wall, and the seneschal started to draw Kira's leg out. The heel dragged at the carpet and her breathing quickened as her balance was eroded.

The woman stopped and tied off the rope, leaving the ankle directly below the cuffed wrist. The position was awful, and Kira grimaced as she tried to get used to it, to tell herself that she should be revelling in this. But it was horribly difficult and panic was setting in; panic that she would be left like this. She prayed that her demerit tally be low, for she couldn't take much of this in silence.

'Your first period will be serving time for speaking without permission. Namely, when I was punishing Thanos. There were two distinct counts, but I shall be generous and just punish you once for it.'

'Thank you, seneschal,' said Kira with gratitude, bringing a smile to the woman's lips, as though she had not expected Kira to agree.

When the weapon struck Kira's inner thigh the leg bucked against the rope, and she choked a cry. The use of the weapon confirmed she was in level two, but the furthest reaches of it as far as Kira was concerned, almost meriting redefinition as level three.

The crop slapped its leather hoop to the other side of her thigh, making her sob. Unable to move, only squirm seductively in her bondage, Kira was served up to her chastisement.

The seneschal paced relentlessly about her, laying down a slow and methodical application, dropping the crop to her hips, her thighs and her rear, torrefying Kira's skin with its hot kisses until she broke off her battery.

'Think on your place here, slave,' she snapped. 'You speak only when addressed or given permission, understand?'

'Yes, seneschal,' muttered Kira, and then squawked as a swipe caught the base of her rear. As she shuddered, letting the storm subside, she heard the door shut and was left to herself and her ordeal. Standing in the enforced darkness she pulled at her restraints, well aware that they were immobile. The gnaw of the cuffs into her wrists was becoming intolerable. Her extended leg began to ache similarly, the perching on top of heels at such an angle proving distressing to her feet.

The pain of the position started to rise, making her gasp and pull, trying to find some way of alleviating it. She could grab the chains and help ease the crimp into her hands, the digits already tingling with pins and needles from the impediment to circulation. But when she did it lifted her up and carried her to tiptoe, making the position even harder on her leg, and making her arms heat with the strain of holding her up. Muscle fatigue started to continue to rise, eating away her strength until she had to give up and hang loose again. Having let her wrists recover it was time to slump indolently, to give her leg a tiny portion of slack and find a shade of ease.

Again and again she went through this routine, finding it harder each time and the rewards less discernible. The general ache in her physique overwhelmed any relief.

Her bound leg throbbed from being kept cooped up, and any struggle to give it some hint of life only made the crotch rope scrape at her sex.

She wanted to cry out for help, to call for mercy, but she had to hold on. What sort of slave would she be if she broke only moments after being placed in the punishment she herself had earned?

With her head dropped back she gasped and continued to pull and drag, seeing if there was a way to unravel the plexus of rope, to get a leg free, just to alleviate the mayhem being heaped upon her. But the ropes were secure, and her long struggle and twisting did nothing save frustrate her and provide a few minutes of distraction from her trial.

How many demerits did she have? What else had she done? Speaking without permission was her first crime, but how many others had she unwittingly perpetrated?

Half an hour ended when the seneschal strode back in and stood before Kira. 'You are now going to serve a duration for breaking out of your uniform and damaging the property of her majesty,' she decreed, taking a new weapon from the wall. 'I know you were attacked, but that is no excuse.'

The black rod was thin and flexible, the tip spilling out dozens of slender rubber strings. She began to swing up into Kira's pudendum, the underhand swipes gently delivered, but searing in their effects because of the sensitive flesh it targeted. Hot shocks leapt through Kira's womb, making her whimper and writhe. The seneschal applied a dozen strokes, launching them into Kira to have her gasp and whimper until she had been deemed punished sufficiently.

'You will respect the property of the queen. Aggression will not be tolerated. You are here to serve. We have warriors, we have assassins, we do not require slaves to adopt the traits required of these castes,' stated the woman, and again left Kira to dwell on her crime.

How she wished Thanos were here, to make love to her again, to let her feel his raging sex pounding into her. It had been an experience of superlative delight that was burned into her mind. She didn't know whether it was love or just obsessive lust, but there were other things that attracted her to him. He too was besotted with queen, just as she was to Cassandra, who in turn treated them both to her contempt. Also, they were trophy pieces, set apart from the other denizens of the palace.

Her hands and feet were numb by the time the seneschal next entered, her body wracked by shudders of distress. She couldn't take any more, she just couldn't.

'Now, slave, the next part of your punishment is for that episode with Thanos. I don't know exactly what went on, but for concealing it from me I am going to give you a full hour to think about your felony.'

The crop began to attack Kira's breasts with skimming touches, sending hot flashes through the flesh, making the orbs bounce and sway as Kira struggled. She mewled in shock as she was spanked so cruelly, the rest of her body being further pained by the bondage as she fought the restraint.

With Kira's breasts pulsating with havoc, the woman ceased her maltreatment and reached out, cupping one of them in her gloved hand, massaging it with admiring gentleness.

'You will always tell me the truth. You will not hide anything from me, slave. I own you, I own everything about you, even your memories and your deeds. If I want to know something, anything, you will reveal it without hesitation, distortion, or exaggeration. Is that understood, slave?' she said, her words becoming severe, and her caress became a fierce pinch towards the end of her speech. The clamp of leather digits made Kira whimper and scowl, grinding her teeth in endurance.

'Yes, seneschal.'

Kira weighed up her choices as the woman strode for the door. Should she speak? Should she ask for mercy? It was sorely tempting. Yes, she had to, it was worth the risk. She was sure that if she applied herself to pleading in earnest, the woman would take pity on her.

Opening her mouth, she was stopped as the door closed, her frightened meditation on the subject having made her miss the opportunity. Cursing her weakness she started to sob as she continued to hang, her body filled with mayhem.

The hour that passed was like a year, every second drawn out by her continuing and rising pain. It was purgatory she couldn't bear, and her pledge to be utterly obedient from now on was made with all her conviction. She couldn't face this again. Her mistakes had been accidental, but if she'd only been aware of the severity of the demerit sessions, then she was sure she would have remembered and evaded making these errors.

Just as the bondage was eroding her sanity and making her delirious, the door opened suddenly.

'Please, seneschal, please, I can't take any more! Show mercy, I'll be good, I'll never disobey you again, I'll do anything,' she stammered, tears soaking the blindfold.

Kira let out a yell of pain as the crop stung her inner thigh. The weight leant to the stoke made her head roll back as she sobbed, the pounding welt continuing to make itself known to her in great clarity.

'I was coming to set you free, slave, but since you have opted to speak without permission, I can see you need more time to learn your lesson.'

'Seneschal, *please*,' she sobbed, distraught at the prospect of more time in this hell.

'Okay, you've just earned yourself another demerit, taking it to another hour in here. Do you want to go for one and a half, or will you do as you're told?'

Kira snapped her mouth shut, her lips quivering as she bit on her words, fighting to keep silent, her body wailing for her to continue, to plead, to seek freedom, lie, do anything she could to get free. But the seneschal was merciless, and would continue to extend Kira's sentence as long as she refused to show complete obedience.

The seneschal listened to Kira's hesitant reticence for a short time, tempting her to continue, a tease she refused.

'Good,' she stated flatly, the clink of wood on wood sounding as she gathered some anonymous implements for use. 'Now, slave, instead of a beating, I'm going to give you something to help you remember for every second of this next hour.'

The taste of leather came to Kira's lips as the woman took hold of them, pinching them together and pulling out a little before capturing them in a peg. The compression squeezed them tight and held them shut.

Again the seneschal squeezed her lips before laying another peg in place, the second resting against the first.

Another was set on the other side and Kira moaned, the bite of the pegs as they crushed her lips making her sob, unable to open her mouth and release her cry.

A fourth and fifth caught the last edges and sealed the corners of her mouth, stopping her from doing anything save groan in futile rasps.

The cold pound in her flesh started to grow more stern with every passing second, and she wondered how she was to endure this for a full hour. The seneschal stepped away and deserted her, the stabbing thumps of sensation in her lips now rising to rival the keen ache that plagued the rest of her form.

The hour she spent in bondage was the longest hour she had ever known, and she wept tears of dismay as she was left to face it alone. Slowly she grew more used to the pegs, feeling only a slow heartbeat through her crushed flesh, making the bondage position the far more terrible of the two to endure.

Eventually, after her eternity of travail, the door opened and the seneschal stepped before her. Hands brushed her blindfold and it was taken away, revealing the woman still clad in her police uniform. Kira looked across the shimmering latex and the crisp shirt, aching to kiss and fondle it, enslaved by her beauty and unrelenting sadism.

'Have you learned your lesson, slave?' she quizzed.

Kira nodded weakly, offering her agreement as best she could.

'Very well, we'll see if you have or not,' she decreed, and removed one of the pegs. Kira released a murmur of pain as the flash of returning circulation made her scowl. Another came free, and another, each loss being announced with the same nova burst of distress.

Licking her dry lips, she sucked in each one and mulled over its aching membranes, comforting them in her mouth.

The seneschal leant down and opened the ropes at her foot, setting it free. With a maximum effort Kira tried to bring it under her, but it would hardly move, so used had it become to this single position.

With several hissing drags she managed to get it under her and with a shove she managed to take up some of her body weight, letting a little relief enter her strangled wrists.

The woman opened the crotch rope, releasing it, letting Kira's foot plummet and drop beside the other. Wobbling on her heels, it further aided in standing upright, to wait patiently as the woman inserted keys and simultaneously popped the locks of her wrist cuffs.

Her fainéant legs folded under the new weight, unable to handle it. She collapsed into a twisted ball, her hands and legs resounding with prickling riots of restoration. Holding them to her she wept in a pitiful fit.

The boot of her tyrant stepped before her eyes, and obediently she leant forward and kissed its smooth leather surface. Now she was free she felt wonderful. The alleviation of such stress threw her to a new high, the act of merely being loose such a contrast to her pain that it was an intense pleasure.

'Thank you, seneschal,' she muttered with genuine appreciation, glad to have been trained, in having been shown the error of her ways and rededicated to obedience.

'Good, slave,' she said softly, letting Kira adore her footwear as strength slowly returned to her limbs.

Lapping at the soft leather, Kira rolled her tongue up and down the firm calves, down the heel, encircling the towering dagger as the woman loomed over her like some avenging seraphim of darkness.

'Now let's get you back into your uniform,' she stated, applying a leash to Kira's collar and walking away, towing Kira from her position on all fours.

Scampering in her wake, Kira's eyes were locked to the image of the walking Seneschal, her mind seething with possibilities of what she wanted to do. To lap at the latex stems of her legs, to be smothered under that glorious rear, to suffer pain as she had just endured, just to earn the right to take a single lick at her sex.

The latex was mesmerising as its stretched lines tilted one way, then another. The fabric of the skirt rolled upon her muscles, her legs taut with her bold strides beneath the black shell that was impermeable to Kira's touch. The rigid lines of her skirt and the authoritative attire added to her already imposing regnant.

Leaving the discipline chamber they entered the passage beyond, where they saw a maid with dustpan and broom, grooming the carpet with attentive effort. Sealed in a latex catsuit, a skirt revealed through its tightness the bulges of her chastity belt. A short hobble chain connected her ankles, and she was perched atop ballet boots to make her lot more difficult. A white apron and matching head-dress completed the attire. Her features were emphasised by dark shades, and her long blonde hair was tied into a rigid plait that was itself tied with red ribbon, the only hint of colour to her monotone appearance. She stopped as soon as she saw the seneschal and adopted a humble kneeling pose, her head lowered in respect.

The woman paused and extended a boot, letting the slave kiss the toe. A lick of the crop sank into her rear, making her whimper as the seneschal continued to pass, applying capricious spite to keep the girl dedicated to her job. After a moment of tensed recovery she went back to her task, watching Kira from the corner of her eye.

The main room was exposed to Kira once more, and at the clapping summons of the seneschal the males once more emerged.

'Yes, seneschal?' they said, bowing again and kissing her boots with reverence.

'Put this slave in her chastity belt, and install a new pup uniform,' she ordered, moving back and settling into one of her nest-like chairs, lounging to watch the process unfold once more.

Again Kira beheld the steel confines of sexual incarceration, her eyes closing with dismay at the sight of it.

Lubrication was applied, and as she stood still and accepting of the will of the seneschal, they applied the waistband, and then pressed the crotch band into place, making her cry out at the feel of its entry.

A latex uniform was brought out, and again the males started to put her in the sleeves and stockings, sliding her into the garment, locking it in place, stealing away her manual dexterity and trapping her on her knees.

When they withdrew from her she was again a latex-bound canine, but one considerably more broken-in than before.

Kira looked up with adoring eyes as the seneschal slithered from her nest and walked around her quaking pet, studying her, confirming that all was in place before again taking up the leash.

'With all that commotion and distraction I never made it to my meeting,' she revealed, speaking more to herself than her pet. 'The head slaves will still be waiting, though; they would not dare leave until I arrive.'

With a tug to the lead Kira was drawn out of the room, scampering on her knees. Shown through the labyrinth she was delivered to a set of double doors, the portal spreading itself to reveal a meeting room. The bleak walls of the heptagonal chamber were barren, but in each corner a female slave was strapped inverted into the angular shallow. With their arms stretched out before them so that fingers could just graze the floor, their heads were sealed within tight hoods, a pipe spilling from the mouth and snaking into the wall. Other than their cuffs and collar, they were naked save for one final and functional addition.

Into each rear was sheathed a large candle, the angle of the waxen staff letting the drool of the light drip down their buttocks and spine, each woman's back encrusted with frozen trickles of solidified black wax.

The legs of the living candelabrum were bathed in the amber glow of their candle. Their bodies were cloaked in shadow as they were left to their isolation, serving the needs of the palace as furniture.

A seven-sided table, the black glass surface rimmed with a wooden lip, dominated the middle of the room. Before each face was a large divan, the leather cushion large and soft, accommodating the comfort of its main occupant.

In each divan, lying on her back, was a bound slave. The males and females were cocooned in a sheath of rubber, their bodies compressed into a single stem, leaving only their mouths exposed.

Their legs were hauled up into the air, a ring at their toes setting a chain up to connect to the ceiling, keeping them bound thus. A living part of the divan, the true guests of this chamber had seated themselves on these fawning maws, relaxing into them and tasting of their dedications while using their raised legs as a back rest.

Head slave Strafe reclined in her red catsuit, a zip at the crotch showing that this was a different one to that which Kira had seen her in. From the woman's presence she could guess that all six of the other women her head slaves, each representing one of the castes of the royal palace.

Standing to one side were a row of five waitresses of the variety Kira had seen when first arriving in the palace. Their nipple and nose rings helped balance a tray laden with blue crystal glasses, the goblets filled with warmed red, the sustenance giving off small curling lines of steam as they waited to be called forth again.

Kira was drawn towards the only seat left vacant. It was one with a slave of voluptuous physique, her alluring breasts and rear straining at the sheath, and during her approach she noticed the labels.

Etched into the wood of the perimeter and filled with silver, each tag named the position of service held by the woman who was to be seated at that place. No names were given, suggesting that the places were set for whoever currently held that rank.

The ruler of the livestock was a young woman with long tan hair, her strong form sealed within a uniform akin to that of a riding mistress. Tight white breeches slithered beneath tall polished boots with spurs strapped to them, the garment making it difficult for the slave beneath to attend her adequately. A leather bolero jacket hung open, revealing a crisp white shirt beneath and a studded belt at her waist. The open collar exposed the metal band of her slavery, the silver strip marked as all the others were. It illustrated well that even though these women were appointed tyrants, all of them including the seneschal were still nought but property of the queen.

Her dark green eyes were lazy and passionless, as though she were only half-aware of her surroundings or was merely indifferent to them.

The curator of the feed banks, whom she knew to be named Gherth, was an older woman, her slender body dressed in penurious attire. Her auburn tresses hung as a loose bob around a heart-shaped, delicate face, a strange visage considering her placement in such a place of dread. Kira expected her to be some brooding devilish harridan, not this fragile beauty.

Dressed in gloss shorts and knee high patent boots over fishnet, a matching bra cupped her breasts, and gloves rolled to her elbow. Her collar had been armed with a wicked starburst of spikes that encircled her throat, but left the fastening of her ring and the symbols of her ownership and identity bared. She reclined leisurely upon the face of her slave, the zip of her shorts dropped, the open crotch mesh tights allowing access for the supplicant.

The trainer responsible for the servants had a mane of curling dark hair that wreathed a pretty and carefree face, one stiffened with a stern glower.

Clad in a latex dress, the laced plunging neckline sank almost to her waist where the mini-skirt moved slightly with the work of the slave buried within it. Her bare legs were covered from the knee down by stiletto leather boots, the same fabric used to create her opera gloves.

The manufacturer responsible for the furniture and function slaves which all of them were currently enjoying was a small butch woman, her hair cropped to a short pelt of spiky brown. She was clad in what appeared to be a leather business suit. A white shirt lay over her collar and was pinned beneath a buttoned, close-fitting jacket, the sleeves giving a hint of her white cuffs laying beneath before leather gloves coated her fingers. Figure-hugging leather trousers fell from her waist with a plain belt holding them, and tall thigh boots covered her legs again, setting her atop low-heeled boots.

The woman responsible for the harem slaves was a gorgeous woman who wore a vindictive expression, her tall body accepting a cascade of golden hair that fell wildly to her waist. A strapless bra of latex surrounded her chest, the cups small, the fastening strips almost like cord. Other than latex leggings that emphasised her towering legs and the added height of incorporated high heels, she wore only her collar.

The seneschal stepped up and slid into her seat, showing Kira's awed eyes that she was without underwear, her loins free beneath the skirt and stockings. With a soft shudder the woman settled into position, the faint sound of suckling emerging from beneath her.

Laying back into the woman's soft legs, the seneschal ordered forth the refreshments, the slaves wandering the table edge and showing relief as their burdens were lightened with the removal of drinks.

'To her majesty,' toasted the seneschal.

'Her majesty,' they all replied, raising their glasses and then taking a deep draught. The women sighed and lay back, some of them revealing growing fangs, their teeth emerging at the taste of blood.

'An excellent vintage, Gherth,' stated the head slave of the harem. 'My compliments.'

'Thank you, Gabrielle, I have a few choice youths in the banks I've been saving. Now seems as good a time as any to start on them.'

'You'll have to send me a few bottles,' said Gabrielle.

'Of course, I'll have a slave bring them to our quarters once we're finished here,' she replied.

While this exchange of pleasantries was conducted, the seneschal merely lay into her seat, devouring the attentions of her slave, her eyes closed with pleasure. How Kira envied the slave beneath her. She would have done anything to take that position, to taste the seneschal, to please her.

'To business,' she snapped, bringing herself from her warm torpor. 'What is the status of the farm and kennels, Sykora?' asked the seneschal, looking to the woman in the riding outfit.

'I have prepared the report, seneschal,' replied Sykora and reaching behind her into the cushions she handed over a pre-prepared hard copy of the data.

The seneschal opened it and perused the contents, turning the pages and commenting as she went. 'Mares, Colts, Fillies, good. Though we should get some more into training.'

'Yes, seneschal.'

'What of the pain slaves?' asked the seneschal, glancing to Strafe as she took another sip of her beverage before smacking her lips and setting the glass on the table.

'As you predicted seneschal, the visiting Asian dignitaries have placed a number of their private property in my care,' she replied. 'I am using our best ordeals on them as we speak.'

Kira smiled to herself, hoping that the suffering of the cat that had attacked her would be long and excruciating.

'Excellent, the clan holds accomplishment in the field of vice with the highest regard,' said the seneschal, revealing the importance of Strafe's work. 'An impressive display may well ease negotiations.'

'Servants, Ditta?' she questioned of the woman in the latex dress with leather extremities as she shifted and repositioned herself on her slave's face.

'I've had an extra twenty in training since last meeting, and as a precaution, some of those with less spotless records have been placed back in intensive training, just to polish up their skills and obedience.'

'Excellent,' commented the seneschal. 'Double all demerits assigned to servants who fail to perform as expected.'

'Is that wise, seneschal? That will deplete our numbers.'

'Then deny them any choice save the most strenuous to work off their tallies. That should keep you at full strength, and besides, it will work out better in the long run because you'll have less serviles with faltering dedication to their duties. Now, what about furniture, Kristen?' she bade of the woman in the leather suit.

'A new wave of ghouls are being installed in various guestrooms, and I have another fifty in training right now. My trainers are under strict orders to ensure that they produce only the finest furniture slaves for duty.'

'Good. I want no repetition of that incident with the Russian delegation six years ago.'

'Please, seneschal, that was not my fault, it was—' Kristen attempted before being interrupted by the abrupt words of the seneschal.

'I don't want excuses, I want furniture that stays put and does what it's supposed to. Ten percent of all demerits assigned to furniture slaves will be worked off on your tender hide. Is that plain enough to understand? Or do you have anything else to add, head *slave?*'

'No, seneschal, I apologise for my words, I meant no disrespect,' she said meekly, lowering her gaze and keeping quiet until the seneschal changed the subject.

There was a knock upon the door and Kira turned to face it, wondering who it was, for surely a guest or denizen of this place could simply walk in. Did the doors only open for those of standing? Were slaves such as she unable to get access through them? She could guess that it was something to do with the collars.

The bands might well be fitted with something that doors detected, making them refuse access or open willingly depending on who was seeking entry.

'Enter,' firmly stated the seneschal.

The door clicked and a moment later, after acknowledging the voice, opened to let a female enter. Her arms were trussed up behind her back, her mouth spread wide by a ball-gag. Shuffling in hobbles that held her knees and ankles, she tottered on her heels, her body smothered by latex that left only her eyes and breasts free.

The woman turned about, revealing a naked rear, an envelope clasped in the cleft. The seneschal removed it with a tug and paid the messenger a tip in the form of a swift stroke of her crop. The girl staggered forth a step and then straightened to attention once more, the red smudge darkening with each passing second.

The seneschal opened it and read the contents before crumpling it into a ball. 'I am to attend her majesty immediately. Is there any other business?' she asked, making the girl stiffen as the litter was absently forced through her sphincter and into her anus.

'I believe that's everything, seneschal,' offered Sykora, looking across the others to see if there were any disagreement.

'Good,' said the seneschal with a tight smile, rising from her seat and straightening her skirt. 'Strafe, take Kristen to the pain blocks, set her up in third level bondage, cane her regularly until she's worked off, oh, lets say five hours. I think that'll get the lesson across.'

'Yes, seneschal,' replied the woman, walking over and hooking a finger through the head slave's collar ring. The girl looked to Strafe with sorrow, clearly dismayed that she was going to have to suffer so much.

Strafe started to draw her away for torment, and with another swat the messenger was sent scurrying off.

The seneschal took up Kira's lead and left the meeting, making for the throne room.

CHAPTER 15

Sitting on the slab, Thanos dwelt on what had happened. Kira had surrendered herself to the abuse of the seneschal for him, suffered her wrath to preserve him from her venom.

She was gorgeous, a girl of beauty and strength he never thought to encounter in any facet other than the queen. He would be ecstatic if he could gain access to her, if they could be enslaved together, performing for the amusement of others.

His time on the stage with her was unbelievable, watching her squirm in her bondage as the latex nuns wracked her body with intense sensation. It had almost made him climax just to watch the show. He would love to look on again and again as Kira was punished by their mutual owners, and then to suffer alongside her, to both be trained and held in chastity until they were given a spontaneous reprieve.

His hand enclosed his shaft and he shut his eyes, dreaming of tasting Kira's delicious flesh once more, of following her smooth curves, of burying himself deep into her, hearing her mewl and purr beneath him.

The door opened and he stopped his slothful onanism, jerking his head around to see who it was.

The pair that stood before him were a bizarre sight, one of the many teams of wandering punishment slaves that meandered through the winding depths of the palace, adding to the general wicked ambience with their plight.

A young vampiress ambulated on the verge of collapse, deprived of sleep for many days. A short metal pole lay horizontally at the centre of her spine, her arms draped behind it and her wrists brought forth to be connected at her belly. A dress of thin rope had been fastened about her, incorporating the metal strut into its web to hold it firm. Her breasts were strained through woven jaws, her chest compressed, her arms captured by numerous hoops.

A pole was fitted between her legs, the tip shaped into a phallic spear that had driven into her sex. The shaft descended between her legs, throwing out short chains that grabbed metal bands above and below her knees, and at the base another set snapped to her fetters. With the pole anchored into her, she could neither get off it nor wilt from her standing position, lest it push deeper than she could accept.

Her clit ring was teased and played by a small bell fastened to it, while similar examples had been set on her nipple rings, causing the girl to air soft melodious chimes as she staggered.

A ball-gag was forced into her mouth, straining her jaws wide. Her cheeks were streaked with tears, and her long hair had been tied into a ponytail that swayed against her back.

A clamp had been snapped to the flesh of her left breast, the pinch of skin serving to support an envelope. The use of such slaves to deliver mail was a usual one, the offer always being that maybe the letter they bore would satisfy the recipient enough to warrant their release. It was unlikely, but it was the only hope they had for early freedom.

The girl was haunted by a rubber wraith, the curves of the male emphasised by a complete suit of dense rubber. The comprehensive garment included his stiletto boots, a hood that gave him nothing save eye-slits, and a sheath that held his erect penis.

His forearms were connected along each other behind him, the suit merging to keep them trapped, his fingers lost within the single sleeve.

From the exposed ring of his smothered collar a chain had been fastened, the leash reaching forward to the centre of the pole that was responsible for containing the girl's arms.

Connected together, the only distraction for the male was to plunge himself into the girl's rear, attacking her at random, able to only get the most minute satisfaction through his stifling condom of a suit. He could thrust away with all his maniac hunger, but had no hope of achieving release, making him more frustrated and more eager to try and ease this torment by hunting for elusive climax in the girl's tight rear. The vampiress, on the other hand, was doomed to simply wander, hounded from behind by her faceless persecutor, the latex ghost filling her regularly.

They stopped before Thanos and he removed the envelope, tugging it off to make the vampiress gurgle at the added stress placed to her clamp.

Opening it, he found a summons to attend the queen in her private chambers. It probably meant that he was going to be subjected to her training again, several days having passed since his last period of tutelage under her.

Removing the clamp from the girl, she aired pips of shock from the extraction, the clamp having been set on her for some time. The sight of the strangled breast had him look upon it with a new light, and reaching out he took hold of the smooth flushed mound. The girl tried to back away, seeing what he was intending, but Thanos merely dropped a crooked little finger through a nipple ring, forcing her to stay put. She shuddered and stared at him with wide eyes.

'Scared of the lupine are we?' he scowled, adopting a fake tone of threatening to intimidate her, scare her a little, for he was of the race that butchered vampires without remorse, and this neophyte to the palace would still be utterly terrified of him.

No one would know if he had a little fun first. He would earn it in time, because the queen was no merciful trainer.

Drawing her in by her nipple, she was shaking as he looked up at her, peering through the valley of her breasts and into her innocent face.

Taking hold of the pole with his other hand he jiggled it, making her stiffen in fits as he laughed to himself. 'Would you like to have a werewolf ride that cute rear of yours?' he asked, making her throw her head from side to side. Thanos laughed and set free the cilia of power within him.

The collar had been left deactivated, so he was free to change. Ordinarily it shocked him if he tried to shift to or from the form demanded of him, but for now he could do as he wished.

The girl shrieked into her gag as he arose before her, spreading his body outward, gathering his full form, shedding it in fur and muscle, adding claws and fangs to it.

Grabbing her about the throat he held her firm and stepped behind her. The male kept his distance, as much as the chain would allow, for he too was terrified of the werewolf, a creature that could so easily end his un-life.

The girl was wailing in distress as Thanos took hold of her hips and rubbed his stiff length in the cleft of her rear, teasing her with it. She clenched with all her might, trying to deny him, but he merely smiled and placed his thumbs to the soft cheeks. With a forceful drag he parted the barricades and nuzzled against her sphincter.

'Open wide,' he mused, and forced his entry, making her gasp and snort, writhing as she was lifted to tiptoe by the trespass.

Thanos began a dilatory molestation, savouring the feel of her tight anus squeezing in bursts to his intruding shaft. He dreamt of it being Kira, but for now he was satisfied with this slave's opening.

In moments the girl was changing her tune to one of delight, her fears allayed, her relish in being so massively filled turning her from a quailing wreck to a writhing slut, begging for more. She cried out with a mixture of pleasure and pain, stretched to her limits by his length.

Quickening his pace, he reached around and groped at her breasts, his hot breath rasping across the cold skin of her neck. With a hissing growl he launched his seed into her, treating himself to further thrusts to drag out all his bliss as the girl shook as though being electrified.

Pulling free, her rear clung to him until it was able to close, the interior slick with his semen.

Turning about with a sigh of satisfaction, he patted the smooth head of the male. 'You'll find entry easier now, my friend,' he derided, and sat back down.

The male continued to stay well back, keeping the chain stretched tight while the girl rested against the plinth, panting. With his goal lubricated it was even more unlikely to find release, and besides, Thanos' presence still kept him at bay.

'Maybe you need some help?' purred the lupine, and lifted himself up, moving towards the male. The vampire tried to escape, pulling at the chain, the girl refusing to move, her body a dead weight he could not shift.

Thanos snatched him and pulled him close, turning him around and keeping one arm locked about the male's neck, his strength vastly superior to the undead while he wore this powerful anatomy.

'We lupine can be generous, as well as lethal,' he chuckled, and grabbed the male's shaft in a vice grip. 'I've pleased your partner, it's only fair I do the same for you.'

The vampire bucked, whimpering softly as Thanos began a savage masturbation, throwing his fist back and forth, the squeeze defeating the thickness of the rubber. Despite the pain, despite the fear, the vampire was soon squirming against the wall of fur behind him, his eyes rolling back with delight that he would at last find climax.

The feel of having full control over the male's pleasure and the reigns of fear Thanos held over him started to seduce the werewolf. The feel of this power had him swelling with lust once more, making him hungry to take the sense of might further.

'No, not yet,' purred Thanos, stopping the stern shuffle just before orgasm. The vampire pushed his hips against the fist, trying to acquire the last movements that would end his frustration.

A talon danced at the rear of the suit, opening a hole, and steering himself in, Thanos fought for access. As he drove through the frantically barricaded buttocks he found the sphincter tight, almost virginal, but it was clearly just a façade. The decadence of the palace made the denizens within heedless of gender, they sought only pleasure, and thus, the vampire was resisting just to feel himself be defeated. And Thanos was happy to oblige.

'Come on, you can take it, you know you can!' he growled, letting the pain being visited onto his length by using it as a weapon increase his savagery, the rear fighting his will.

'There we go,' he hissed with his success, finally sliding in. The vampire screeched with silent pleasure into his gagging hood, his anus being stretched, the lupine stuffing his rear with a vast intruder, lifting him to tiptoe. The feel of such acute penetration made the male quake in spasming fits, his delight prevalent over the shock of such trespass.

Riding back and forth, Thanos' hips rocked to churn the male's insides. So as not to deny the male his full quota of bliss, Thanos once more grabbed the vampire's shaft and started to pound upon it, the brutal onanism conducted with spiteful virulence that only stoked the male's libido further.

'Are you ready to be filled like your girlfriend there?' he asked viciously. 'Well are you?' Thanos growled when there was no response, and thrust harshly.

The force carried the vampire from his feet, holding him in the air, mounted on a werewolf's length, spitted by it, his booted feet kicking at the air. The male spasmed, the hidden hints of his mouth stretched wide with his shriek of violated pain and absolute pleasure.

Dropping him back down, Thanos slammed him against the plinth next to the girl and continued stabbing harshly, bringing out another pain-enhanced orgasm for himself, his spare hand fixed to the cross section of forearms. The feel of the penetrated slave fighting impotently against him was massively arousing - the subjugation of another through strength, even though it was a secretly willing defeat. The squeak of the slave's latex body against the stone as he struggled joined Thanos' hissing breath as he started to ride deep, a warmth spreading through his shaft, the feel of explosive release beckoning. Thanos stiffened, slowing his rate as he poured a new wash into the rear of the slave. The spine of the slave jerked, the injection of warm seed into him shattering his paltry rebellion with delight.

Once Thanos had captured all his bliss he left himself inserted and sped the rhythm of his hand. Watching as the male shook with harrowing and pleasure, he felt the small grips of the slave's sphincter to his embedded shaft, the squeezes of response to the uncaring attention, the gratitude of such an enactment of playful molestation. The vampire was resisting him, trying to avoid succumbing to the encouraging hold, sneakily attempting to best Thanos, to have his resistance broken. He clearly wanted to end his all-consuming frustration, he wanted to feel the rhapsody of climax, but his need for punishment was more driving after the sodomy. Thanos smiled and played along, adopting stern tones of authority over his subject.

'Don't think you can deny me, corpse!' he scowled, increasing the ferocity of his hold, increasing his haste, a wide smile peeling back his lips, his hot breath washing over the head of the latex-bound vampire slave. 'Give it to me! I want to feel this dead flesh come!'

The sodomised servile jerked with spasms at his own release, filling the sealed sheath of his penis just as his own anus had been tainted.

'There we are... happy?' Thanos mocked, patting the slave's head before he strolled away, withdrawing from the male, causing him to arch back with the shock of its sudden flight from his tender membranes.

Pulling back his lupine form, Thanos restored an ordinary visage and set off to attend the queen, leaving the giddy serviles to relish the memory of their use and the sight of their eternal partner being similarly taken.

He strolled the passages by memory, the route so well known he barely needed to keep his eyes open. Thinking heavily on Kira, he entered the throne room and marched behind the huge chair of his owner.

Touching the wall, a section gave several muted clicks and swung open, exposing the secondary chamber beyond. A vast vault door dominated one wall, waiting to accept his palm, his retina, and a sensor scan before allowing him in, the queen guarding her most private sanctum with fanaticism. She had not reached her current longevity by being careless.

With booming tones the locks were drawn back from where they drilled into the walls, ceiling and floor, and the polished metre thick portal started to glide back.

Stepping through, he settled onto his knees, regarding the white corridor that stretched forward, the walls hidden by red drapes, the ceiling a curling fresco of spiralling designs.

The enslaver of Thanos entered the hall at a brisk march, and without word rapidly clipped a leash to his collar before towing him in her wake. Scampering on all fours, he wondered if she knew about Cassandra's attack upon him, and though he ached to inform, he knew that by speaking aloud he would only bring even harsher retribution upon himself.

He barely saw the lush domain that was her home, his gaze so mesmerised by the tyrannical overseer. Her abdomen was gripped by the sheath of a latex mini-skirt, a vest top displaying her breasts beneath a smothering layer of gleaming rubber. Shoulder length gloves turned her arms into smooth rods, and fishnet stockings, the suspenders peeking out from under the hem of the skirt, rolled down her legs to enter stiletto-heeled ankle boots.

He was fascinated by her. When she was with him he could do nothing to resist, she had seen to that, her training having cultivated this obsession.

A door opened and he was led within. The bleak chamber bore some sparse furnishings, and was already occupied by two female slaves, who each hung from the ceiling by a single ankle. The sex, anus and mouth of both women were stuffed with candles to provide illumination.

The queen brought him beneath the two widely spaced cuffs hanging from chains in the centre of the ceiling and pulled up a chair. Sitting down, she crossed her legs, the creak of her clothing making Thanos ache to caress himself.

'Lick,' she ordered, and Thanos jumped forward, dropping to his knees, his tongue spilling out to adore her boots, his mind heady with the pleasure of serving her thus.

'I can see that your time with the clan has not eroded your libido any, slave,' she commented, flicking a glance to his raging length.

'Well, if satisfaction is your goal, I am currently dispositioned to grant you it. Does that please you slave?' she asked, lifting his chin from his task so she might see his face.

'Yes, your majesty,' he simpered, his smile wide. His hand strayed over to enclose the hard rod, the taste of two vampire rears having failed to dwindle its voracity.

'No, not like that, I have a different method for you, slave,' she smirked, letting him know full well that it was to be a punishment rather than a reward.

'Stand up, slave,' she crooned, causing him to rise, trembling slightly.

With her possession standing, she arose from her chair and sauntered over, her body slithering within the latex skin, graceful and alluring. Reaching up, she presented his wrists towards the cuffs and then slipped them through. With a squeeze they locked in place, the heavy reinforced bands designed to house the most distraught struggles of mortal or supernatural beast. As the queen bound him her latex skin brushed his body, making him start to stiffen further as the smell of her reached his nostrils, kindling his lust, turning his sex to a pillar of stone.

The queen continued her restraint, walking to the wall where she flipped a concealed switch. Immediately the chains started to retract, being drawn in, hauling him from the floor, the metal shackles stretching his arms wide and leaving him hanging cruciform in the air.

The ascent stopped, and the vampiress took a bundle of slender cord and some other objects from a small table as she watched Thanos dangle by his wrists, his toes unable to even brush against the floor.

The queen knelt down, released her cache where he could not see it, and began to use the slender cord to tightly bind his legs together, forming them into a single meshed stalk. The criss-crossing lines pulled in the skin, squeezing it in a choking hold.

Tying a lead cylinder about his ankles, she placed yet more strain upon his already throbbing arms. Thanos scowled slightly and kept his head lowered, watching her from under a furrowed brow as he strove to endure.

She moved closer and let her hand stray to his collar, clicking on the lock, depriving him of the option of chancing into a form more able to resist her.

Putting her fingers to his lips was the unspoken command for him to lick them. He obeyed with fervour, breathing heavily because of the strain of being so cruelly stretched and suspended.

Watching with a licentious expression, she had her servant suck the digits, treating each one like a small latex phallus.

'Would my slave like a gag?' she asked, pulling her fingers slowly back, making him strain forward to continue until he could no longer reach them.

'Yes, your majesty,' he whispered.

'My slave impressed the clan, so he deserves a reward,' she commented, and stepped back.

Thanos stopped breathing and stared awe-struck as she smiled illicitly and reached up under her dress. Pulling down the thong she stepped from it and lifted it, presenting it to his mouth. He flashed his jaws wide to gather the material, but his efforts were blocked with a finger across his lips.

'No, not yet... first, smell,' she stated softly, and then gently placed the fabric across his nostrils, holding it there, letting him drown his senses in the smell of her and the rubber aroma set upon it.

Thanos closed his eyes and quaffed deep snorts, breathing out through his mouth, sucking in every portion of the scent he could before it was lowered and stuffed into his mouth.

Leaving it there without further addition she stepped back. Both knew he would not let it fall, his tongue too eager to taste it, to keep it as a trophy.

Taking hold of his penis, she lifted the swollen member and cupped her hands around the testicles. Anxiety and fear glistened in his eyes, and he winced as she squeezed them. The vice-like grip rose in ferocity and he wriggled, making the weights dance, and the pain in his stretched frame heighten. Rasping through the gag he looked to her with imploring.

'All that exercise has made you sweat, and smell. I think a little perfume to mask it is required, don't you, slave?' she pondered maliciously, Thanos well aware of what she planned from painful experience.

Maintaining her hold, the queen picked up a bottle of cheap aftershave, and ignoring the dismal stare of the slave, began to liberally sprinkle it onto his scrotum, massaging the burning fluid in.

His shrill cries were stifled by the gag, but his pain manifested itself in intense quivering. It felt as though his groin were soaked in petrol and alight, and no matter how much he fought, the waves of fire continued to bore into him. Yet he was in ecstasy from it, solely because he was suffering for the queen. Once she had been mistress, now, with the city hers, she was his queen, or even his goddess, the deity he worshipped but could not possess, only amuse.

She took a cane from the wall and began to lambaste his buttocks and thighs, casting his suffering to new levels. Thanos could not help but struggle, and this made his situation worse, causing panic to rise as he thought his wrists might dislocate from the abuses visited upon them by his own involuntary throes. No matter how many times he was caned he could never remain impassive towards it. The weapon and the skill with which the queen deployed it always befuddled any hope of quiet stoical endurance.

After a dozen severe strokes the queen stopped and his body became languid from overexertion. The queen smiled and ignored his fatigue, caressing his burning groin until he was erect again. She recommenced the masturbation with swift strokes, making him moan, inflicting pleasure with each shuffling movement.

Despite the torment, he was being tended by the queen, her rubber-sheathed hand handling this act, and his instantly rekindled frustrations could see a means of escape. With a squeal of suffering he finally came, his penis raw and tender, misty orbs spilling from the end as he shuddered in his bonds, his head thrown back, his mouth sucking on the intimate gag.

After milking him dry of all she could gain, the queen moved back and placed her chair before him, settling into it and watching him dangle.

The regal and all powerful vampiress simply sat there, his eyes locked to her gorgeous latex-smoothed body. For another fifteen minutes he was left to hang and dwell in the stringent bondage pose, his eyes teased cruelly with her salacious physique.

Thanos kept himself dedicated to this study, following every line and curve, aching to lick them, to grovel at her feet and drink in the taste, texture and smell of her. Such diversions easily made him ignorant of the stress of his bondage, the ache in his arms, the pain that grew in his hands and his wracked legs.

Standing up, she wandered over and released the cuffs, sufficiently pleased with the extent of his torture. He collapsed to the floor, his arms throbbing as circulation returned.

'Come, slave,' she ordered, and had him drag his weighted and bound legs, shuffling after her on his hands.

Led through into her bedroom, the empty chamber held only the vast altar upon which she slept. The circular mattress was supported in a cradle of curling towers that reached inward overhead like clawed talons, a nest of organic black spires, covered in winding veins and crooked thorns. A single aperture permitted entry onto the satin sheets, the perimeter dotted with pillows.

Thanos stood and watched with glee as she settled on the edge of the mattress and laid back, propping herself on her elbows, her legs dangling over the side.

'Take them off, slave,' she whispered, watching him from beneath her brow.

Settling on his knees before her, his erection throbbing with heat and desire, his hands brushed the patent smoothness, his fingertips gliding on the material. Reaching in, he drew down the zip, the soft cackle as it descended churning his thoughts with rampant licentiousness.

'We've found your big sister, slave,' she mused, watching him as he worked. 'Little Corin has been most anxious to find you.'

Once the zipper reached the bottom he reverently cupped toe and heel, drawing gently to let the footwear slip from her stockinged foot.

'She's been searching relentlessly, suffering great hardship in this personal quest. Even her elders have forsaken her. She's alone, desperate, miserable.'

With equal devotion and utmost respect he removed the other boot, the softest scent of their interior making his head swim.

'Now the stockings, slave,' she commanded, and with a slight tremble of excitement to his fingers he started to undo the fastenings, taking a sly chance and delight in being able to touch her bare thighs.

'I think she deserves a reward too,' the queen went on. 'I mean, all that stress, all that fighting and bloodshed. It would be wrong to just kill her. I think we should give her precisely what she wants.'

Thanos knew she was planning to ensnare Corin in her sexual enslavement. Would his sister succumb? He had been easy to train, because of his penchant for female domination, but Corin? She was rigid and inflexible, disdainful of any vice, and he wondered if she had even ever lost her virginity. How then would she react? He knew she would be broken by the queen, for no creature could resist her charms; she was too well-versed in such methods, her ancient wisdom and skill unsurpassed.

One at a time he drew down the fishnet sheaths, knowing he was being rewarded for his show, that this was his gift, and it was one he felt exquisitely honoured to receive.

'I want you to assist in her capture. To bring her to me so I can enlighten her, relieve her of all these foolish noble thoughts, set her loose to finally enjoy herself.'

Stripping to reveal the elegant limbs beneath, he left the milky-white flesh naked to his gaze, holding her stockings as though they were holy artefacts.

How could he participate in Corin's arrest? It was not so much the abduction of his older sibling that bothered him, it was the fact that the queen would then devote a massive amount of time to breaking his sister - effectively deserting him. Besides, to bring her down, to reveal his shame to others, that would be a humiliation beyond all others. Yet that was probably precisely the reasoning behind it.

The assisting and orchestrating of his sister's capture after she had spent these years methodically fighting to find him, to be shown as a broken and seduced pawn of dark powers and their ancient enemy, it would be the final chapter in his training.

Once this deed was done he was doomed to servitude forever. It did not bother him, but it was a strange sense of finality to be able to see the end approaching, the absolute point of no return. At present he might harbour some hopes of flight in his weaker moments. After this, such dreams would be useless to hold any more.

'Take out your gag and lick them, slave,' she crooned, lounging back into the sumptuous folds.

With verve he dove forward and started to lick the cool flesh, letting his tongue drift between her toes, engulf each one and suckle on it until each and every one had been fawned upon.

'That will do, slave,' she commented, and used the attended foot to push him back, the toes pressing across his nose and cheek.

'Hand those to me,' she commanded, making him offer up his collection of delicate garments.

Taking the panties and one stocking, she placed the wet thong into the fishnet and pushed it back into his mouth. He accepted it willing, closing his eyes and savouring the degradation. Taking the other stocking she looped it around his head, tightening it so that it would help hold the other ball in.

'Of course, if you fail in her abduction, I cannot have her running around any more. When we were destroying the other houses she made a valuable diversion and assistant to your assassinations, but now I need peace in my city. If you fail, she will have to die,' the queen stated, the words almost unnoticed, Thanos' mind fixed to his task, all else lost. She had taken away his obligations to his tribe, to his people, to Gaia; all that was left was devotion to her. She was revealing this to prove that fact, his lack of contemplation on such grave topics just showing him how little they meant in his mind now. Truly he was trained, truly he was hers, forever.

His stiff length was pounding as she retreated back onto the bed, and after reaching under a pillow she retrieved latex replacements. With a teasing show she started to slip her shapely legs into the opaque stockings, drawing them into place and adding the suspenders to them.

'Come here, slave,' she ordered, slithering back against the sheets, beckoning him forth.

Thanos softly crept up onto the mattress, staring at her body, aching for fulfilment, to lap at her and toy with himself.

'Lay face down,' she said, causing him to spread-eagle himself upon the luxurious sheets.

Thanos looked to the aperture that had provided him access, his mind racing with possibilities.

Another set of her underwear was produced and set across his nostrils, letting him dwell on the scent as she continued her work, retrieving her items from under the pillows, her armaments already placed ahead of time, awaiting the arrival of her slave for their use.

Lengths of metal wire were removed, the thick cable more than adequate to contain his struggles, its severity as a device for restraint making him concerned as to what he was going to face here now that he had gained his rewards. There were always prices to pay for everything the queen gave, the most minute favour or blessing always requiring a stern repayment, the interest factor high for any act of her charity or his pleasure.

She started by tying his ankles to the posts, spreading them wide, stopping him from escaping her, not that he would ever do so.

With harsh hoops and knots she bound his elbows and then his wrists tightly together. Affixing two lengths of rope to the connection between the joints, she cast them behind her.

Taking hold of the two excess coils she sat behind him and pulled on a pair of surgical gloves prior to methodically working a scoop of lubricant into his rear, liberally applying it and covering him both inside and out. The delve of her digits had him snorting with delight, the feel of being opened and explored by her, of being so thoroughly used.

Smearing what remained over the toe of her right stockinged foot, she removed the gloves and wrapped one of the ropes around each of her hands. Drawing in the slack she started to exert a tremendous pull. His torso rose from the bed and the wire bit painfully into his wrists, yet his suffering was made all the worse by the knowledge that this was not the torture, merely a method to make its application easier.

His rear erupted with blazing pain and he writhed in torment as she slowly began forcing her foot into his orifice, slowly stretching the opening with patient but scathingly administered rocking movements. He snorted in gasping breaths through the panties, pulling frantically, resisting more to feel his defilement than any coherent attempt to escape.

The queen chuckled malevolently and fought his desperate tugs upon the rope, keeping her hold strong and shifting her bodyweight so that every manic haul he made only aided in driving her foot in.

Gradually, after long and ceaseless working, his rear began to accommodate her invading foot, and with less than gentle pressure his anus finally swallowed the width of her heel. With a smile of victory she glided in, Thanos unleashing a croaking moan of bliss and suffering as his sore sphincter shrunk to place a loose squeeze upon her ankle.

His pained muscles gripped against her intruding flesh as she drew it in and out. Using the appendage as a battering ram she continued to molest him with it, penetrating with shuffles, making his rear utterly compliant to its constant insertion and retreat.

After working to free her foot while Thanos grizzled and sobbed from the burning effects of the trespass, she renewed her attention. Now she was setting to keep the muscular ring lax so that she might withdraw her foot entirely and then as the slave strove to deny her ingress with a clenched orifice, she would plunge mercilessly back in.

The heel rode in and out, her toes popping free of his aching sphincter and granting a hope that she had finished before she started again, forcing her entry as he moaned. Again and again she slotted her foot totally in and then took it out before returning it, sheathing herself in him repeatedly.

When she took her foot from him for the final time and released her reigns to let him lower back to the bed, he could only lie in phased torpor, unable to comprehend the mental machinations that conjured such acts. But he was glad that she was so fiendish, that her abuse was so effective for it kept him in his place, made him more appreciative of the few pleasures she granted.

'Did my slave enjoy that?' she asked, removing the latex stockings and unfastening his gag.

'Yes, your majesty,' he panted, his words uneven, his rear pulsating.

'Would you like these as a trophy, slave?' she asked, draping the gag across his back.

'Yes, your majesty,' he whimpered, knowing precisely from previous experience where he would gain it.

With squeals of fortitude he bit his lip and muted his cries as the garments were put to his rear and injected with a shoving thumb. Once they were almost in she forced her fingers deep, stuffing him with the attire. His rear closed and he could feel them within him, slowly travelling deeper, losing themselves in the twists and turns.

'Because you've been such a good and obedient pet and slave, I'll give you another little treat,' she professed, unfastening the ankle bonds and turning him over before reapplying them, his hands now trapped under his body.

'I'll be back for you later,' she crooned, leaning over him, his eyes glistening as he looked across her breasts, hanging over him within their latex walls. 'I have matters to attend to, so enjoy, my slave.'

'Kiss,' she offered, lowering a little, making him stretch his neck up until it smarted, and his lips brushed the subdued point of her smothered nipples.

'Good slave,' she said, and with the rustle of fabric and latex, she left the bed and moved from the room.

Thanos lay upon the sheets, wondering what she was planning, the image of her, the taste of latex in his mouth still strong as he ran through their session again and again. When one act or part stood out he rolled it through his memory, repeating it like a favoured scene in a film, rolling the same images and feelings through his mind's eye, reliving the memory alone.

His examination of the recent events was even more erotic now, for the pain of application was gone, making the memory sweeter to relive. He wished his arms were not so effectively tied, for right now he was desperate to exact a little pleasure for himself.

At that moment the doors opened, and four women strolled in with seductive strides. Naked save for their golden collars, Thanos had seen them before, he had watched them pleasuring the queen in one of the longest and most stressful nights of his life. Their images were strong in his mind, for he had been bound at the foot of the bed and watched the lesbian orgy unfold for hours and hours. Aroused beyond comprehension he had been filled with frustration, and could only watch impotently, gagged and restrained.

The women were part of her royal harem, and the reasons were obvious.

Each was a tall, slender creature, her head and every inch of her body shaven to the skin, her eyes rimmed with dark, her lips painted ebony black to match her pointed finger and toenails. Each nipple and aureole was also painted a midnight hue, making them stand radically against their snow-white breasts.

Their willowy limbs and pouring feminine curves made his palms sweat with the need to brush his skin against their marble flesh. Their bodies and their faces were unnaturally beautiful, as though someone had projected the image of utter perfection and made four identical copies, so pleased had they been with the initial success.

The faint impression of chastity belts was still on their skin, fading after a long companionship. The hunger in their eyes was like lightning, making their gaze flash as they looked across his supine body, like a smorgasbord of meat to devour in a rabid banquet.

The mattress sank under their weight as they climbed on. The first curled herself by his head, lowering her mouth to his and initiating a kiss. Her lips were like spun silk, and Thanos melted into them, their tongues riding out and curling against each other.

Cool hands grabbed his tumescent shaft, holding firm, squeezing but not moving. Aflame with desire Thanos lifted his hips, pushing into the grasp, creating his own masturbation.

Lips brushed his testicles and the orbs were taken into a cool mouth, a deft tongue rolling around them as she suckled and teased. The hand started to ride slowly up and down and Thanos sank into the sheets, the woman's tongue tasting the furthest reaches of his mouth. His heart was pounding in his chest like a stampede of cattle, his mind flooding with adrenaline.

A weight straddled his chest, the wetness of her sex cold to his skin. Breasts were spread in the hands of the fourth woman, and together they worked to have his shaft enclosed and manipulated within the soft valley.

Thanos was almost insane with bliss after only a few seconds. A woman was riding his chest, her hands stroking his hips as she kissed the woman responsible for holding her breasts, cupping them to his penis and bobbing them up and down.

Another was working his testicles, devouring them like succulent fruit as her hands traced his rear, sliding a finger in and out as the other tickled his splayed inner thighs.

The first female decided to step up her motions and lifted her hips, swinging them over. Thanos opened his eyes to see her loins descending, her thighs splayed across his face before he was smothered by them. His eyes peered up across the smooth white fields of her belly to her breasts, the woman caressing and massaging them in her own grasps, the black nails and nipples contrasting the whiteness of her flesh. With her head lolling back she gasped and moaned as Thanos started to lick, her pudenda like nectar.

Croaking into the smothering womb he stiffened and jolted as the underwear and stockings were snagged and slowly drawn out, rubbing against his sphincter until they were pulled free and set aside, robbing him of them.

The woman entrapping his length removed herself, instead letting her face drop down, devouring his shaft, her tongue flashing around, tickling him with the most educated of attentions.

Having had the breasts she was deploying removed from her grasp, the other woman took hold of the orally attentive female and pulled her from Thanos' torso. With her hindquarters exposed she immediately buried her features into them, sinking her tongue into rear or sex as the mood took her, her hands reaching through the portal of her thighs to tease her hanging breasts.

With a pair of hungry maws devouring his genitals, Thanos' tongue was alive with spry action, plunging and flitting, thrashing within the woman atop his face. He could feel the heat of his orgasm rising relentlessly along his penis, he wanted to hold on, to hold it back, to partake of this for longer, but against the four nymphets he had little hope of denying them.

Spasming wildly his seed was extracted, the vampiress gulping it down, suckling, dragging free every droplet she could as though it were the source of her un-life. Her features lifted away and the lips deserted his balls before flashing to the mouth of the sated female, plunging her tongue in, their fervid kiss allowing her to taste of her partner's feast.

Swinging herself across, the vampiress tending the sex and rear of the other scampered in and straddled Thanos, facing his legs, guiding his length into her humid womb. The velvet tract swallowed him up and he groaned and twitched, the feel so exquisite even after having been brought through climax a few seconds earlier.

The kissing females circled like vultures and entered the exchange again, each of them locking to one of their partner's nipples as they bobbed with her ride upon Thanos. Tending the teats, one of their hands took and massaged one of Thanos' testicles, while the other ferried in their own sex, teasing their clits.

The woman atop him started to flash with orgasm, clasping her own breasts, compressing them with forceful grips, punishing them for her own pleasure. She drank of his devotion for a lengthy time, relishing it. With a flushed sigh she slipped free and slumped aside, clutching her well-licked tracts, comforting them.

Leaving his mouth free she moved around and behind the other three, sitting between Thanos' opened legs. Her nails ran up the skin and then she arose between the breast-fixated females to start kissing the one currently atop Thanos.

Thanos strained his arms against the bonds but could do nothing save lay opened to their attention. It took longer for them to work him to orgasm this time, but their beauty, their skill, their relentless pursuit would not be denied. The vampiress on him mewled with glee, her nipples being eaten by a pair of masturbating vampire maidens, her lips adorned with the lips of the last female.

Gasping, his shaft raw and tender, he let out a prolonged cry as her tracts grabbed at him and hauled free another ejection of fluid. With some twists she sank down and then pulled at him, dragging out every portion of ecstasy for herself.

The woman toppled aside, dropping into the mattress. One of the women dropped onto her belly, nails pinning down her thighs, offering the moistened orifice to her appetite. Delving in she lapped and sucked, devouring the contents, making the woman squeak and thrash from cunnilingus applied so soon after penetration.

Inspired by this sight he felt a head emerge between his legs, hands on his thighs, stroking them as a tongue slithered in through his rear, making Thanos arch and murmur with rapture. The feel of the wet organ pouring into him so deeply had his eyes rolling back, his thighs flashing with tensed flicks.

The last female sat astride his chest, lowering down, her hands beside Thanos' head, placing her breasts onto his face. He could not resist the sight of them, so perfect, so delicious, and controlled by his urges he started to lick and kiss, taking one nipple and then the other into his mouth, unable to decide which one to stay with.

Croaking cries began to emerge again as the woman he had filled was torn through clusters of climax by her attending partner, carried through and then deserted, her body limp, twitching occasionally.

A fist enclosed his shaft once more, the flesh wilting, sore from such prolific use. He tried to moan for them to stop, but the breasts filling his vision were effective gags and only garbled mumbles seeped through them.

The woman with the languid partner found new purpose, drawing the female from his rear, her hand leaving him. For a moment he thought he was going to be allowed rest, for he heard them kissing, their tongues rolling over each others' bodies, exploring their partner with hunger.

Then he felt one of them take hold of his shaft once more, squeezing the flaccid organ and starting a slow shuffle, her lips reaching in, lapping at it, tasting the women who had already attended it. Thanos tried to resist, but there was a more primordial mind at work within him, and against his wishes he was growing stiff yet again under her expert caresses.

Rendered adequate for her needs she sat across him once more - hovering, pausing. The other woman replaced the hold, starting the masturbation, keeping Thanos erect as she set a squirming tongue lose in the hovering anus. With deep laps she lubricated the woman and then let her descend, steering Thanos into the puckered opening.

The tight orifice rolled down his length and settled into position, the muscular ring giving soft grips before she started to ride him towards fulfilment. Again he tried to ask her to stop, but the pleasure of her, the feel of her tight rear dancing upon his length, was an ample compensation for the discomfort.

The breasts in his face moved up, leaving him and presenting him once more with a pudenda to taste. As she settled into position Thanos attended his task with harried intensity, hoping to pleasure her enough to sate her. Had this woman already taken him? Was she back for more? He had lost track of who was who. Were these women even satiable? Would they continue to take him until he was screaming in agony from the effects of their chafing attention?

The duration required to get him close to climax was lengthy, and served even further to contuse his penis, the skin raw, feeling like sandpaper with every shuffle. Howling into the woman atop him, he was brought to orgasm once more, the woman sighing with glee as she felt herself being injected with a paltry amount.

With soft moans the female on his head started to mimic his peaks of rapture, shuddering, holding to his hair and grinding him deeper into her. Only once she was fully fulfilled did she lift herself away.

He sobbed as his aching penis was deserted, the woman moving back into the arms of the other exhausted female, the two of them cuddling together, kissing gently.

Thanos looked up and dropped back as he saw the last two returning onto him, their predatory gaze still very much in need of him.

A mouth grabbed hold of his ailing member, her tongue an expert trickster, able to conjure forth erection even against the most stalwart defiance.

His protests where hushed as soft pale cheeks were opened and a rear was placed across his mouth, his nose falling into the cleft of the female's womb.

With no choice left to him he started to force his tongue through the restricted hole, driving deep, the damp sex rocking upon his nose, trickles of juice spilling down his cheeks. Airing a dismal groan into the sphincter, he felt himself being guided into a damp womb, the female mounting her restrained partner and starting to extract her pleasure.

She tweaked and twisted his nipples as she worked, rising until his tip almost fell free and then dropping to the root with increasing speed. Whimpering, she spent her time working him towards climax again, the pain in his length making him sob and shake. But still there was enough stimulation to facilitate her purpose.

With a distressed squeal he felt himself come, the amount produced meagre when compared to the first doses he had distributed, his reservoirs drained.

The woman continued until she had successfully pleasured herself, and with a slothful movement she entered the embraces of the other satisfied women.

The vampiress on his face removed herself and shuffled back to his flushed and pulsating member. Taking hold of it she felt its strength ailing quickly, and with a swing she set her loins over his face.

Looking into the crease of her rear, Thanos was forced into cunnilingus once more, his tongue aching, the muscles pulled from over use.

A cool mouth enveloped him again, and with tears in his eyes he felt the fellatio commence. The women were expert in the carnal arts, and even in pain as he was, drained as he was, and exhausted as he was, there was to be no denying them.

The woman worked tirelessly, being ferried into orgasm numerous times during her long toil upon his shaft. Finally though, Thanos stiffened and wailed, his penis feeling as though it were passing stones through it, the feeble spit from the tip swallowed in one go.

The woman rolled aside to her fellows where she was welcomed into their close nest, leaving Thanos still stretched on the bed, drained of life and semen.

Closing his eyes, he was wafting into sleep in seconds, the exhaustion of mind and body complete.

CHAPTER 16

Entering the vaulted halls once more, Kira beheld the queen dressed almost tokenly in a latex dress and thigh boots, her crown absent. The two attendants were gone, and there was no Thanos, a vacancy in his place making Kira a little forlorn, for she had wanted to see him again.

Settled into the arms of her throne, the vampire queen watched them approach and nuzzle at the first step, Kira forming into a ball, Cassandra bowing deeply.

'Arise, most trusted seneschal,' she decreed after a short pause to remind Cassandra of her subservience.

'You summoned me, your majesty,' she replied, looking up at the aloof goddess. Kira kept her head low, watching the queen from under her brow.

'Yes,' she stated firmly. 'You will take my pet and whatever other forces you require, and conduct the abduction of this Corin were-bitch that rampages on my city.'

'Has your majesty considered that perhaps it would be wiser to simply slay this creature, for she would make an ideal scapegoat?' offered Cassandra, her words strained, affected by the prospect of yet another distraction for the queen. Already Kira's training had taken up much of her time, but it was time that would have been lost anyway because of the visiting dignitaries. Once they were gone though, the queen would be free to continue her regime of self-gratification, and if this new lupine were captured, then such attention would certainly not be for Cassandra.

The queen arose from her throne and started to descend the stairs with a majestic tread, retorting as she did so, the click of her heels echoing through the solemn hall.

'I do not want the carnage wrought by my pet to be blamed on this female. I want the vampire houses, and every other quarter of power to suspect my involvement. I want them to be worried, to be unsure of my motives and my strength. Allocating blame for my rise back to power upon some independent lupine wastes what could otherwise be a substantial strength to my assets,' she revealed calmly, detailing her reasons to her seneschal as her feet dropped onto the flagstones before Kira.

From her humbled pose she stared at the midnight stems, fighting the urge to shuffle forward and lick them. The two most divine females she knew were here together, talking freely above their demeaned pet, and Kira started to curse the chastity belt once more for its impediment to her wishes.

'But, your majesty, I—' began the woman with protest, her hands shaking slightly, her body tense.

'If this is too much a burden for you to handle, seneschal, I shall have to replace you with someone more able,' warned the queen, looking upon the keeper of her house with firmness.

Cassandra's eyes were faced down to her owner's boots, clearly afraid that her queen would discover her true motives written in her countenance if she allowed herself to be scrutinised.

'I am sorry, your majesty, I merely sought to advise you,' she said dejectedly and softly, sagging with resignation.

'Your consideration is appreciated, but my decision is made, seneschal,' she decreed, the words causing Cassandra to shift for a moment as though she had thought of a new ploy.

But she sank to her knees before the queen, humbled and full of sorrow, her latex-sheathed legs releasing soft squeaks against the stone. Looking up, Cassandra beheld the gaze of her owner.

'Majesty, if I have offended, allow me to make amends,' she begged, her hands clasped across her latex shirt, squeezing the leash and the crop in the hope of being given permission. 'Please, allow me to service you.'

'An apology that would no doubt please you more than it would me, seneschal,' accused the noble vampiress.

'I seek only to serve you, majesty,' rebuked Cassandra, lowering her head, foiled in her plot and infuriated by it. The queen, however, had clearly seen through the deception and was going to excite her slave's frustrations as a lesson in etiquette.

'Then maybe I should test your skill at training my property, and have this fine pup perform for me?' she muttered, walking over to Kira and stroking her hood and ears, the touch making her wilt with longing. To bury her tongue in the queen, it was a glorious dream come true. She had done it before, during their night together when she still bore life, but now she could appreciate it even more, having thrived in her wondrous realm.

'Please, your majesty, she is not ready, allow me to attend you,' hissed Cassandra, while throwing a look of inveterate bitterness towards Kira.

If the queen did indeed allow this cunnilingus, Kira would find herself agonisingly punished for it. If she disobeyed, then the queen would be furious with this disobedience, and Kira did not wish to risk ending up in the feed banks.

'Maybe I should see for myself, seneschal,' continued the queen, opening Kira's mouth and pulling her tongue into view, examining the organ she was thinking of taking for a test drive.

'As you wish, your majesty,' murmured Cassandra, giving up, knowing the queen would do as she wished because she was the all-powerful ruler here, and while she bore authority, Cassandra was still a slave. With that fact stamped upon her, the queen desisted with pursuing the deception, releasing Kira and arising tall and proud, her legs filling Kira's hungry gaze.

'But no, I have details to clear up, and you have your own mission,' she stated, and cupped Cassandra's chin, running her fingers along the smooth jaw. 'But you may lick my heels before you go, seneschal. And if you perform your task well, we shall see to a more substantial reward for your loyalty...

'Sweet seneschal,' added the queen with an appreciative smile, and then released her hold, letting Cassandra wilt and lap with dedication upon the queen's heels, her tongue spiralling around the daggers as she quivered with humbled delight.

Kira was livid with envy, but knew she had been fortunate. Cassandra would still see to her needs of punishment and occasional release, but if she had taken this prize from her the vengeance would have been more than she could stand.

Kira did not want to alienate the woman; she was too besotted with her. Of course she wanted to serve the queen, to adore her, but Cassandra was a far more devoted partner. The queen was frivolous, her enthusiasm for one subject waning easily as Thanos had discovered to his cost, and now he pined for what he could not have.

Kira would prefer to evade that trap, to love and worship the seneschal for all time, and never know the agony of losing this most gorgeous and captivating of depraved deities.

The dominance of these women was a powerful drug. The seneschal was more readily available, but the queen was far more potent a concoction and far more addictive. Yet the queen was a scarcer commodity, and to taste such highs would only spoil every other. Never would anything else come close to reaching such heights, and thus disappointment and longing would corrupt her life evermore, wishing for what she could not attain, and bored with what was on offer as inadequate compared to the peak she had acquired.

Without further word, the queen turned and started to ascend the stairs, vanishing behind the throne as they awaited her departure. Once she was gone the seneschal cast Kira a threatening glare, and then drew her away with sharp tugs to her lead. Kira smiled to herself, satisfied with her lot. She had everything she could ever have wanted, and all the time in the creation to explore.

With a cruel vampire mistress, an eternal goddess presiding over them, visiting creatures of strange and esoteric tastes, and a secret lupine lover, she wondered what else she would come to experience in this dark underground world.

More vampire erotica by Bruce McLachlan...

Moonslave, the sequel to Kira's adventures, is also available to order as a paperback at **AMAZON**...

Kira's hungry eyes panned down the short latex skirt gripping her owner's body and for her own gratification she lingered down the burnished rubber stockings that revealed her contours before vanishing into knee high leather boots. Perched atop them, she seemed even more powerful because of this authoritarian influence to her attire.

Moonslave sees Kira still serving as the rubber-bound pet of the regal and cruel Seneschal.

Kira accompanies her owner on a mission to abduct the vengeful Lupine Corin, who is subsequently captured and started on her training in submission. The fiendish lessons are studied and aided by Kira, who soon begins to relish dominance almost as much as her slavery.

Served to the appetites of the Palace and its supernatural guests, Kira finally wins the heart of her true love, and is formed into the Seneschal's personal maid. Finally, through perseverance and obedience, she gains ownership of her own harem of slaves, in which she finds three girls she has long wanted to have at her mercy.

www.ingramcontent.com/pod-product-compliance
Lightning Source LLC
Chambersburg PA
CBHW020405130626
46549CB00006B/2445

* 9 7 8 1 7 8 0 8 0 7 0 3 4 *